ROSEHEART

{a novel}

catherine dehdashti

Causy Taylor Literary Publishing
St. Paul, Minnesota

Names, characters, places, and incidents either are the product of the author's imagination or are used fictitiously.

Acknowledgement to Forough Farrokhzad (1935-1967) for excerpted stanzas from *Rebirth* (1964, Iran), and to translator Dr. Maryam Dilmaghani (2006, Montreal).

Dehdashti, Catherine, 1969-
Roseheart / Catherine Dehdashti.—First American edition.

ISBN 978-0-9863686-7-7 (paperback)
ISBN 978-0-9863686-8-4 (ebook)

Library of Congress Control Number 2015901342

www.catherinedehdashti.com
Facebook: www.facebook.com/CatherineDehdashtiAuthor
Twitter: @cdehdashti

Causy Taylor Literary Publishing
St. Paul, Minnesota

For my family, and for all men who sew

To Kathy –
all my best

In my little,
lonely room,
my heart is invaded—
by the silent crowd of love.

I am keeping track of my life:
the beautiful decay of a rose, in this antique vase;
the growing plant that you brought;
and those birds in their timber cage.
They are singing every hour,
up to the full depth—
of the view.

—From *Rebirth (Tavallodi Digar)*, by Forough Farrokhzad

Translated from Persian by Dr. Maryam Dilmaghani

PART I

Table Thirteen

The curse of the Midwestern work ethic has me driving a compact car through a March storm to get to my waitressing job. The café I'm risking my life to get to this frozen Saturday in 1994 is in the University of Minnesota neighborhood called Dinkytown, so it's called the Dinky Kebab.

You can cringe at the name, but business isn't bad.

My little black Honda with summer tires slides everywhere. From the air, I must look like a hockey puck being knocked around on a pond. I never know when I press on the brakes if I'm going to stop, slide, or spin doughnuts.

SUVs speed by, but even at a crawl, I lose and regain control over and over, rejoicing every time I narrowly escape hitting a punk-rock pedestrian as I skate my way through Uptown. The brief trip down Highway 94 toward the university is better because the highway is gritty with salt and sand. Once I hit University Avenue to make my way into Dinkytown, the salt and sand disappear.

A blue Honda CRX is in front of me, clipping along even though it's as light and flimsy as my car, so I speed up a little too, thinking that if another little Honda is doing it the road must be better than it looks. I'm already thirty-three minutes late for work, so I'm hoping to make up time.

With three blocks to go before I reach the restaurant, the CRX—in a split second—goes from twenty-five miles an hour to a dead stop in front of me. I react by stomping hard on my brake, but only the front of my car stops and the rear of it spins out in front. Before I know what's happened, I've pivoted until I'm facing backward and my car's bumper end swings into the CRX.

After this brief thrill ride, I'm motionless. I blink my eyes, look to my right, and see a gray cat finish its sprint across the street.

It doesn't look like any other cars are coming to join the party, so I just sit there for a moment, savoring the odd moment of peace that comes from how we Minnesotans think when this happens. I don't even know yet if my car is damaged or not, but I know I'm alive and unharmed, so I close my eyes and thank God. When I open my eyes a second later, the sleet has stopped falling and the sun peeks out. I realize I've turned my car off and that means no heat.

When the driver comes to my window, I recognize him—it's one of the regular customers at the Dinky Kebab, an Iranian guy with a mustache. I try to get out, but he tells me to stay put. "Are you hurt?" he asks with a slight Persian accent. "You shouldn't move if you are hurt."

"I'm fine," I say and then I open my door and stand up, but I'm shaky and the road is bumpy from layers of ice.

He holds me by the elbow of my short wool coat and walks me to the side of the road, then goes back and drives both of our cars off to the side where I'm waiting. We inspect the cars. Mine is unblemished because my big rubber bumper was what slammed into his car. His car has a pretty good dent, but it's drivable.

The gray cat skulks along the sidewalk, watching us. "My car can't stop that fast on the ice," I say, as much to the shivering cat as to the guy.

"I'm sorry," he says. "That cat ran out in front of me so fast—it was just an automatic reflex. I shouldn't have stopped." Then he looks at me closer. "You work at the Dinky Kebab."

I'm wearing a big fur-lined hat that covers both ears and I don't know how anybody could recognize me, but I look down and realize my burgundy apron is sticking out of the bottom of my short coat.

"I hope I haven't made you late for work," he says. "And that you don't have whiplash. Maybe you shouldn't go to work—do you want me to drive you back home?"

"I'm fine," I say again. This little spin-out couldn't have been as bad for my back as waitressing, I think, and I can't make it all this way and not go in for my shift.

The guy gives me his business card that states his title as Professional Engineer at Nielssen Parking Consultants. His name is Naveed Shushtari. And the phonetic pronunciation of his last name is printed right on his card, (Shoosh-Tar-EE). I stick the card in my coat pocket.

I offer him my insurance information, but he says he will get in touch if he needs it. I tell him he knows where he can find me, and then I get back in my car and drive three more blocks to the Dinky Kebab.

Now I'm forty-seven minutes late, and I punch the clock, my knuckles white and my hands still shaking. When I tell my story to one of the owners, Kaveh, he says I could have called in because we won't have many customers in this weather.

But we do have customers, because Minnesotans can't keep off the ice, and Naveed Shushtari is one of them. He sits down with a friend who happens to be here alone, sitting at table thirteen. *He's bad luck*, I tell myself.

He looks at me with concern as I try to seat the people who come through the doors in twos and threes. Another waitress arrives before I start taking orders, and I let her take half the tables, including Naveed's. But when Naveed and his friend's kebab platters come up, I bring them out. His friend gets up to go to the bathroom as I head toward the table.

"I really am sorry," he says. "I wouldn't have even been out on the icy roads, but I had to drop off a package for my mother at the post office before it closed at noon. Then I thought I might as well come in and eat lunch."

"Sure, blame your mom," I say. "She couldn't wait for a package to arrive a day later?"

He looks confused, so I smile to show I'm just kidding.

"Let me take you out for dinner tonight to make up for the accident," Naveed says.

"Sorry, but I don't date customers," I say. "Plus, I have a boyfriend." My boyfriend's name is Quentin and he's a stockbroker in Wayzata, with his office overlooking Lake Minnetonka. Lingering, I make small talk with the engineer. He's not flirty, just nice, and I realize he's cute under that mustache.

At the end of my shift I bundle up to go out to my frozen car. But before I leave, I fish my set of keys out of my coat pocket, pull out the customer's business card along with it, and smile. I don't think I need to talk with him because my car is fine, and I'm fine, and he will get in touch with my insurance if he has to. But he had warm, dark eyes, and I remember the tickle I felt when he grasped the elbow of my wool coat.

I throw the card in the oversized kitchen garbage and make my way out through the loading dock, warm up my car, and drive home.

Tomorrow night Quentin is taking me to a play at the Guthrie Theater. He has season tickets with main-floor seats, and this will be my third show with him. When the cordless phone rings at my apartment, I think it might be him because he calls me every day and hasn't called at all for two days now, which is very curious. But it's just Kurt wanting to know if I want to go drive around Minneapolis with him. He says, "Come on, I'll smoke you up."

I'd meant to do my tax short-form tonight, but what would you do? Cruising around town in my old college boyfriend's Nissan 300ZX Turbo will do fine. Not that we hang out for long—after we're good and baked, Kurt has to get back home to his girlfriend.

Personal Phone Call

The next day, Sunday, I'm leaning against the stainless steel counter at the Dinky Kebab. It's between lunch and dinner, and I'm drinking tea from a tall glass with two cardamom candies melted in. I'm just waiting for the dinner shift waitresses to arrive so I can go home and get ready for the play.

The Mexican kitchen workers are still washing the silverware from lunch, which I have to wrap for the dinner shift before I can go. Everything else is ready. The sugar cubes are piled high in bowls on every table. If Kaveh's cousin, Niloofar, can balance even one more cube on top of one of my sugar mountains for each of the thirteen tables, I will fail her inspection. Jars of tart, red sumac powder are full, ready for shaking over kebabs. (This is not the North American sumac, as I learned on my first day working here.) Ketchup bottles are filled and ready for all the Iranian-American kids who want french fries instead of basmati rice with their kebabs.

The mini market looks neat and enticing. Pistachios and other nuts, with saffron-tinted shells—a big tin scoop in each barrel—are lined up next to the case of olives, dates, and feta cheese. I've dusted the shelves that hold tea, bottles of rosewater, quince jam, and other groceries. About half of these items are unique to such a market. The other half are things that could be purchased at Byerly's or any other grocery store, but the customers like to buy them here, in little cans and jars that have traveled from Iran, or at least from the Iranian factories in California. Persian language newspapers and magazines are stacked on the counter. These are published in Los Angeles, not Iran; these are not the voices of *the regime*. These magazines feature photos of self-exiled Persian celebrities—debonair men, and women with perfect make-up and no headscarves. Other features are modern Persian poetry, presented in Persian and English, and anti-regime commentary.

When the phone rings, I go to answer it, expecting a to-go order. But it's Quentin. I like his voice, and after not hearing from him for two and a half days, I'm happy to hear it. It's deep and strong, like a documentary film narrator you trust to tell you the truth. Who wouldn't invest their fortunes with him? I look around to see if the owners are looking—they do not approve of personal phone calls.

"Hi sweetie," I whisper. "I can only talk for a second. What time are you picking me up tonight?"

I hear him take in a breath instead of just giving me a time. "Has the plan changed?" I ask.

"I didn't want to wait to tell you," he starts, "so I'm sorry to do this while you're at work. I went out with somebody else last night. I'm sorry. I really like you."

"Oh," I say. I'm slow. I'm not sure if he's breaking up with me or not. Is he confessing a mistake? Is it up to me now to decide if I want to see him again or not? I'm waiting for him to say, *It was only dinner.*

"Are you there?" he asks.

"Oh," I say again. "Did you meet somebody new? Are you going to see her again?"

Duh, I tell myself. It's obviously somebody new. I know it wouldn't be his psycho ex-girlfriend, Dori, because he's told me all about her drama. If he just went out to dinner with somebody else, maybe I could handle that. After all, I hang out with Kurt sometimes—just as friends, but still.

"I went out with Dori," he says. "We're going to try to make it work again."

I'm silent, in shock. "Dori? But you said she's psycho."

"I wasn't being fair to her," he explains. "We have a lot of history."

The history I know about with Quentin and Dori is that she had been calling him since they broke up, crying and making him feel sorry for her. He finally had to buy something called "Caller ID" so he wouldn't have to answer her calls anymore. She had been driving by his house at night, which is no coincidence because he lives on a peninsula on Lake Minnetonka. It's not like she just passes by on the way to pick up milk. But I thought she had recently stopped all that—I thought she had finally moved on.

"So you answered her call and you met her last night? Why?" I ask, thinking maybe I didn't understand the "make it work" part right and maybe he just needed closure.

"I called her," he says. My grip on the receiver weakens and I drop it to my shoulder.

Kaveh comes in from the loading dock and sees me limply holding the phone, obviously not writing down a to-go order. Normally he would try to shoo me away from the personal phone chat, but instead he gives me a nervous smile and goes to put the wet wood chips on the kebab grill—that's how he gets the good flavor with the gas grill.

"*You* called *her?*" I say, puzzled. A customer comes in the door and waits by the podium where we keep the menus. "I have to go."

"Are you okay?"

I'm so stupid that I almost ask him if we're still going to the Guthrie tonight. Just to be sure. But the customer is waiting to be seated and Kaveh goes to hand him a menu, which he doesn't need because he always orders the soltani kebab.

I hang up, and Kaveh asks if everything is okay. I nod, suck up the tears, and go take the regular customer's obvious order. The kitchen guys bring me the silverware, and as soon as I've wrapped napkins around a few sets, a customer comes in, and then a couple, then a four-top before one of the dinner-shift waitresses arrives.

It's good, I guess, getting hit with a lot of customers right now. By the time I have a few minutes to think about Quentin, I'm able to remind myself that I wasn't so deeply in love with him anyway. He's a millionaire with a Mercedes worth eighty thousand dollars and a condo in West Palm Beach. I tell myself I was more into those than I was into Quentin himself, and those are just things.

So why do I want to cry?

Maybe I liked him more than I'd realized. He was funny. We laughed together. No, it wasn't just that. I don't know when it happened, but I'd become attached. I'm surprised by the bruised feeling in my heart, and the shame of being dumped, and I can't stop a few tears from falling.

There's no way Quentin would have called Dori unless I had failed to keep his attention with all of my whorish efforts, including being a "cool girlfriend" who acts like she never expected a commitment in the first place. It hurts to have to wonder if I'm even more pathetic than crazy Dori, who hooked him with her simple game. Once she stopped calling and driving by, he called her.

Why did you stop stalking me?, I imagine him pleading with her to tell him.

As soon as the four-top's order is clipped to the cook's row of green tickets, a swarm hits. Niloofar has left, and the second waitress hasn't arrived. It's still early—we don't usually get so many customers before five on the weekend. So Kaveh helps seat people, smiling and laughing with them, while I help the only dinner waitress take orders, retrieve beverages, and wrap more silverware bundles until the tardy waitress rushes in. Finally, I can leave to go home and do nothing.

This is how it is in restaurant work. Long periods of busy work are interspersed with customers that blend into each other so quickly that it seems I will never serve them all, never be able to remember who ordered an extra kebab and who just needed a straw.

Melinda

It was the sunny living room overlooking the pool that first attracted me and Melinda to Joppa Lane Apartments in St. Louis Park.

It's just on the border of Minneapolis, walking distance to Lake Calhoun, which Melinda walks around almost every day.

We're the land of ten thousand lakes (more, really) in Minnesota, as you know if you've read our license plates. Lots of them have Indian names, and more than a hundred and fifty of them are called Long Lake. Some even have French names after the voyageurs from long ago. But Lake Calhoun is named after an 1800s pro-slavery politician from the South Carolina. Melinda has been part of some movement to have the name changed.

The pool won't be open for a couple of months, but the setting sun is beaming through the window this evening, and Melinda is bounding around the apartment whipping it into shape and getting ready to go out at the same time.

It's a Jewish part of town, and several of our neighbors have mezuzahs marking their doors. Our next-door neighbor, Mrs. Finklestein, who does not have a mezuzah, looks like a rich old lady because of how well she takes care of herself, but I know she gets Meals on Wheels. Sometimes I get caught up in long conversations with Mrs. Finklestein in the hallway. She does most of the talking—she's always looking for someone who will listen to her. But Melinda is swift and strategic about avoiding the neighbors.

It's our fourth apartment together, if you count our dorm room at the university. Neither of us can afford our own place. And since Quentin has, I think, broken up with me, it looks like Melinda and I will be here together for a while. Melinda is involved with Roger, who is from New Mexico, but they aren't ready to live together. And living together is getting old—again. For Melinda too.

She's begun leaving 3M Post-it notes around the apartment. For example:

- "Valerie, please scrub sink."
- "Valerie, please squeeze water out of sponge after using."
- "Valerie, please sign this petition to change the name of Lake Calhoun."

I make up excuses when I see her in person this evening. "My mom never told me that you have to squeeze the sponge," I say. Then I go for the sympathy timing. "Quentin broke up with me today. On the phone!"

She completely ignores this important new information.

Melinda and I became friends at Wayzata Junior High School. We'd met earlier, in fifth grade when she'd moved here from Philadelphia, but we weren't friends. Once you know how we became friends, well—I'll have to explain that later. It's not exactly a heartwarming story.

But once we really were friends, we talked about boys, and fashion. We pored over *The Official Preppy Handbook* together—Wayzata got a mention in it as one of the preppiest places in the country. So at age fourteen we tried hard to live up to that, even though we lived in the part of Wayzata with the small houses, a good mile from Lake Minnetonka and all of its cake eaters. We didn't say cake eaters in a derogatory way; we aspired to the name. Sometimes we met kids from nearby suburbs and when we said we were from Wayzata, they called us cake eaters, and we stood a little taller for being associated with the Wayzata bluebloods.

You have to understand that Wayzata thinks it's special because it kind of is. Lake Minnetonka is a sprawling body of water with many bays and peninsulas. Its name means *big water*, and it's been called Minnetonka since before white men came. But while a town like, say, Excelsior, has its main street

heading up from Lake Minnetonka, Wayzata rests majesti-
cally upon it.

Wayzata's Lake Street travels the distance through town
along the shoreline, so restaurants, shops, and financial
firms—even Meyers Bros. Dairy and the historic train depot
built by James J. Hill—all regard the lake's splendor. Then
the town climbs a gentle hill, like a wave cresting, so another
parallel layer of homes and the library and post office have
their sense of the lake and perhaps a democratic sliver of
a view. Even our childhood school, Widsten Elementary,
looked out upon the water from the tower above the audito-
rium, where many sixth-graders had their first kiss.

"The refrigerator kind of stinks," Melinda says now. "Can
you throw away that Styrofoam container of eggplant dip
yet?"

I take out my Dinky Kebab leftover appetizer and sniff it.
"Did you even hear me?" I say. "Quentin dumped me. Now
I have no plans tonight."

Melinda pets me on the arm. "I'm sorry, I'll hang out
with you tomorrow night and cheer you up. I'm going out
with Roger tonight."

I dump the eggplant dip in the garbage can under the sink.
"Not a big deal, really. Have fun."

Now that Quentin has exchanged me for his old girlfriend,
I imagine she will be sitting in my seat at the Guthrie tonight.
Or was it *I* who had sat in *her* seat these past several months?
I wonder if she's looking forward to the Tennessee Williams
play. I wonder if she even knows anything about Tennessee
Williams.

As Melinda puts on her beaded earrings then leaves for the
evening, I lay out my black pants, white shirt, and burgundy
apron for work tomorrow. I should clean the apartment, or

call and check in with my mom, who is having knee surgery in two days. But instead, I write until I'm half asleep. The guilt of unclean teeth forces me out of bed to go brush.

As I walk down the short hallway from the bathroom back to my room, I realize that tonight Dori will probably be walking past the authentic Andy Warhol silkscreen of Marilyn Monroe on the way to Quentin's bedroom overlooking Lake Minnetonka. Not me. And while my heart is going to take some time to heal from Quentin, it might take even longer to get over that Marilyn Monroe.

Clan of Mama Bear

Running is just in some people's blood. My mother, Eugenia, had surgery on her left knee for the second time, due to a running injury. Her boyfriend isn't there to take care of her after the surgery because he's running a marathon in Tennessee. Six more states to go and Bruce will have run a marathon in all fifty.

So my sisters and I take shifts. Laura—also a runner— took her to the hospital for the surgery and drove her home, and Courtney is going to help out after I get her through the first twenty-four hours when she isn't supposed to be alone.

Courtney also bought her some magazines and the newest *Clan of the Cave Bear* book imposter. Mom's been waiting for the next book in Jean Auel's series since the last one came out in 1990. It's been four years, so now she's sating herself with all the Jean-Auel-wannabees.

My main job is just to make sure she stays put on the couch with ice on the knee and the leg elevated. As a bonus, I give her a nice foot massage with lotion to try to get her to relax. She already wants to get up. She's only supposed to get up to go to the bathroom, and I'm supposed to help her. But when I run out to my car for something, that's when she decides she can go to the bathroom on her own.

When I come back in, she's on the floor with her leg twisted under her, her thick white hair fanned out on the floor, blending in with her white carpet.

"What happened?" I yell.

"I had to go to the bathroom," she says. I crouch down to the floor to help her get into a sitting position and to see if she's wet herself. She looks indignant. "I fell on the way back," she says. "I think I tore it." The discharge papers with the doctor's phone number are on her kitchen counter. The nurse I talk to says if I don't want to call an ambulance I'm going to need to get her into the wheelchair and back to the hospital for an x-ray.

Kurt, who's a weightlifter, answers my call for help and comes to carry her straight to his car and take us to the hospital. Mom is still drugged enough from the surgery to get away with gazing up at him and saying, "I don't know why you two don't get back together. You would have made beautiful children."

Kurt and I give each other wry smiles. "Off we go," he says.

While Kurt watches T.V. in the hospital lobby, I'm taken to a tiny office and Mom is wheeled away for an x-ray. When my mom and the nurse come back to the room, I face an inquisition.

"Were you there when she fell?" the nurse asks. I explain that I had stepped out to my car for just a second.

"What position was her leg in when you came back inside and saw her on the floor?" she asks. I explain that she was already trying to get back up, so I'm not sure. My mom tells the nurse that she's a nurse too, and she can answer the questions herself.

By the time we get home and Kurt carries her to her bed, I'm pushing my mom to take pain pills. Getting her to sleep might be the only way to keep her from moving around. I threaten her that if she doesn't take her prescriptions, her knee might not get better and she might never run again. But Mom is a recovering alcoholic—maybe seven years sober—and she doesn't want to take the narcotics. She says that she had Laura hide the bottle anyway. Laura had only left one pill out, in case our mom absolutely needed it, and I don't know where she put the bottle. Mom says the ice is good enough. And maybe some more foot massage.

"Hey, if you don't want the drugs, I'll have them," I joke.

"No, you will not."

Mom acts like she's oblivious to my bad habits, even though she's found my paraphernalia before, and even though it was in the newspaper when Kurt was busted once back when we were together. She still adores Kurt too, and believes that it was all a mistake about the bust. He was just in the wrong place at the wrong time, I'd told my parents, and my mother had accepted that.

I can't stand to see her wincing as I try to help her with her nightgown and robe and get her leg in a good position in her bed. We've done the ice, the Advil, and more massage, but she's still in too much pain to fall asleep.

"I guess I could take one pill," she says. But then she looks so beaten. "I didn't want to."

"Sometimes you gotta," I say. I give her the pill, which she holds out in front of her like a piece of rotten fruit, while I go to get her a glass of water.

When I get back a minute later, Mom is sound asleep, still wearing her cerulean blue velour bathrobe over her nightie. I kiss her on the forehead, trying to remember how long she's had this robe. I know she had it when I was in elementary school, because I remember her in it sending me off to the bus stop.

The pill sits atop her cave-people novel, like a big orange rock from the future that has landed at the feet of the Cro-Magnon woman and Neanderthal child.

For a minute, I think about taking the pill. I could just zone out through my heartbreak over Quentin. But I need to be lucid next time Mom has to go to the bathroom, and Mom needs to know that she didn't take the pill, so I leave it there. However, Kurt left me a little bud of Hawaiian, and I go out to my car to smoke it quickly, hoping Mom doesn't wake up and take another fall. Then I go back inside and eat chips and nap in my mom's bed next to her until the next day, when Courtney comes for her shift.

Needle Arts

There's one Dinky Kebab family that visits every Sunday. Today, the daughter is wearing another crocheted dress. The multiple colors of yarn spin a rainbow as she twirls around to show it off to me.

"Another beautiful dress! What talent your grandma has," I say to the little girl. The grandmother gives me a routine lift of the chin, as if to say, *I made it with one hand while canning marmalade with the other.*

"My grandma knitted my *baba* a sweater-vest too," the girl says. I look and see the father has a brown cabled vest, not nearly as delightful as the rainbow dress with its crocheted shell patterns and popcorn stitches.

Only the mother is wearing store-bought clothes, fine garments that could be from Dayton's Oval Room, or perhaps purchased while traveling to New York or Los Angeles. A cream-colored silk suit and high-heeled brown-butter leather shoes with the narrowest stacked heel I've ever seen—just dots of wood piled one upon the other four inches high.

When I applied to waitress at this Middle Eastern cafe, I imagined women in chadors as customers. Those are rare though—and never the Iranian—otherwise known as "Persian"—women, although sometimes the Arabs wear chadors or scarves. Students are rare too in this college-town restaurant—the Dinky Kebab is more expensive than the student hangouts, and they don't have a beer license.

As I serve the father tea, the girl's mother asks for water only with her meal. After the meal, she'll drink her tea and also order tea for her mother-in-law, who had motioned to me that she would not take any. The wife knows best—which is that her husband's mother always drinks tea after her meal, even though she always refuses to ask for it.

This family has never come in here without the grandma, who speaks no English. They are bound to her, as if by crochet needle and the skeins of yarn that cover the girl and her baba, tied to her with all of these decorative stitches.

Zoom

Melinda is making a necklace for her mom's birthday and watching a drama show that I never watch. She offers me some corn chowder she made. It's spicy and rich and I eat a big bowl of it.

"Do you want to hear a few lines from my story?" I ask her. It's for the last class I'm taking at the university, even though I've already graduated. I'd always wanted to take a fiction class, and my dad didn't refuse my request for a few more credits worth of tuition. He often tells me, as his mother told him: *Education is always worth it.*

"Sure," she says as she slips another bead onto the wire.

I offer her a hit off of a joint that I got from Kurt. I read a few pages of *Shoedog* to her.

Melinda takes a few little tokes of the joint and gives me some thoughts. She still doesn't get the title, even when I explain that the characters, shoe salespeople, are called shoedogs because they go fetch the shoes from the backroom and bring them to the customers. I know—I've done that job. She still doesn't get it, and I finally give up on reading it to her.

Then she turns down the T.V. and tells me the latest on Roger, who is moving back to New Mexico for a new job.

"Did Quentin call tonight?" I interrupt.

"No, and I'm glad he didn't," she says. "Face it, you guys are over."

"I'm not sure. I think Dori guilted him into taking her back. She probably threatened to kill herself or something."

Melinda gives me the wan look for which her perfectly smooth forehead may be credited. "I'm glad you two broke up."

"You're *glad* that my boyfriend broke up with me?" I say.

"You were starting to dress like a Harvard grad on a weekend to *the Cod*. I thought we both left that preppy look behind after ninth grade."

I smirk. "You mean...on a weekend to *the Cape*?" I ask.

She darts her eyes, a brief loss of confidence. But then I'm laughing so hard at how she just called Cape Cod "the Cod" that she can't help laughing too even though she *hates* to be wrong.

"The *Cod!*" I scream. Stoned, we both laugh so long and hard that she has to put down the necklace she's making because beads are rolling everywhere. Finally, Melinda composes herself, touching her face as if to iron out any laugh lines waiting to set in.

It's ironic she would insinuate that I was dressing for Quentin the stockbroker, when Melinda is the one who dressed and did her hair like Barbara Eden in *I Dream of Jeannie* when she was dating her last Arab boyfriend.

Roger is her first boyfriend who is both white and American-born *ever*. Even though she's so pretty, no boys in Wayzata liked her. She's tall and big boned—maybe a little plump too. All the popular boys in Wayzata liked only skinny girls, like me, and Melinda wouldn't have dated a guy who wasn't popular back then.

Each *objet d'art* Melinda has lying around this apartment is an artifact of the homeland of the guy she was dating at the time she acquired it. There are, for example:

- Turkish hamam antiques
- Spanish Lladro figurines
- Italian mouth-blown glass
- hand-painted Kashmiri papier-mâché boxes
- Algerian tapestries
- a Jamaican kitchen witch
- Liberian beads
- French paintings

I love the Jamaican kitchen witch—I was camping on the island with her when she got that one. I still have the photo of her with that lover, Jesse. The Rastafarian stands next to the big, blonde, white girl in front of a wooden door that reads: *JAH. Black man know yourself.* I had the tent all to myself many nights on that trip.

But that was then. "You should meet one of Roger's friends," she says now, "since nobody else has been asking you out lately."

I wasn't going to bother telling her about my customer at the Dinky Kebab, but this goading forces me. I can't resist—her antagonism brings out my news like the golden truth rope of Wonder Woman.

"You didn't tell me you got in a car accident," she says, genuinely surprised because it's not like me to keep anything from Melinda.

"I spun into him, but no damage to my car," I say. "Anyway, I'm not going to go out with him. I'm just saying, it's not true that nobody has asked me out."

She's not impressed. "Oh good," she says. "I can't tell you how *real* it feels to be with someone from the same culture. We hum the same tunes, literally!"

I zone out while she babbles about how they both started humming the theme song from *Zoom* at the same time one day, and how that never happened with Omar or Giles or Jesse or whomever.

"And I'm worried those connections wouldn't happen with this guy for you," she concludes. "Plus, a Middle Eastern man won't marry a non-virgin."

"Who said anything about getting married anyway," I say.

"And maybe I will go out with him," I add, just to be contrary. "I have friends, like Savi, who didn't grow up humming 'Zoom-a-zoom-a-zooma-zoom.' We still have things in common." Savi is from the Caribbean island of St. Lucia. Her great-great grandfather arrived there in 1849 on a ship from India, one of thousands of Indian laborers to work the sugar cane as an indentured servant after African slavery was abolished there.

"That's just an example," she says. "Plus, Savi…" I interrupt before she can diss Savi.

"I probably would go out with him," I say, "except I threw away his business card and I don't know if he'll ask me again." I ladle some more corn chowder into my bowl and start walking back to my room to work on my story.

"Well I hope not, for your sake," Melinda, expert of all things in love, bellows at me as I disappear down the hall. "I'm just afraid it would end badly."

The Sunglasses Spa

One of the first signs of spring in Minnesota is that people with disposable income buy new sunglasses. They buy them in winter too, especially if they ski. But the first week in April is when they start lining up—even if there's still snow on the ground. When the sun comes out and it's not below zero, it's time for shorts and sunglasses. April and May are the only months of the year when I earn more money in commission at my Sunglasses Spa job at Southdale Mall than I earn in tips at the Dinky Kebab.

When I come back from getting a twice-baked cheddar-jalapeno potato at One Potato Two for my late lunch, customers are waiting, so I have to set the potato aside. The first one I help spends fifteen minutes trying on every pair in her price range and not letting me help anyone else at the same time. She leaves without buying anything. But then I hit it big with one of the teenaged heirs to the Cargill Inc. fortune, who tries on and buys the $280 Revos *and* two pairs of Oakleys.

As I'm ringing up the sale, I see my Dinky Kebab customer Naveed Shushtari walking by with a gigantic rectangular shopping bag. The Sunglasses Spa is a kiosk in the middle of the mall, so there are no walls and Naveed sees me. He heads my way as I begin ringing up another customer.

Naveed looks at the Ray-Bans until I'm free, and then he tells me he was here to pick up a poster he had framed at Prints Plus. I might vaguely remember telling him that I work here, although I'm not sure, and the framed art is a pretty good cover if he did come here looking for me.

"Did you get your car fixed?" I ask, wondering if I'm going to have to pay anything or if my insurance rate is going to go up.

"I have a buddy who has a body shop," he says. "It's all taken care of."

"Cool," I say. Good for me, too. I don't know what else to say because I'm not too clever with small talk, so I suggest he try on the Ray-Bans he was admiring.

Naveed refuses to try on any sunglasses. "I don't want to be your customer," he says, "because you said you don't date customers. I was hoping you would go out for dinner with me tonight."

It's not entirely true that I don't date customers. I mean, I don't date customers at the Dinky Kebab, but the Sunglasses Spa is where I met Quentin. He bought Persols.

"Well, you're still my restaurant customer," I say, looking up at those gorgeous eyes with pretend innocence through my wispy bangs. "But we can go out as friends. I get off work at six."

Date

Christos is a Greek restaurant in South Minneapolis that is better than the Greek place near Uptown where Melinda and I sometimes eat. I've only been to Christos a couple of times, back when I was seeing Kurt and he was raking in the money with his business selling large amounts of pot and small amounts of cocaine. It feels different here with a parking ramp engineer, but comfortable. We share almond-garlic dip, peasant salad, mousakka, and lamb shanks with artichoke sauce. Naveed also orders souvlaki, which is really similar to Persian kebabs. I try to eat all lady-like, but the food is so good and I just keep eating and eating. I don't worry about the quantity I'm tossing down because I'm very thin. People always tell me I can afford to eat a lot.

I learn that Naveed came to the U.S. right at the beginning of the Islamic Revolution, and got his student visa from the American embassy in Tehran just weeks before it was taken over by the revolutionaries.

When Naveed was starting college here, I was a sixth-grader at Widsten Elementary, counting the days that Iran held American hostages. We kept track on a small paper-covered bulletin board, framed in a yellow card-stock border with a yellow bow at the top. Each day, a student would be selected to change the number card pinned to the board. There were yellow ribbons everywhere. Naveed's mother in Iran, he tells me, was worried about what people would do to her son here.

Naveed tells me about his childhood, and asks me about mine. As we talk I notice how he looks kind of baby-faced, and also how he's wearing too much cologne. I have a headache coming on. After a dessert of sweet cheese in filo dough, we leave in our own cars. I barely make it home before my headache becomes a migraine and I start throwing up my dinner.

By the next day I've associated Naveed directly with my headache, but I tell myself that's not fair. It's just that he would have been plenty attractive without the cologne. When he shows up at the Dinky Kebab that night and asks when we can see each other again, I whisper that I'm still think-ing of us as friends, and that if we go out again he can't wear so much fragrance. Although I really emphasize the *if*, I quickly make sure Kaveh and Niloofar aren't looking, and then I write down my phone number on an order slip and slide it to Naveed with his bill.

Gyp

For our second date, Naveed picks me up at my apartment. He compliments all Melinda's gilded gold Catholic iconography, my marbleized silk pillows, the trinkets and the art, and the antique armoire that holds Melinda's killer stereo system and my T.V. None of this is mine, I confess, except for the pillows and the T.V. I don't really have a decorating style, and I'm unlikely to ever develop one with so much of Melinda's global-bazaar style dominating my living space.

We have a small glass of wine and sit on the scratchy loveseat, which is also mine—or rather I'm borrowing it for the long term from Savi. Unlike me, Savi is a real writer. Sometimes I sit on her couch when I'm writing. I pretend I'm her and have both unique ideas and the focus needed to write all kinds of good stories for both my own creative satisfaction and paying clients.

I'm not sure what I should think of this guy. Although I've liked looking at him and talking to him at the restaurant, I'm not sure I should be sitting on the loveseat drinking wine with him in my apartment. He's eight years older. And he's an engineer. My father is an engineer and I never thought I would date one.

I never thought I would date anyone with a mustache either. At least he has cut out the cologne, which I later learn was *Bijan!*, the brand worn by many proud Iranian men because the designer Bijan is Iranian himself. *Bijan!* smells horrible in the large doses it is usually applied.

The restaurant we choose is an Afghani one that serves food that's a lot like the food at the Dinky Kebab. I'm partial to the Dinky Kebab and notice how the Afghani place's rice and kebab portions would never do for most of my customers at the Dinky Kebab. The prices are about two dollars higher on each dish too.

Naveed notices the price and portion differences too, and says, "What a gyp."

"Oh please say 'what a rip' instead," I beg him. "Gyp is so racist, although I'm sure you didn't know that. It comes from *Gypsy*, and is an unfair stereotype. It's no better than saying *Jewed*."

"Okay," he says, and he quietly lets me tell him about another job I have, writing for the only Gypsy serving on the council of a major human rights organization in Washington D.C. The guy lives here in Minneapolis, and I met him when I wrote a paper about Gypsy stereotypes in literature, movies, and T.V.

Part of my job (my third job, although this one I call an "internship" since I don't get paid) is to be vigilant for these slurs and stereotypes, and to write letters to the perpetrators and letters to editors, which occasionally get published. I use these opportunities to tell who the Gypsies really are, that they call themselves *Romani*, that they have been both contributors to society and victims for thousands of years. The Holocaust, for example.

My family is only interested in this work I do because of its amusement potential. They like to quiz me on if it's bad press for Norwegians when the Minnesota Vikings pillage another team. They ask me if the Pope has asked me to write a letter to the owner of the St. Louis Cardinals.

But Naveed admires my sincerity about the persecution of the Romani people. He looks at me inquisitively, seeing how I'm more than a waitress and sunglasses sales chick.

The lighting is low and romantic, and as I sip my wine I start to see Naveed's thick, long eyelashes. When he takes me back to my apartment, we kiss in the car and he holds me by the elbow again like the day of the car accident. He's going to New Orleans with his friends, and tells me he wants to see me when he gets back.

I have the rest of that bottle of wine, and because I have rented *Under Siege* for myself but it seems like a good guy movie, I invite him in.

We keep to our own sides of the scratchy loveseat for the opening scenes. Sometime between the scene when Tommy Lee Jones's helicopter lands on the ship and the scene of his mercenaries trying to kill Steven Seagal in the ship's kitchen, we start kissing. I still have Melinda's voice in my head, asking me why I think he would ask out a young and lowly waitress except to get laid. "You have to go home now," I say. "But bring me something from New Orleans, some little souvenir."

"Some Voodoo potion?" he asks.

"Sure, something Voodoo-y." I walk him out of my apartment.

It's late, but my mom never goes to bed before midnight on a weekend, especially now that she's sober and divorced and can do whatever she wants to do—except for drink. I call her.

Mom is in bed reading and eating Whoppers malted milk balls. She's supposed to be taking it easy for a few more weeks while her knee heals, but she tells me about her long walk today. She crutched all over a big park while Bruce ran ahead and back to her over and over until he'd gone ten miles and she'd crutched almost two. I never even walk two miles.

I don't tell her about Naveed, even though it's probably why I called her right after he left. Although she hasn't had a drink in years now, I notice that she sounds a bit drunk. She slurs her words sometimes when she's feeling depressed, and I know that she's depressed because Bruce has also been going jogging with another woman.

Like me, my mom lets men be too much a part of what makes her happy. I must get this from her, although my sisters are much more independent. Her voice clears up and she sounds better when I ask her what she's going to plant in her garden this year.

She says she already has pansies in pots and all her spring bulbs are up and in bud. "I'll get tomatoes and cucumbers in the ground as soon as we've had our last frost," she says. Then she starts slurring again and adds, "If I'm still alive by then."

Roux

I'm trying to make that spicy corn chowder that Melinda made. Since she started dating Roger, she's been cooking a lot of southwestern cuisine. She has a cookbook called *Hot Spots*, and the chowder is one of its chili pepper-inspired recipes. But the book says "make a *roux*," and since Melinda isn't here and I don't know what that is, I call my mom.

She makes shrimp and crawfish bisques, sometimes even lobster. "It's what I do when I make the bisque," she says. I have no idea what she's talking about and then she moves on to start talking (and talking and talking) about something else instead of giving me the directions. She's never actually taught me how to make her bisque. Maybe she's changing the subject because she remembered she's keeping it a secret. But now at least I know one part: it has a roux.

I call Laura's fiancé, Ty, who tells me, "Stir a smidgeon of flour into butter on the stove until it takes on the color and aroma of roasted chestnuts." Ty loves to cook, which is good because Laura does not. I don't know why my mom couldn't have just told me how to make the roux.

Mom is from Georgia, but she's now spent more years in Minnesota than there. She has the gift of gab like Grandma Vivian. Still, her cooking is mostly Minnesotan, since she was married to my Norwegian-American dad until two years ago. The only southern things she makes are fried chicken (the best), spicy sweet potatoes, chicken curry salad with apples (which Savi says is *not* how you should treat curry), and pecan pie. And the bisque, of course. I love all of those things, but that's all she will do for me. The rest of her cooking is what my dad likes, or now what Bruce likes.

Sometimes I craved the southern flavors so much that I poured Tabasco sauce on pieces of bologna and stuck them under the broiler for a snack before Mom's meals of boiled potatoes and baked fish.

I wish Mom cooked all kinds of Georgia low-country food, and could teach me. But she never even taught me how to make the bisque. I'd spent years trying to figure it out and didn't even know about sautéing the onions first until Melinda told me how sautéing brings out the flavor in everything.

I'm always telling Melinda she should write a cookbook. She cooks a lot, usually the cuisine of the guy she's dating at any given time. Since her college career was like one long Festival of Nations, I've learned some things from her about international cooking. But the relationships never lasted long enough for Melinda to master the cuisine, so I never picked up much.

Brain Surgery

The Sunglasses Spa at Southdale inconspicuously occupies the lower level rotunda, so when two dozen red roses arrive for me there I hear a lot of hooting and hollering about it from fellow mall workers. They like to tease.

Quentin sent me flowers all of the time, but never red roses like these. "Pink, for excitement," Quentin once had the little card inscribed to read when he'd sent a dozen perfect pink roses.

"Pink for pussy is more like it," Melinda had said when I showed her the card. "You know how guys think."

I don't know how old Dori is, but even though Quentin is in his thirties, he never dates "anyone whose biological clock is ticking." That should have been my first clue. I guess I just get blinded when I'm in a relationship. I hope that isn't what's happening to me again now.

My coworkers see the red roses, and guess that Quentin and I have moved to the next level instead of that he has moved to the next level with his old girlfriend. In hindsight, I see his lack of commitment. I see that he is not going to call. And, as if the big glass sunglasses case is my crystal ball, I suddenly see that Dori is probably not going to get his commitment in the end either.

Naveed sent these red roses, probably by making a simple phone call from New Orleans. There's a typed card that reads, "I got your souvenir. A hint—it's something *Voodoo-y*." I imagine him telling the florist to put *"Voodoo-y"* on the card, and it makes me smile and think about him for the rest of my shift.

When I get home at night, Melinda shakes her head about Naveed and the roses, but she overcomes her desire to tell me again how good it is when cultures don't collide.

Instead, she says, "I'm going to show you how to hang your roses upside down to dry. I was tired of how you always left your roses from Quentin in my antique vases until they rotted." I remember. She'd left me a Post-it note on that once: "Valerie, Remove dead roses and clean vase."

"I know how to hang roses upside down. It isn't brain surgery," I tell her.

"I'm going to show you how to do it *properly*," she says, like Martha Stewart although Martha's television show isn't on the air yet, "so they will last a long time and look beautiful in our apartment." Martha does not exist to us. We're still that untapped market of status-hungry young women for whom Martha has launched a business that just hasn't reached us yet.

I nod, pleased that I can contribute something to the decor, and grateful that there's only one Post-it note today. It's a recurring one on the bathroom mirror asking me to wipe down the vanity after using the sink.

I have a little bit of pot, and we smoke it together from my marble pipe while Melinda, her blonde hair pulled up in a Southwestern-looking beaded barrette, shows me how it's done. She wraps a rubber band around the stems to hang the roses from a banana hook sitting atop three phone books into a bowl of white powder on the table. The white powder will absorb the moisture from the petals quickly, so they can dry before turning black.

I don't know where she learned this. "This actually *is* like brain surgery," I say. "What's the powder?"

"Silica." She folds over the top of the bag of white powder and puts a paper clip on it. "It acts as a desiccant." She pronounces *desiccant* so casually, like it's a word she uses frequently, although this is probably the first time she's ever said it.

I think we're done, so I decide to watch a rerun of *Cheers* while I glance over an article about Iran in my *New York Times*. Since I met Naveed, Iranian stories catch my eye more than they did before, even though I've worked in the restaurant for two years. So I can see how it happens to Melinda—how she gets into things as they relate to her newest boyfriend every time.

Melinda goes to work on another necklace and tells me she might try selling jewelry again. In college we made neon clay jewelry together and sold it at a gallery in Butler Square. One morning when I was still asleep my mom called and told me to run and get a *Star Tribune*. One of our pins was on the cover of the Variety section for a story about artsy jewelry by female designers. After that we had a flurry of business, but we let it slide.

Now she has the bug again. I just don't know how she can work with those little beads if she's as stoned as I am. I like to marbleize silk fabric with paint, but I don't make jewelry anymore.

I will never understand Iranian politics, I decide, so I toss the newspaper to the floor and laugh along with the laugh track on *Cheers*, just briefly acknowledging to myself the privilege of being able to abandon the "story" on another country.

Melinda and I hang out a lot for the next few days, like old times. Roger is in New Mexico. Melinda turned down a dinner date with her old boyfriend, Omar, who is promising her that he got out of his arranged marriage in Palestine, and that he is madly in love with only her. But Melinda tells him she's happy now, being with an American. She recommends he marry the woman his family has chosen for him.

Voodoo

By the time the red roses have dehydrated in the silica and been arranged in Melinda's greenish-gold vase, Naveed is back from his trip and inviting me to dinner at his house. I'm excited to see Naveed for our third date. He's reminded me over the phone that he has souvenirs for me and I can't wait to see what they are. I hope for something really good.

I get my highlights touched up and it feels great to be blonde again, as always, even though it makes my long hair frizzy and fly-away. My skin has broken out and I work hard on popping pimples and applying my prescription adult acne lotion.

I put on jeans that show my flat belly and a short T-shirt, feeling confident as long as I can sneak into a bathroom to touch up my concealer every hour. I drive over to his house, following the directions he's given me over the phone.

The house is a 1950s brick rambler in South Minneapolis, near the border to the affluent suburb of Edina. When I pull up, Naveed is outside helping his neighbor across the street unload bricks from his car and bring them around to the side of his house. He introduces me to the guy, who is also Iranian, and I go sit on the front steps. It's cold this May evening, but mainly because of the wind.

When Naveed tries to open the front door for me, it sticks and he has to turn the knob just so and then give it a little kick. But I'm instantly more comfortable than I ever was in Quentin's Lake Minnetonka chateau with his majestic double doors with their leaded glass windows, satin-nickel handle set, and electronic entry. Naveed is clearly happy to see me—he tries to lay me down on the couch for a long kiss, but I stiffen. I want to see my presents.

My souvenirs turn out to be:

- a voodoo rag doll with pins
- a jasmine-filled pillow
- a mechanical shark-shaped back scratcher

Dinner is some sort of tomato-based split pea stew called *gheimeh* that has homemade french fries on it and is served on top of rice. It's Persian food, but not the kind of food they serve at the Dinky Kebab. It's great, and I'm impressed that he made it himself and has even lit candles.

The movie Naveed has rented, *The Firm*, is suspenseful and engrossing. But he's made a fire and positioned us against backrests on the floor in front of it, and by the time Tom Cruise's character accepts the too-good-to-be-true lawyer job, we're talking more than watching. By the time it dawns on Tom Cruise that his wife Jeanne Tipplethorn was right to suspect his new employers, we're kissing on the floor, backrests cast aside. We stay on the floor in front of the fire. I'm the one to remove the clothing, mine and his, deciding not to take the slow route or pretend to be a virgin as Melinda had advised I do if I want any chance at this being more than an affair, which she still insisted was a bad idea.

Afterward, he moves to my side and holds me in his arms. "So this is what making love means," he says.

"Haven't you made love before? You had girlfriends."

"I'm sure I have, but you've made me forget," he says. I know this answer is extremely corny, but I fall for it anyway, laying my head on his broad chest and breathing in sync with him.

We lie in front of the slow-burning fire and talk until the middle of the night. I already know he had a serious girlfriend once for three years and was once "almost engaged" to an Iranian woman he was set up with by his mother and someone else. But now he tells me the rest: the recent girlfriends and the wild 80s. I tell him about my own wild 80s and early 90s. Well, not all, but I don't pretend to be a twenty-four-year-old virgin.

We make love again, and then we take a long shower and go to sleep in his bedroom. His bedroom is very 80s bacheloresque and I imagine him on the black lacquered waterbed with an unknown number of women who preceded me. There's a black onyx panther staring at me from its perch on the headboard shelf—maybe it's kept track.

In the morning Naveed lends me an extra toothbrush. I wonder if he keeps them in stock for one-nighters. But looking at him now, that's sort of hard to imagine. He stands in front of the bathroom sink in a striped robe and bunny slippers that seem incongruent with the style of his black lacquered water bedroom set.

After he brushes his teeth, he kicks off the bunny slippers and changes into a fishing resort T-shirt. Then he's off to the Byerly's in Edina for apple fritters and orange juice to bring back to his house. I wait here, alone.

Snooping is a part of my nature, inherited from my diary-reading mother. It was the best part of babysitting. After kids went to sleep, drawers would be opened, master suites would be explored, and I would scrutinize everything: Some husbands used condoms, which I had never thought of as birth control for married people, and some families seemed to drink a lot, while others had not a drop of alcohol anywhere. I sometimes found porn in my conservative middle-class neighborhood, and once found some cocaine in the desk of a Wayzata car dealership owner.

The challenge with gathering information in an Iranian immigrant's house is that much of the writing is in Persian, and I can't read that, so I don't know if anything I see is incriminating or not.

What is somewhat disturbing is the mess of strange collections in two of the rooms. One room is a second bedroom, and it's a quarter full of gadgets: tools, picture frames, things that look like they're from the reject pile at Brookstone. There's a bed in there, but it's covered with paperwork—copies of bills and photocopies of articles that, at my childhood home, my father would have filed in neat folders in his big mahogany desk.

The other room, I realize, should be a dining room. It's right outside of the kitchen, but it has a pocket door that matches the kitchen's pocket door, instead of a regular bedroom door. Naveed served our dinner in the kitchen last night, so it hadn't occurred to me that he had a dining room.

There's no dining set in here, just a brass chandelier above a bed where there should be a dining table, and there's open shelving for dishes rather than a regular closet. This room has stranger collections yet: clothes, fabric, and a sewing table. There's a vanity table with a mirror and brush next to an old calendar notebook. I open the drawer and find special soaps and lotions.

At first I think: Could he be married? Is his wife out of town? But then I look at the vanity table again, and something—or someone—sort of registers.

His mother.

He's told me about her. The mirror and brush are sitting on something very pretty and white. It's a delicate lace doily, crocheted with complicated tiny shells and popcorn stitches.

Gruff

When next I see Naveed at the Dinky Kebab, I boldly ask Niloofar, "Could you wait on this customer? I don't want to wait on my *dates*."

She's confused for a second, thinking I'm saying something about the giant sweet Medjool dates we sell at the counter. But then she gets it. Niloofar's other cousin, Jamsheed, is standing by, but he leaves this conversation to her. He knows he has no right to comment. Still, he stands close enough to listen to me tell Niloofar that Naveed and I are dating. There's just a hint of a blush on his face. Jamsheed and Kaveh treat me with a great deal of kindness and concern all of the time. They're proud of all of their college-girl waitresses, whom they treat like their own little sisters.

Niloofar, like a bossy older sister, comes straight out with her concern. She's always the first to say if one of the waitresses could use a little lipstick, or has some on her teeth. From what she's seen, she thinks this Naveed is a little "gruff." He isn't very charming. And no, she does not see the warmth in his eyes that I see. I don't know how she could not, but I'm glad that his eyes don't smolder like that for everyone.

She doesn't mention my reputation, but there's that too.

"He's hardly even polite," she whispers. "Certainly not the example of a refined Persian gentleman." I glance at him. He's pretending he doesn't know me to try to keep me from getting in trouble with my bosses.

"He's not gruff," I say. "I don't know where you get that. Maybe just a little clueless."

"Ah, just like you." Niloofar turns to go seat him and his work colleague without menus. She knows what they each always order.

I have to take the next three tables. Niloofar is leaving after lunch and still needs to work on the schedule for next week. When I go to look at the schedule hanging up in the kitchen later, I see she's only given me two shifts.

Less money, I think, with concern because one of my sisters' birthday and my mom's birthday are coming up and it's hard enough to pay rent *and* buy good birthday presents.

But also, I think: *More time to do other things.*

Naveed and I feel bold. We need some things from the Dinky Kebab's market the next weekend. Already we're together so much that we have to tend to housekeeping chores together, like grocery shopping. One of us could just go alone, but it's almost summer and I haven't yet taken a ride on Naveed's rarely driven motorcycle. I've only ridden on one a couple of times before, with my motorcycle-cop Uncle Andy, in Atlanta.

The roads are clear and the air is exhilarating. I wear the only helmet and put my arms around Naveed while we ride into Dinkytown. We pull up in the lot and I take off my helmet. Kaveh is on the loading dock, and when he sees me, he goes back inside. We don't see him again. Jamsheed rings up our olives, bread, saffron, and feta cheese with polite small talk and a blush on his princely sculpted cheeks.

Intersections

I don't want to be all dramatic about my parents' divorce. I didn't even cry a lot when it happened, only when we had to sell our house and I said goodbye to my childhood bedroom

I shared with Laura. But to me right now, it seems like my dad, Neil, has spent most of his free time for the last twenty-plus years on the golf course, and that he didn't seem to mind an awful lot of traveling for work. It didn't seem to me like it was such a big loss for either of them.

So, there isn't much to dramatize, but still I decide to put Mom and Dad, with made-up names instead of Eugenia and Neil, in my *Shoedog* story, maybe just for filler because I'm a little stuck on some of the retail team members' lives.

Melinda is playing her CDs loudly, but I want to read some of my story to her, so I turn it down a little and then I read:

> "Linda wanted more affection, but Carl thought she was content with her ladies bridge group and her drinking and all she did to take care of Megan. Of course, she was sober for years before they separated, but sobriety didn't bring them any closer.
>
> Megan wouldn't want a marriage like that. But still. She picked up her squirming terrier mutt. She asked herself, 'Oh, why, after this long, can't they just stick it out?'"

"Stop right there," says Melinda. "That's over-the-top. And what does Megan want them to stick out?"

"Don't you remember?" I ask. "When my mom asked for the divorce, my dad said, 'I thought we were going to stick it out.' And my mom said, 'You go stick it out.'"

"Your mom has a weird sense of humor," Melinda says. And again, like the term shoedog, I have to explain to her why "stick it out" belongs in the story. I have to remind

Melinda how after my dad gave up on the counseling, Mom started flirting with other men at the YMCA, and noticing that they flirted back. When one recently separated man with a very un-Neil-like hairy chest and a very un-Neil-like tight ass played footsie with her in the Jacuzzi, she thought maybe she didn't want to stick it out with Neil.

"Okay, fine, keep reading," Melinda says. So I read:

> "Myrtle Beach was going to be golf heaven. Carl's two best buddies since high school were living there. Linda was getting an apartment in Minneapolis."

"Your dad didn't move to South Carolina!" Melinda calls me on the fact that my dad is moving a half-hour east to St. Paul with his new wife, Wanda. And that my mom moved to a suburb near Wayzata with lower home values.

"It's fiction—I'm just using some things from my life. Megan isn't me," I insist. I read some more:

> "The new family would be moving into the house in three weeks. Megan needed to get an apartment again instead of what she had been doing, sponging off of her parents since she returned from her study-abroad program. Taghato's was hiring in Women's Shoes."

"Taghato's? Is that what you are calling the department store now?" Melinda asks. "I thought it was just good old Dayton's in your last draft."

"I renamed it for the story. I learned that *taghato* means crossroads in Persian. Working in Dayton's Women's Shoes in downtown Minneapolis was like being at the crossroads of my life."

"It doesn't seem like you've crossed the road yet."

"Thanks for reminding me," I say. Melinda is very seriously building her "network" and scrambling to get a salaried position. She paid two thousand dollars to work with a career specialist, and she's joined Toastmasters. It's true that she's crossing an intersection I haven't yet reached. I didn't even send in my tax form on time.

"Isn't Megan going to have two sisters, so you can explore your problems as a middle child?" Melinda asks. Melinda is an only child. She likes to explore what birth order means for people with siblings, and imagine how she would be different if she had a younger or older sibling or both.

"No, Megan isn't going to have any sisters," I say. "That would make the story too complicated."

"Well, think about it," Melinda says. "According to what I've read, the oldest girl always attaches to the father and the youngest to the mother. The middle child is neither here nor there, never attaching or taking much of an interest in people."

"That's so untrue. And how does that make for a good story?" I ask.

Melinda twists her amethyst beaded necklace around her index finger. "The middle child is most likely to become a sociopath, basically. Think of Jan Brady all grown up. Doesn't that give you any ideas for character development?"

"Thanks," I say, looking at her necklace, imagining the string of beads wrapping itself tighter and tighter around her neck. "But my main character doesn't need any sisters."

"Just like that *Brady Bunch* episode when Jan wished she didn't have any," she says as she rises to turn the music up again.

Then I think, but I don't say, *Maybe she won't have a best friend either.*

Golf

My mom has lent me her Lady Callaway golf clubs, which are two decades old, but she swears they are the best brand, and always calls them "My Lady Callaways." Laura and Courtney have new Lynx clubs.

We've come to play this nine-hole course after Courtney and I just got fitted with paper dresses at the seamstress's house. Laura and Ty are getting married in a few weeks. Laura isn't too concerned about the lack of progress on the dresses, though. She's more worried about our mom. We went out to dinner with Mom last night for her and Laura's birthdays.

Bruce just broke up with her and took the woman he'd been jogging with to Hilton Head. I could say I know how she feels, since Quentin dumped me, but it's different for Mom because she's still hurting from the divorce. Bruce was numbing the pain, and now he has just doubled it.

"I know," I say. "I actually called the suicide hotline because she was dropping hints. They said she has to call them herself, and that we can't do anything unless she's in the middle of attempting. Then they can arrest her because it's illegal."

"It's illegal?" Courtney asks. "That's absurd."

It's Courtney who looks slightly absurd, wearing pajama pants with a polo shirt on the golf course. The girls just a few years younger than my high school class started this trend. Pajamas in public—the ultimate win for the id over the superego and the ego. It's a good thing we play at a public course. This would not be allowed at Wayzata Country Club.

Laura disagrees. "Suicide is basically murder—just of your own self."

Still, Laura thinks I'm overreacting. She was away at college during Mom's worst alcohol years, and she's never quite believed that our high-achieving mother even had a problem. Mom seems pretty together to her, running races and settling into her new house. But Laura knows Mom is beyond blue.

Courtney, as usual, switches from agreeing with me to agreeing with Laura. "Yeah, I mean—I doubt mom would kill herself over a male nurse."

Bruce doesn't really match anybody's stereotype of a male nurse, but I laugh anyway. This is still a time before so many men go into nursing, so it's still funny. Most of our mom's nursing colleagues have been women, so when she met Bruce and found out he was a nurse she was a little hesitant. It didn't take long for her to realize there was nothing feminine about him. I still can't imagine him having any bedside manner.

"I hope Mom and Dad get along okay at the wedding," I say. Laura drives the ball from the tee and it lands a few feet from the green. My ball goes into a thicket of ornamental shrubs that I'm sure weren't there a second ago. I go into the thicket to get my ball, and come back out with a rip in my shirt from a thorny branch. Laura looks at me with sympathy, but I know she's getting impatient.

"Ty is making a fabulous dinner tonight. I can't wait," says Laura. "He's been cooking with porcini mushrooms a lot lately." Courtney rolls her eyes, probably because she doesn't think porcini mushrooms and Italian lamb sound any better than McDonald's burgers.

I can't hit the ball again. I whiff it and hit it ten feet to the right until the group behind us asks to play through. I decide to quit and just walk the rest of their game.

When I get to Naveed's house, he sees my ripped shirt and brings me inside to that extra bedroom/dining room where all the sewing stuff is. He gets out a thin needle and some thread that matches my pink shirt.

I tell him about my golf game and my sisters, but he says, "I can't sew when you talk, so please be quiet for just a minute."

I sit on the bed in just my bra and jeans while he stitches. His big arm makes light, graceful swooping motions as he sews.

When he's done, it's impossible to see where the shirt was ripped. Like a wound that has healed without a scar.

"You are full of surprises," I say. "Do all Iranian men know how to sew?"

"Maybe more than you think," he says, and tells me how his mother had her own sewing school. He grew up helping thread needles and rip the seams of all the students' projects that didn't meet her teacherly expectations.

When he's done, he starts handing my shirt back to me, but then pulls it away and I have to fight for it. "You have a rip in your jeans, too," he says. "Hand them over."

He pulls them off of me, and I don't get back any of my clothes until well after the sun has gone down and we realize that we've made no plans to eat dinner at all.

Moving On

After two weeks with no shifts, I consider myself an ex-employee of Dinky Kebab. A waitress did ask me to take a shift she couldn't work, but I didn't feel like it. The place where I once felt such belonging now gives me a feeling of shame. The owners never said dating customers was against the rules, but all of us waitresses knew that it was.

My dad thinks this is a good thing—that I no longer work there, that is—not that I've shamed myself by taking a customer as a lover. Not that we talk that often, but I did mention it to him when I called him last time. He said maybe now I'll study for the LSAT and become a lawyer, or maybe I should become a public relations manager like Laura, and then I can quit working at the Sunglasses Spa too.

Naveed, by the way, also thinks this is a good idea. Not that the two men have met, or discussed my future together, but they feel the same way—that it's time for me to do better for myself, you know, and give up the burgundy apron.

Speaking of the apron, my resignation (or firing perhaps) is so gradual and unofficial that I don't even turn that thing in. I remember one waitress cried when she turned in her apron on her last day, so it's just as well I don't create such an opportunity for myself. I liked working there, and admired Niloofar and her cousins so much. I can't be sure I wouldn't cry.

Soon, I quit the sunglasses job too, thanks to a cash gift from my father, given just for the purpose of paying rent while finding a job more congruent with the amount of money he has already paid in college tuition. The human rights org council member I intern for goes to Bulgaria for a couple of weeks, and Naveed goes to North Dakota on a parking ramp job. I ask him if there are even enough people in North Dakota to merit a whole ramp. Maybe a surface lot.

Paris

Quentin wants me back. I get my first letter from him the day Naveed leaves for North Dakota. I'm excited to receive it if for no other reason than getting personal mail. Girls and women of the future may never know what it's like to get that envelope in the mailbox, to open it and see man-writing, to know that their lover had touched that paper. But we don't even have email yet, so I don't know what a shame that will be for the people of the future not to have real mail, how much more titillating it is to hold that paper in your hands than reading electronic type.

Quentin says he can see us getting married, and that he is finally over Dori. He says it was a very unhealthy relationship, but we will have a healthy one. Now that he knows what he wants. He seems to assume that what I want is him. I don't know what I want in life—maybe just to fit in somewhere and have my freedom at the same time—but I don't think I want him. Not anymore.

Notice that he doesn't actually write, "Will you marry me?" but just, "I can picture us married." I don't write back or call like he has begged me to do. He then calls Laura and Ty and tells them he really has to talk to me. It's important.

So I call. Because I do still think about him sometimes. It creeps up on me to realize how much I liked him. Of course, I also think of him when I imagine being rich and living in his house on Lake Minnetonka with all those boats, and the maid doing my laundry. And doing his laundry, so I never have to complain about my husband leaving his socks on the floor like I always hear married women say.

But although I imagine all the dinners and vacations, I also remember last Christmas when I spent two weeks embroidering a velvet pillow for him, and he gave me a VCR. He never let me forget how much more expensive his gift was than mine. It's not generosity if it comes with reminders.

On the phone, he tells me he wants me to go to Paris with him. For a month. Right away.

I *love* Paris—I went there in college. And yet, maybe I'm not as shallow as it must seem I am by now. Because I say no. Definitely not. It's somehow easy for me to say no to him right now, no to wealth and travel, no to a *normal American boyfriend*. No to a month in Paris!

But then, I've been there.

Diversity

I finally go to turn in my apron at the Dinky Kebab, because I don't want the owners to think I kept it on purpose—as if anybody would steal their stupid waitressing apron. Kaveh tells me to come back to visit, to eat, that I'm always welcome if I want to come back to work. His kind words make me feel more like I resigned than got fired, although I'm still not really sure. Probably, this is all just part of his usual *politesse*, but it's unlikely I would come back begging for my apron and a pad of order tickets. It really is time for me to move on.

Even though I'm job searching, I do have more time on my hands. I've been writing in my journal with this extra time, three pages every morning, just as I learned in a book Savi gave me called *The Artist's Way*.

Savi doesn't work anymore because she had two babies and Matthew said he just wanted her to stay home with them and have lots of time to write since she's so good at it. Except that staying home and taking care of two small kids—one boy and one girl—didn't leave her with that much time for writing. But the boy is in preschool now, and she's sending her daughter next year, so maybe she can start writing more again. She does freelance work for clients, and her own creative projects.

And then she has her freelance "diversity column" in her local newspaper. She's the only non-white person who had ever been published in the suburban paper, so they asked her if she could write once a week about her life as a non-white person, and about the lives of other non-white people. The white people of Eden Prairie love to read her column, except a few who write hate letters.

She and Matthew have a good marriage, I think. He liked her more at first, I could tell. For her birthday the first year they were together, he built her a massage table and learned shiatsu. She's crazy about him now too.

I meet Savi in Dinkytown for coffee one day, and her son and daughter play with toy cars in a corner while we talk. I give her a full update, about looking for a "real job," about *Shoedog* and my other story ideas, and about Naveed.

I also tell her about Melinda. After all of her experience, Melinda has concluded that foreign men are a way to experience the world, but *we are not supposed to marry them*.

Even though Savi hardly ever says a negative word about anybody, she's incensed that Melinda would say such a thing. She even looks like she wants to slap me for having such an obnoxious—she even uses the word "racist"—friend.

"She doesn't have your best interest at heart," Savi says, "if she even has a heart."

I look down and take a second to think about how I'm going to change the subject to avoid fighting with Savi when she's just being a good friend. Because this last statement of hers has brought out the Melinda loyalist in me. You can call her a racist, neo-colonialist, orientalist, or just an obnoxious bitch. But never say she doesn't have a heart.

Positive Feedback

Shoedog

The closest Megan ever felt to Carl was when she was just big enough to go with him to the driving range. He would buy a bucket of balls and she would watch him hit each one so far that it went out of sight before falling to the ground. If Megan got bored, Carl would buy her a grape soda and a frozen Marathon bar and she would knock back and forth on a creaking glider bench on the clubhouse porch. Finally, the summer after third grade,

Megan was big enough to try golfing
herself. Most of her swings missed the
ball, the club whiffing air. Or land-
ing with a big chop too early, sending
grass and dirt into the air. Carl said
she could improve if she tried. He
stood behind her, his arms around her
arms, his hands adjusting her hands.
He wasn't the cuddly type of dad, but
she felt secure like this with his arms
around her, guiding her swing.

"Okay Valerie, I didn't interrupt," says Melinda. "I liked
that. It was really sad. Do you want any feedback?"

I shrug.

"What if you added just one of your sisters? Then you
write about how Courtney became the youth champion at
your dad's favorite golf course and got all his attention for
it. Then it could be even sadder."

"Thanks. But no. No sister stuff."

"Okay. So, anyway, what about the shoes? I thought this
was going to be about selling shoes at Dayton's…er, Taghato's.
Are you going to describe all those beautiful shoes, like the
Robert Clergeries and the Stuart Weitzmans?"

"It's not really just about the shoes," I say. "But I'm getting
there."

Chantilly Lace

I'm always running late these days. Naveed and I are so in love we're on fire. He has even said that to me in Persian—*Asheket-am*—I think it means, "I'm on fire."

We're late for everything, even my sister's wedding, and I'm a bridesmaid. Laura and Ty's wedding is the first big family event Naveed attends, and I prep him to meet everybody. I even convince him to shave off the mustache, but I can't stop him before he splashes on *Bijan!* aftershave lotion, which burns my face when we make out before we leave. My red face will be forever evident in the wedding photos.

But everybody looks happy for this daytime wedding; even my mom has rallied for this. Maybe she doesn't look ecstatic, but she's managed a smile that at least looks pulled together, next to my dad's smitten smile at Wanda. My dad seems proud to walk Laura down the aisle, while Wanda looks on with her smarmy cat face.

And Naveed is smiling brighter than I've seen, although it could just be that his irresistible dimples stand out more now that the big mustache is gone. He looks so beautiful. And yet I'm getting a migraine headache, triggered by the *Bijan!* fragrance.

It's a perfect wedding at the church we went to when we were growing up. After Laura and Ty have said their vows, they light a single candle with two smaller candles and then they leave all three lit, to symbolize that they're both still individuals as well as a united couple. The pastor says it's to remind them that they don't get extinguished when they form a bond as a married couple. I look at Laura and she's following the script that she rehearsed yesterday. Even though I think the candle thing is really corny, I notice that in the candlelight with her lace dress and blonde hair swept up, she looks like supermodel Kim Alexis in the Chantilly Lace perfume ads from the 1980s. When it's over, we step out of the dark sanctuary and into the sunny spring day, and my migraine throbs.

Wanda keeps my dad's attention at the reception and he doesn't react much to the presence of Naveed. I've brought lots of guys around over the years, so maybe he thinks this is just another casual date. Not that he ever imagined his children would date someone who wasn't a European-American. But he is surprisingly normal about it, and then Wanda takes his arm and leads him to the cash bar as soon as the men have said five words.

At Naveed's house after the wedding, his neighbor, Milad Zand, and Milad's wife, Yasmin Noury, are outside with their daughters. Naveed asks Milad to take pictures of us because it's the first time we've dressed up together. I'm still in my bridesmaid dress, which after all those measurements still doesn't fit my chest or hips right, but Yasmin comes close enough to tell me she loves my dress.

Yasmin's youngest daughter trails directly behind her, her eyes stuck to me as she peeks out from behind her mother. She says, "My name is Parvaneh. It means *butterfly*. What's your name?"

"I'm Valerie," I tell her, squatting down to be closer to her height. "It means *strong*."

"Then you look like a strong princess," she says bashfully before she runs back to her older sister.

I don't feel strong with my head throbbing like this, but I run after her to give her my wrist corsage. Parvaneh wraps the elastic twice around her wrist and curtsies for me.

Naveed is in a black suit, green shirt, and purple tie. We pose next to a fire hydrant in his front yard. In later years I will say those photos look *so 90s,* and I will remember both my migraine and that precious butterfly child curtsying to me. After we come inside, Naveed showers off the aftershave for me and disposes of the whole *Bijan!* fragrance collection in the garbage can outside.

But not soon enough. While he's in the shower I have to come into the bathroom and throw up right there in front of him because it's the only bathroom in the house except for downstairs in the renters' apartment. *How humiliating and disgusting,* I think. But Naveed quickly turns off the water and dries himself off so he can tend to me. He gives me Tylenol and massages my temples and my neck until the headache subsides. We stay in for the night, with nothing to do but talk and be close.

"Is it just a coincidence that Milad Zand across the street is Iranian too?" I ask.

"Nope," he says. He and Milad were best friends when they bought the houses for cheap at auction right after college. They had a falling out and didn't talk—except when they played soccer or basketball with all of their mutual buddies—until the day Milad asked Naveed to help unload materials off the truck for a gazebo in his backyard. Now they're in a period of détente. Naveed asking Milad to take our photo was another building block toward a potential peace.

"What was it about?" I ask.

"Nothing that should have been anything," he says. "We're good now, so that's all that matters."

We talk about a hundred other things as he massages away my headache and cooks me a Persian soup. By the time we're ready to sleep, I confess to Naveed that I wasn't so sure I liked him at first, but that I didn't think it was that way for Laura and Ty either.

Ty liked Laura first. I'm happy about this, how this guy liked my sister so much and how he cooks for her. And why wouldn't any man cater to a woman who looks like Kim Alexis? Some of his smitten generosity extends to the rest of the family. He even had us all over to his house once for wild boar and stuffed mushrooms—and pear liqueur—and some card game that I didn't know how to play. Of course Laura fell in love with him eventually.

"How did you get me to become so crazy about you?" I ask Naveed.

"I pouffed magic dust on you," he says. "It was all I had." The wedding, despite the migraine, has made me feel romantic. Although it's maybe premature, I imagine myself up at the altar in a lace bridal dress, kissing the groom. Naveed and I are entwined for the rest of the night.

Goodbye Kurt

When I was in seventh grade, I couldn't sit still. Previously an introverted kid who just liked to read and obeyed the teacher, I became the class clown. After months of disrupting class, I was diagnosed as "EBD"—Emotionally and Behaviorally Disturbed.

After years of internalizing all of my feelings, it was as if I had suddenly turned myself inside out. This "externalizing disorder" got me a lot more attention than I'd ever gotten before, but eventually I learned that internalizing disorders are much more acceptable and I went back to holding every-thing in.

That was the 80s. Nowadays, anybody would just give me some Ritalin. But nobody took me to a drug-prescribing psychiatrist (just a couple of counselors). I don't like pills anyway. Smoking pot seemed to even me out fine.

I can't get the pot anymore though because Naveed and I agreed that we don't see anybody else now, and that includes Kurt who always gives it to me. Too bad, because I love smoking pot. I like the way it smells and tastes, and how it makes everything seem funny. Except for all the sadness in the world, but I don't think about all of that when I'm high.

I guess I've been meaning to quit anyway because I don't want to smoke pot for my whole life. Sometimes I get chest pains when I smoke it. And also, Melinda says we have to be careful because we could get smoker's wrinkles—especially around the mouth from all the toking.

But I don't really like being *told* that I have to quit, or that I can't see Kurt anymore.

I've remained friends with him, and not just for the ganja, throughout my last three or four relationships. There's noth-ing else there anymore; it's not like Kurt and I are going to get high together and start doing it. Maybe we'd get high and get the munchies together and go to Figlio's in Uptown for pizza and pasta. Maybe I still like seeing his deep blue eyes, and his big bicep through the rip in his Coca-Cola shirt. But that's about it.

Since we broke up, we've cared about each other more than we did in the five and a half years we were together in high school and college. Back then, we fought all the time. I used to lose my patience with him and hit him, sometimes in the car when he was driving. I would hit him so hard he would have to put down the bong to steer.

Breaking up with him was hard, but once he found his new girlfriend, Chantal, I knew we weren't getting back together. I guess he sort of signaled that to me when he brought Chantal to Dayton's Women's Shoes to meet me. She was an eighteen-year-old girl-woman with a toddler on one hip. I tried to baby-talk the little girl, and she kicked me with her tiny white sandal.

Chantal had put up with our palling around for a while, but she's run out of patience with that, plus with Kurt's habit of smoking and selling pot and getting arrested. She's sort of a "personal responsibility" Republican type of single mother, and Kurt got an ultimatum to either grow up or get out. I don't think he told her the truth the last time we hung out, but he didn't feel good about that either.

So the timing, at least, is right. Naveed's jealousy and Chantal's ultimatum coincide to mean that Kurt and I won't be driving around getting stoned and going out for vindaloo and naan at Tandoori India together anymore.

I'm also the jealous type. Naveed and I both watch for each other to check out another person for too long and then call each other on it every time. One time it even happened at a traffic intersection. The woman turning in front of us was really pretty.

One night we went to a party at Laura and Ty's and I was jealous because Naveed engaged in a conversation with a beautiful woman about how their grandmothers removed bitterness from cucumbers. Her grandmother was Russian and cut the tips off first, then rubbed them in a circular motion against the main part of the cucumber. This description seemed dangerously sensual and I went on guard. Naveed replied with his grandmother's similar cucumber method, which seemed equally superstitious. I inserted that my Norwegian grandma soaked the slices in vinegar for fifteen minutes, and that it actually worked.

Naveed and the woman looked at me blankly and went back to talking about their grandmothers' various forms of kitchen magic. I was annoyed he found this pretty woman so interesting and also certain my grandma's method was the only one with any scientific merit. And if they were *really* talking about cucumbers, they would have agreed. I told him so on the way home—the whole way home.

I'm also jealous because Naveed rents out a separate apartment in his basement to two young women, and both are pretty. He says he's had many renters in the basement, and hadn't noticed that the current ones were anything to look at. Uh huh.

So we're both the same. I don't like anything that seems like flirting, and he doesn't like me having ex-boyfriend friends. Or smoking pot. "It is illegal," he reminds me, "so it's not like I'm just making up rules all by myself for no reason. You shouldn't be doing it anyway."

I nod and wave, as if to say *yeah, yeah.*

"You could be anything you want to be if you get a little more serious," he says. "You're smart. You could go to law school, or start a business. We could do something together. But if you would rather be a party girl for a while longer, let me know now. I need to know now."

I guffaw at "party girl." I have never been a party girl. I'm perfectly happy getting high all by myself at home. I hardly drink. I don't even like parties.

Law school sounds dreadful, but maybe the idea of starting a business isn't bad. I agree not to see Kurt again, not for any reason, and not to smoke pot or use any other drugs. I haven't used other drugs for a long time anyway. Kurt and I snorted a lot of cocaine one summer, but quit because we hated the come-down. Plus, someone Kurt knew died from just one line of coke because he had a previously unknown heart defect. That made me give it up until I snorted some with Quentin a couple of times in West Palm Beach.

Still, I make it clear to Naveed that Kurt has been my friend for more years than he was my boyfriend, and that I'm only ending the friendship for his sake.

Then I ask, "Don't you ever talk to any of your ex-girl-friends?" He says no, never. "But what about the one you told me you were almost engaged to?" I ask.

"Sure, I run into her, but she is so happily married now and I respect that."

"But you care," I goad. "Are you sure you don't still love her?"

"I love you," Naveed says, for the first time.

I'm sorry that the first time he says this to me is in response to my insecurity. But he repeats, "I love you. And I wonder why it's always so damn hard for you to believe that you are loved."

I say, "I love you" back to him. Because it's true. I love him most.

So, here is this guy, who is a law-abiding and handsome engineer. Who is not a dope-selling failure, like Kurt. Who doesn't seem to be commitment phobic, like Quentin. Who loves me—dope-smoking, emotionally and behaviorally disturbed, sloppy me. It's hard to believe, but I have to try.

He recently asked me if I knew something horrifying. My last name, *Kjos*, (pronounced nothing like how it looks, but like *choce*) is the word for "fart" in Persian. Not just any fart, but a really smelly one.

I'm horrified because I worked at Dinky Kebab for two years and said my last name all the time. I'm mad at Kaveh and Jamsheed for not telling me. At least Niloofar could have said something, like when she told me I had lipstick on my teeth. She could have just whispered: *Don't tell people your last name—it's embarrassing.*

It's been hard enough to have this last name which sounds nothing like how it looks my whole life. But now this!

I have to ask myself, would I date someone whose last name was Smellyfart? Something must be wrong with Naveed if he loves me. When will I find out what it is?

Wrinkle

Mom limps over to the stove to put green beans in a pot, a big frozen rectangle of them from the Green Giant box.

I may think that the world revolves around me, but my mom does not. She's asked me to come to her little house for dinner. For a moment I imagine she'll want to hear all about what I have been up to. My new temp job in the fraud department at St. Paul Companies Insurance, for example. I had to get something, even though I'm still trying for a communications position. My bosses are detectives who clandestinely shoot photos of disability clients riding their ATVs and chopping wood for their fire-pit leisure time.

Maybe she'll ask me about my deepening relationship with Naveed. Or maybe she'll want to know if I've talked to my dad lately so we can gossip about Wanda. But Eugenia Randolph—she's gone back to her maiden name, and I sometimes now think about changing to Randolph too—is not in the mental state these days to mother her girls. She's got her own train wreck going on, I can see. And not just because of her knee.

Since the divorce, she's been serious with several men. Her prematurely white hair that she refuses to dye has not turned them away, perhaps because her face still looks so young.

There have been, in the past couple of years, for example:

- scuba-diving Sam
- some creep with a nice Porsche
- a Jewish poet who was 'too sensitive'
- Bruce, male nurse
- my internship boss, the Romani human rights guy

How I regret letting her meet that last one, because it's hard to work with him now. She didn't give him a second date, and he kept asking me about her, and I finally sort of quit working for him.

If there was ever any doubt, I know where I get it from if I'm too focused on men instead of getting my own act together. Mom could just put more enthusiasm into her job or one of her many interests and friends. But no. Bruce breaking up with her has undone her.

But actually, tonight, she seems okay. Her wheels are back on. And this is why I wonder what new man is in her life. Because I know that neither she nor I know how to put our wheels back on ourselves.

It turns out that someone else is homing in on her in her time of need. Someone has helped her with her wheels. Mom puts me on salad duty while she mashes potatoes and tells me about Charlie.

Charlie is an older man, she says. Mom is forty-six. I'm thinking "older" means fifty-five or so.

"He helped me remove all that 1960s metallic wallpaper in the dining room," she says. "And those mirrors that covered that whole wall! Remember those mirrors? They're gone!"

I peek into the dining room. It looks nice, walls smooth and painted.

He's done some flooring work too, I see. And he's advising Mom on what to do about the odd little stage in her tiny living room. "He thinks maybe it was a piano stage," Mom says. "He wants to take it out so the whole floor in there will be even."

"He sounds great," I say. "You do need a lot of work done around here. You can't do it all yourself." But something isn't right. I see she wants to talk to me about it.

"He wants to borrow six thousand dollars," she says. She knows this isn't a good sign. I don't *need* to tell her that.

"That's not a good sign," I say.

But this is my mom, Eugenia. She isn't stupid, but she's generous to the point that she's almost a vulnerable adult. The guy has done two house projects and wants to even out the wood floor in her living room. How can she turn him down when he needs the money?

I don't even ask why he needs it. But I do ask, "Why can't he borrow it from one of his kids?"

"He only has one daughter and she doesn't talk to him," she says.

"That's not a good sign," I say again. She says I sound like a broken record.

We sit down to eat Mom's pork chops and Green Giant vegetables and the rest of this well-balanced meal. This is the kind of meal my dad loved, I think to myself, Good Seasons Italian salad dressing and all. It's good to eat dinner at my mom's, to feel cared for by her, even though I'm lecturing her as if I'm the parent.

Finally, exasperated from having to be the mother in this conversation, I greedily turn the conversation from her new relationship to my own boyfriend.

"Haven't you learned from any of Melinda's experiences with Middle Eastern men?" Mom asks. I would be irked by this question, but frankly, I'm happy to have turned things back around to having Eugenia be the worried mother again.

I say, "Naveed is Iranian and Melinda hasn't dated any Iranians. Only Arabs, Frenchmen, Turks, Liberians, Spaniards…"

"Well, have you read *Not without My Daughter*? That's a true story, you know. Horrifying." If we ever marry, she says, we should have a signed agreement that he would not take the kids out of the country.

"I want to go to Iran," I say, "Maybe we should have a signed agreement that he *will* take me there."

"Now isn't a good time!" Mom says, not pausing before continuing the barrage of questions. "If you marry him, will he let you work?" she asks.

"His aunt runs the ancient family business making rosewater and other rose stuff," I say. "His sister is an entrepreneur. His female cousin in Chicago is a prominent cardiologist, and the one in Houston is a computer programmer for NASA."

"Well, that is surprising," Mom says.

"I know," I answer. "They're more successful than any women *we* know."

Will he let me *not work*, I wonder, as I perhaps could have *not worked* if I had married Quentin?

"Did his mother work?" my mom asks.

"Yes, she had her own sewing school."

I know Yasmin Noury and her husband have two daughters who go to a daycare center while they both go to work every day. I've seen this only because of my increasingly frequent sleepovers at Naveed's house, so I don't tell my mom about them. Yasmin is always dressed in a suit and carries a briefcase. I don't know what she does, but she sure looks serious about her career.

I could give her other examples of successful Iranian women, but Mom has given up. She's like the mother, Katharine Hepburn, in the *Guess Who's Coming to Dinner* movie when Sidney Poitier has to be an international doctor to be good enough for her daughter. The women in Naveed's Iranian family have to be rocket scientists to satisfy my mother, a pediatric nurse, but at least she is now satisfied.

"I always hoped you and Kurt would get married," she says. When I'd been with Quentin, she'd suggested that we get married too, but she doesn't mention him now, knowing that it was Quentin who broke up with me. I too had hoped that maybe I would get married to Quentin and that would be that. I'd have stayed home, volunteered for the Girl Scouts, and played tennis while a babysitter would come twice a week to watch our three children. Just like Mom did until I was twelve. Of course, she says all of that time with kids drove her to drink.

Mom went back to school, and work, at a time when the triangular orange signs that read "Women at Work" were losing their novelty because so many women had gone to work. The novelty never appealed to me. Why would you work if you don't have to? Unless you could write for money, but I've always been told it usually doesn't pay and most writers are poor so I shouldn't even consider it. That's why my major was mass communications instead of journalism. I heard it would provide more job opportunities, like Laura's PR job, but I could still possibly write. Except that in mass communications, I mostly learned how to write in bullet points—levels under levels of bullet points, from solid black to a hollow circle to thin introductory dashes.

Mom's hair is pulled back from her face and I can read that she seems to be thinking: *Well, time will tell.* I know she's thinking something like this because of the crevice between her two perfectly curved eyebrows. It's a sharp vertical wrinkle that in about ten years from now will be a wonderful candidate for Botox.

But we don't know about Botox and other miracle wrinkle fixes yet, and I'm getting the same vertical axe-in-the-head wrinkle now too, partly from all of the worrying I have to do about my vulnerable-adult mother. She just seems so desperate, so in need of being loved and cared for.

And if Charlie doesn't work out (and I'm sure Charlie isn't going to work out), she could be on the verge of starting to drink again. She already doesn't go to the Alcoholics Anonymous meetings anymore. I'm afraid for her.

So I have to turn the conversation back to her and tell her this.

"I'm worried that you need a man so much, even when it's not good for you. And I'm scared that if you have your heart broken again you might drink yourself to death."

There, I've said it.

"You're overdramatizing things again, but that's one thing I love about you. You're my most creative daughter. You have such a knack for details and drama," she tells me, as if this very realistic scenario is just my artistic fantasy. But she makes a promise not to get her heart broken and start drinking, and I trust her to keep it.

Aryans

My father isn't calling me back. This could simply be because he's seasonally unavailable due to golf. I let go of worry because frankly I'm too busy being in love. That and doing my temp job at the insurance company. (I'm thinking maybe I should have become an insurance detective—they just sit in cars for hours waiting to get that one "gotcha" photo of a supposedly disabled client outside dividing her hostas.) I don't keep calling my dad.

Finally he calls, and everything is normal. He says Ty, who has taken up golf and been hitting the course with my father, told him how Naveed is such a great guy. Mom and Dad have also somehow learned that Iranians are Caucasians, even when they're brownish like Naveed. This is somehow an important point, that they're the original Aryans, that the word "Iran" even means "Aryan." The pertinence of this is uncertain to me, but I'm trying not to be cynical about it.

Mainly, I'm just happy that my mom has stopped referencing *Not without My Daughter*. And that she seems happy to have something interesting to tell the bridge ladies about. Now, she's thinking of how that will be to add Persian to the family lineage if we get married and have children.

My two sisters and I have always known this list of what we are by heart: Scottish, Irish, English, German (or Prussian—whatever that is), French, Norwegian, and Cherokee Indian. We can say it so fast that it blurs together like Mary Poppins singing *Super-cali-fragilistic-expiali-docious.*

Like all white people who are a tiny bit Indian, we're supposedly related to Pocahontas. I didn't learn until college that Pocahontas was not a Cherokee Indian, so this is something I've tried to clear up with some older relatives, but they don't know. They just know "for certain" we really are related to her, and that's that.

It might be my own lack of a singular ethnic identity, but in Melinda-fashion I seem to be getting interested in all things Iranian since I've been seeing Naveed. I liked these ornate Persian things when I was working at Dinky Kebab, but now I'm starting to notice all the Persian carpet shops around town. Naveed doesn't even have a good Persian carpet—just a fake one made in China.

Savi teases that, before you know it, I'm going to be buying those Middle Eastern slipper shoes that curl up at the toe. She says she doesn't blame me for gravitating to shinier things, because my own white American family's culture is limited to drab department store goods, potluck picnics, and green Jell-O salad.

Of course I thought Savi had a lot of nerve to say that. She was probably just in a bad mood that day because, really, who doesn't like a potluck picnic? And I'm totally offended about the green Jello-O salad. My family has never once in my entire life made green Jell-O.

If she knew us at all, she'd know we always make the red.

Reveal

We've been looking through two old photo albums that sit on the corner table in the living room. I'm going to bring my album over and show Naveed my pictures too—not all the old boyfriend pictures, but the ones of me as a kid, the ones of me canoeing in the Boundary Waters, for example. I look strong in those. And tan.

Pictures of Naveed in the 70s show him as a different person, a skinny teen with a pointy face and an afro, whereas now he has round cheeks and a tiny bald spot that he takes pictures of so he can see if it's getting bigger.

He has his shirt off in one old photo and his ribcage bends over a big brown guitar. In another photo he's camping in the desert of southern Iran with his buddies, cooking a pathetic little bird over a small fire. "Is that a wild desert chicken?" I ask. He doesn't remember.

I flip past some shots of Naveed with the next-door neighbor, Milad Zand, seeing how they used to be so close. In one photo, Yasmin Noury serves Naveed tea from a silver tray. Then, Naveed points to several photos of his mom—some from the 70s, some more recent. Her name is Goli, pronounced like *Goal-ie*. Gol means rose (and also any flower, but especially rose). I guess Goli is like the name Rosie.

*That which we call a rose, by any other name would smell as sweet...*I automatically recite in my head, a result of having to memorize lots of Shakespeare in eighth grade.

In some of the photos, I can see Goli is in Minnesota. She's sitting on the ivory polyester satin couch we're sitting on right now. "So your mom has visited you here," I say, even though I have already surmised that by the things I've seen in the guest room, like the crocheted doily and brush and mirror set. There was a woman's winter coat too, hanging in the foyer closet. I hadn't been sure it wasn't a younger woman's, but I didn't think so.

"She was here for a long time," he says, "because she had two open-heart surgeries at the Mayo Clinic in Rochester." Then Naveed tells me a story about how she came all the way to the U.S. to have heart valves replaced because she thought American doctors were the best. She walked into her first appointment with the surgeon and almost fell over when the Nigerian man walked into the room. But she went back to him for the second surgery.

In the photo, her blouse is black and pine green. The low neckline reveals the scar, a pink track climbing up her golden olive flat chest. If I had my chest ripped open, I wouldn't even wear low-cut shirts, and I admire her for showing her scar as much as I'm relieved to know that she won't be prudishly judging me for some of my shirts.

I realize there aren't many photos of Naveed's dad, just one that must have been taken when Naveed was about five years old. He's sitting on his dad's lap, but instead of seat-belting him in with his arms like most parents would, his arms aren't even touching him.

"You look like you're going to fall off your dad's lap," I say. "That is your dad, right?"

"Yeah," he answers.

"Did he come too, when your mom had the surgery?" I ask.

"No, they don't...Hey, I've been thinking about telling you something very private," he says.

I put down the album. "What?" I ask, suddenly on guard. *Is now when I find out what is wrong with Naveed*, I wonder.

"They don't live together."

"They?" I ask, and then I remember that we were talking about his mom and I'd asked about his dad.

"My parents—they don't live together. But you're not going to tell anybody that, are you?" He whispers it, as if the neighbors, or the girls who rent out the basement, might hear it and be shocked.

My parents' divorce hasn't been any secret, so I don't understand what he means. "If they aren't living together, don't people know that already?" I ask. "Besides, who would I tell?"

"You tell Melinda everything. And you tell your mom a lot of things, I've noticed. And she tells everybody else everything you tell her."

I didn't realize Naveed had known my mom long enough to pick this up, but I can't say it's not an astute observation.

"It's not a big deal," I say, "to be divorced." But he says they aren't divorced. Then he shifts around a little and I don't know if he's going to say anything else about his dad.

Finally, he says, "I wasn't sure if I was going to tell you this, but my dad left us when I was eight. He took another wife, and my mom was too ashamed to stay with him."

"Oh," I say. And then I remember about Muslims and multiple wives—and wonder why I'd never wondered if his dad had more than one wife. "But that's pretty normal there, right?" I ask.

"No," he answers defensively. "Families like ours—modern families—didn't do that." He says it like it might be a black mark against him personally.

"But her friends—the neighbors too—they must have all known. Right? So why didn't she just get a divorce and move on?"

"His other wife lived in a different town. So my mom just told people her husband got throat cancer and died. That it was all very sudden. Only the family knew."

That was a long time ago. The second wife has since died, and his parents are still legally married but they don't see each other. I guess it would be odd for them to see each other now that the second wife is dead, since Goli tells people that he's dead. Of course, they could just do it like in the soap operas and have him come back, saying he was living somewhere else as another person due to amnesia.

Now, Naveed's brother takes care of their dad, which must be hard but he does it because the dad is suffering from some sort of paranoia. His brother has to make sure he takes his meds, and he's forgiven him for what happened so long ago. Naveed says he just doesn't consider him his father, and hasn't for a long time.

His dad just wasn't part of his life for long after he left. He'd even come to the U.S. for several years. It sounds weird, but this guy from a well-off family came all the way to the U.S.—to manage a shoe store.

A shoe store, I think. *He was a shoedog.* Are people who sell shoes always escaping something? Then he went back to Iran at around the time Naveed was coming here, like he was *trying* not to see his own son.

"So now you know," Naveed says. And he doesn't remind me again to not tell anybody, because he knows I'm going to tell my mom anyway.

Well, I don't think I'm going to tell her that Naveed's father died from throat cancer when it isn't true. No way. My mom is a nurse—she would want to know the medical details.

Charlie

Mom has lent Charlie some money. Not the full six thousand dollars he asked for, but enough to get him by. And she's bought herself a new car and given him her old one. He's removed more wallpaper too, and told her how much he loves her and wants to be a part of her family.

So, although I don't want to meet Charlie, I need to. Partly because I need to find out more about this con man. And partly because it's an obligation—the family is invited to dinner with him at my mom's.

He looks like Marlon Brando. Not the young Brando, of course, but the big fat Brando with the bad knees. Like the Marlon Brando who is about seventy years old. He limps over to hug me. I didn't grow up with a big hugger for a dad, and I don't need hugs from this older man, but I give him a chance. He has been good to my mom with all the handyman work, considering that he isn't in such good shape to be doing that kind of stuff.

As soon as we sit down at the table, Charlie tells us three girls, "Eugenia has told me that your father is not very warm. I want you all to know that *I* am a very warm person. I would be honored if you would let me be a father figure to you."

Naveed is here too, but it's just his second or third dinner at my mom's and he doesn't yet have a good understanding of the dynamics of these people I call my family. Courtney and I don't say anything. We're moving into neutral gear, slightly manipulated.

But, score one for Laura. She blurts out a deep and throaty laugh. "My father is very warm," she says, with a buzzsaw no-nonsense voice worthy of Katharine Hepburn. Ty nods his head in agreement. "He's a wonderful, very loving father and I don't need any other dad but him."

Ashamed, I think about how she defended our dad's character just like a good public relations manager—and a good oldest daughter—should. She woke me and Courtney from the trance Charlie was starting to put us under.

Even so, I have to smirk. Describing Neil as "very warm" is a stretch. But I guess it's all relative.

Viv

She's the most beautiful woman I have ever known, with teal blue eyes that match the teal leather interior of her lemon chiffon Cadillac. I'm elated each time someone tells me I look a little bit like her. Grandma Vivian Randolph goes out dancing a few times a week, and even though she's in her 70s and there are women there as young as forty-five, Grandma's fresh blonde bombshell looks and feminine shape get noticed. She has long affairs with eligible men who fall madly in love with her, but they usually end when she won't move in with them or won't quit dancing with other men.

When I was eighteen I visited Grandma Viv by myself and she had me dancing with some men about twenty years older than I was, much to my Uncle Andy's annoyance. Since, at eighteen, I still wasn't over my childhood crush on Uncle Andy, the motorcycle cop, I was secretly pleased at his reaction. I think I would still have a crush on Uncle Andy, but he doesn't talk to his family anymore. His new wife forbids him even to talk to Grandma Viv now, and nobody knows why except that maybe his wife is just a jealous bitch.

Boxes

I'm snooping again, while Naveed is on another one of his morning errands to Byerly's for orange juice and pastries. I think of myself as the writer, but now I have evidence that Naveed can write too. I found a paper he wrote in a class, and finally it's something that I can read, something in English for my searching eyes. It's about the town where he grew up, and how sad he is that he hasn't been back there. It's about how he worries that if he does go back it will have changed so much under the Revolution's regime that it will destroy all the good memories he has.

The key turns and the door is opening. Byerly's grocery bags make a rustling noise, and I quickly stash the composition back into a folder and come out to help get our breakfast ready.

Inspired at how even a parking ramp engineer can write something touching and meaningful, I want to spend the rest of the day by myself, writing in my own room at my apartment. We eat and read the newspaper, and then I tell Naveed that I need a day to myself, at home. He's started to think of his home as my home, as have I, and to think of us being together as a given on any weekend day. It takes him a minute to understand. But, he says, his buddies are planning to meet for basketball and he could go play with them.

I decide to spend the rest of my day working on *Shoedog*, deepening the meaning of the story that is turning into a short novel. But my plan doesn't turn out that way.

When I get home, I just want to go straight to my room. I know that if I start talking to Melinda, who is there with cardboard boxes for some reason, I won't get around to writing anything today. But it's hard not to be pulled into a conversation with your roommate when she's blocking the hallway to your bedroom with moving boxes. You just have to wonder what those are for.

"I just accepted a job offer in New Mexico!" she screams. "I have to get packed—can you help? I'm moving there in four days!"

I'm very confused. I don't know what to say. How can she be packing up and moving? We live here together. We have a lease.

"Huh?" I ask. She keeps throwing things in the boxes while she tells me about the job and how the offer is only on the table for an immediate start date.

I can't afford to live alone, and she hasn't mentioned how she will pay for her half of the rent through the end of our lease, so my first questions are—she believes—a little selfish.

I guess she expected me to give her a big hug and say, *Congratulations! Many successes to you. Let me know when you've arrived safely.*

But I don't say that. I get mad because Melinda has called the rental office before telling me about this, and already gotten permission for us to break our lease. I feel like our lease is also an agreement between us, to each be responsible for half the rent until the lease is up. She hasn't felt the need to ask my permission to break our covenant, or even to act like she realizes this puts me in a bind.

Melinda gets mad because my first reaction to her good news is not happy, is not supportive. No, she says, she obviously does not have the time to find someone to sublease her half of the apartment, vacancy available immediately. She says I should do that.

And didn't I hear her? Didn't I see her, unlike me, job hunting all the time? And Roger had already been in New Mexico—wasn't it obvious that she was trying to get there, get with him? Don't I think, too, that it's time for us to get real jobs, make some money, and stop just sniffing other people's cake when we could be eating our own? Isn't it time to make our own buttercream?

I don't answer the barrage of questions. Each one of them stings and I know I'm going to cry.

She stares into my green eyes with her same-green eyes and holds fast until I say, "What am I supposed to do? Move in with Mrs. Finklestein?"

Before she can tell me to consider it, I trundle off to my unmade bed and stare at the popcorn ceiling through my tears, looking for answers.

After an hour or so of quiet crying and thinking, I realize that an unexpected giddiness has set in. I'm not giddy for Melinda though. I'm giddy for me. Even though I don't know what I will do, I wonder if maybe this is my window of opportunity, my time to push myself from Melinda's nest, to possibly even end this adolescent-formed alliance.

After all, I'm sick of Melinda. For one thing, she's an imperialist of identities. Even though she has enough style, personality, and talent of her own, she has to copy other people too. This is why she copies the cuisines and décor of her boyfriends, even though she already has her own gilded gold Catholic thing going on. This is why she also now marbles silk fabric and sews pillows trimmed with tassels and beads, like I do. Nothing can be just uniquely mine.

Our apartment is full of Melinda's décor, her food, her bookcase full of cookbooks, her music, her Post-it notes. Our apartment is full of *her*, and sometimes it feels oppressive. Like I am nothing, nothing but a subject in the Empire of Melinda.

Of course she's right—I should be happy for her, if I'm a real friend. We have to grow up, and get some confidence and be successful. I just wanted more advance notice that she was actually doing it. I'm confused—excited at one moment about making a break from Melinda and the residue of my messed-up teenage years. The next moment, I'm afraid—not just about the rent, but about losing her.

I've been attached to Melinda for two-thirds of my life. So I have to ask myself:

- Who am I without her?
- What will I do?
- Who will I talk to about everything?
- Will she succeed, and...will I fail?

Adult Lives

The next day, Melinda grudgingly tells me she talked her new employer into paying her half of two months of rent. It won't get us through the lease, but it should give me time to figure out what to do.

As she tells me, she's throwing the last of the kitchen equipment into a box. She breaks off a long section of paper towels from the roll, and wraps up her Pottery Barn tea cups that I like so much. They're yellow, with a sun and palm trees and a monkey. They remind me of our camping trip to Jamaica.

She's vexed about having to ask this of the people who are giving her this new life in New Mexico, and she lets me know how grateful I should be that she asked. I'm vexed too, about her leaving me so suddenly, and not even thinking twice, not even seeming sad.

"This is how it's supposed to be. We get adult lives," she says. No doubt she told her mother that I was giving her trouble, and her mother counseled her to say all this. "I expected more support from you. This is hard for me. I have a lot of shit to pack and a lot of loose ends to tie up."

"Fine," I say. "What do you want me to help you do?"

Melinda asks me to take her Discover bill to Sears, where it's due tomorrow, and can be paid in person.

But I cannot even do this one little thing right. I pay it a day later, which puts Melinda over the edge. It seems like she hates me now. She's ready to give me up for good.

The morning before the day when she moves away forever, I ask Melinda if I can help her move tomorrow, imagining some rented or borrowed truck will come and we'll fill it up. I think maybe I will even ask Naveed to help, now that I have such a handy boyfriend and don't have to ask Savi's husband, Matthew, for help anymore.

But she says, "It isn't necessary. The company is paying movers."

I hadn't thought of that before. "Paid movers," I say. "Wow." We've moved almost every year since 1987 and never have we so much as rented a U-haul, even if we had to take fifteen carloads and ask Matthew and Kurt for help lifting furniture.

We talk a little bit, and for the first time I ask her about the job, her plans with Roger, and where they're going to live. I explain to her that I always imagined that we would grow up and start our adult lives at the exact same time.

We make up a little bit, and say we'll meet at our apartment after my work day. I'll make dinner, and then we'll get ready together and go to the New French Bar for drinks to celebrate her new job, her big adventure.

I don't know how I'll pay for it, but for some dumbass reason I say, "It will be my treat."

I get out of my temp job early so I can make a worthy dinner for us before we go to the bar. I'll have to work faster on filing those fraud cases because they're piling up. I got a company email account today, and access to the World Wide Web a few days ago. The Web is still just a blue or black screen and text, but I can already find myself wasting a lot of time on it, reading the AP newswires and discussion boards like recipes.group.

I print some recipes from this amazing new World Wide Web and then leave work to go to the store for ingredients. I make calamari with olives, veal scaloppini, and fresh pasta with artichoke sauce. She's late, so I start getting dressed up, putting on a gauzy blue skirt and a lavender cotton shirt, tied at the waist.

But Melinda doesn't come home, and I eat the calamari (rubbery, fishy), the veal (tough), and the pasta (not bad!) alone. I write.

I watch *Cheers* (with no pot to smoke to make it very funny), and very late Melinda calls me from a payphone. She's at the New French Bar, but she's already drunk and she says she's sorry but tonight just isn't going to work out. At one-thirty in the morning I hear Melinda and Roger come in and have drunken sex in her room.

Except that it isn't Roger. Remember? It can't be Roger because Roger is already in New Mexico.

The next morning, Melinda is still sleeping when I leave for work, but I'm in the kitchen making tea when Melinda's ex-boyfriend, Omar, comes out of her room and goes into the bathroom with a sheet wrapped around his lower half.

When I come home from work, the apartment is a different place. It's just my stuff now, and a box with some of Melinda's books and beads that she must have thought I might want. And one scruffy antique Queen Anne chair she must have decided not to take with her because the old yellow upholstery is dirty. Or maybe Queen Anne doesn't fit in very well with the adobe homes of Santa Fe.

There is nothing on the walls, no cookbooks, no shiny gold or ethnic décor. For the first time since the day we first looked at the apartment, I notice that the walls are white. The living room and kitchen look plain and sad. There's just my scratchy red loveseat that I've borrowed from Savi, my marbled silk pillows, and my T.V. and VCR, looking bereft outside of Melinda's antique armoire that had held them in such style and grace before.

Of course, the disaster I call my bedroom is untouched. Everything else bears the signs that someone got out fast and with determination.

There's no goodbye note, not even a Post-it.

I pick up the phone, to call whom I don't know because I don't really want to talk to anybody. There's no dial tone. Oh yeah. Melinda wanted to close the account because it was in her name. After my tardy drop-off of her Discover Bill, she was not about to trust me with her good credit again (her mother's counseling, no doubt).

Like a bachelor, I turn on the T.V., smoke the potent resins that line my empty pot pipe, and eat the leftover pasta and a few bites of tough veal. I jump when somebody knocks at my door, and quickly stash my pot pipe, spray some Windex in the air, and go to answer it.

It's the superintendent. He sniffs at the air as soon as I open the door. "I got a call from one of your neighbors who thought she smelled something burning over here. Are you smoking marijuana?"

"Not me," I say, wide-eyed and innocent. "Oh my gosh, no way. I wonder if it's somebody else. Or if it could be my dinner—I burned it a little."

I see Mrs. Finklestein's door opening just an inch across the hall and imagine her standing there listening. Maybe she's the one who called, which is odd because we've smoked pot in here a hundred times. The super just nods and turns to leave. Apparently, there's no fooling him when it comes to the scent of pot resins.

"It's a good thing you're only on a two-month extension," he says. "Because if you weren't moving out soon enough, I would probably kick you out."

Mrs. Finklestein's door moves slightly, and then closes silently.

I gulp and deny my smoking once more and then say good-night before closing my door. The chain slides into place. My eyes sting with tears, but I let it go. Moving out soon, indeed. I'm not going to cry over Mrs. Finklestein narking on me.

Then I go to the hall, to the box of junk Melinda has left me, and I save a couple of books (What kind of person would leave behind a first edition hardcover copy of *The Color Purple*?) and a small box of beads. The rest of Melinda's detritus goes to the dumpster.

When I come upstairs to the apartment, my door is buzzing, and I wonder if it's the super again, but he would just knock instead of buzzing from downstairs. It must be Naveed. I want to be alone, but he'd have seen my car and known I was home. *Argh,* why didn't I park underground? I buzz him in.

"I tried calling, but your phone is disconnected," he says, then looks around. "Wow, she really cleared things out."

I just nod and go to the bathroom, and see how stoned I look. I drink some water from the faucet, and put scented lotion on my arms. I come out, reluctantly.

"It smells in here. Have you been using drugs? Why are your eyes red?" He looks right into my eyes and I just squint back.

"No," I lie, "I'm not using drugs." Anyway, it was just the pot resins in the pipe—who knew they would smell so strong.

"It's probably the smell of the Italian food I just reheated. And my eyes are red because I'm sad that my best friend moved. If you were more sensitive, you might guess that I've been crying."

As soon as I say this, my voice cracks, and it becomes true. I sit down on Melinda's scruffy yellow chair and bawl.

Naveed's brow furrows with worry. He's perhaps not fooled, but sorry anyway. He kneels, head against my thighs, arms around my hips, and holds me up from my center of gravity.

PART II

Visitor

"You don't sound very enthusiastic," I say, when Naveed asks me if I just want to move in with him when the two months of Melinda's rent money are exhausted.

"I want you to live with me," he says, "but maybe we wouldn't do it yet if you had another option."

What hangs in the air is that I haven't been looking at other options. There's nobody else I want to live with, I don't want to put out fliers looking for a roommate, and I can't afford to live by myself. Maybe if I would try harder to get a communications job, the reason I went to college. It's just hard.

"You can take your time deciding what you want to do," he says. "Or we can just make the decision now."

I don't play hard to get, since the offer doesn't seem that firm. It doesn't seem like he's going to insist, or beg me to move in with him.

"Okay, I'll move in," I say. It's not going to be a major move—a lot of my stuff is already at his place and there's not much in the apartment.

"Before you commit though…," he says. "I have something to tell you."

I'm pretty sure now is when I'm going to find out what's wrong with him, why I've been lucky enough to have a decent, contributing citizen be willing to be in a committed relationship with me. Like, maybe he doesn't want kids. Or maybe he already has some.

"My mother is coming for a visit," he says. "My sister, Firoozeh, bought her plane ticket yesterday."

"Oh, great, it will be nice to meet her." I say. "How long will she be staying?"

I know of those extended families that used to come to the Dinky Kebab, but Naveed said the word "visit," so I'm sure it won't be like those families that have parents living with them. I mean, he didn't say she's coming for a heart surgery this time, so it should be short.

"At least two months," he says.

"Oh, wow," I say. I've never actually heard of a visit lasting two months, except a study abroad trip, or a few of the rich kids in Wayzata who went to camp out east for most of their summer.

"At least two months? And what's the max?" I ask.

"I don't know," he says.

I don't understand that answer and so I probe. "How can you not know how long she will be staying?" Once I realize he means at least two months, right here, in this house, the question reverberates in my mind in many ways: How Can You Not Know How Long? *Howcanyounotknowhowlong?* HOW CAN YOU NOT KNOW HOW LONG?

"Because," he says, a little impatiently, "that's not a question that I can just ask. It's considered rude." He says this, I think, in a tone that seems to insinuate that I'm rude to ask.

"Well, it's not a rude question here," I respond. "It's just normal to want to know, to want to plan."

To want to throw up, I add, but only in my own head.

Then I think of the obvious—her plane ticket. "Won't her airplane ticket be reserved for the return flight?" I ask. "We can just look at it, or ask your sister."

"I don't know. I could ask about the return flight if you really need to know," he says. "But it doesn't matter. The dates can be changed anyway."

I repeat his words, "The dates can be changed." Then I add, "I've never heard of such a thing." My plane tickets have always been firm on arrival and departure, as far as I knew.

"Are you going to be okay with that?" he asks. "She's my mom, you know. I'm going to let her stay as long as she wants."

This last statement eclipses me by what he doesn't say, but which I think he really means: *because this is my house*. But I tell myself not to complain. After all, if it hadn't been for his mother, Naveed would not have had to go to the post office that icy March day when I crashed into him.

I think back to that package he had to mail to her, and think, *She's part of my fate*. If not for her, he would have been just another customer at the Dinky Kebab. And, of course, I did not date my customers.

Swimming

Savi and I are at my apartment. Finally, she comes here—she wouldn't come when Melinda lived here since she can't stand her. I'm showing her how to marble fabric and paper, and she's amazed at the strangeness of the process. After an alum mordant is applied to the fabric and dries, I put some seaweed powder in a blender with water and whirl.

The seaweed powder, called *carrageenan*, is the same ingredient that plumps up commercial ice cream. I pour the resulting grayish slime into two plastic tubs, one for each of us. We drop colors of paint from plastic squeeze bottles. The colors swim across the surface of the slime

It's my first time marbling fabric without being high, but I feel high because Savi is saying things that stoned people would say, even though she does not get stoned. She tries to make life into literature, analyzing everything for symbolism and metaphor.

She squints her brown eyes, pushes her black hair back, and says, "So you are done with this wealthy farm boy turned stockbroker, *the classic American.* Along comes Naveed, the dark foreigner, *the forbidden fruit,*" She says this in a whisper, as she drags a comb across the paints, pulling them into swirls.

"Naveed isn't the forbidden fruit!" I swear. "Do you think you were the forbidden fruit for Matthew? Naveed isn't some exotic toy for me, you know. He's an American citizen who wears a dorky little name badge to his boring job. He's an engineer, like my dad."

I almost talk myself out of being in love with him with this defense. Forbidden fruit sounded better.

"Maybe he symbolizes your father."

I stop what I'm doing, which is to dance a stylus through the swirls to make a pattern that looks like a hundred whirling dervishes. "No. He symbolizes nothing. But he's stable, and he's a good guy. And I really, really like him."

"But…" she says.

"But what?" I ask.

"But you said you needed my advice about something."

"Oh. Right. The 'but' is that his mother is coming from Iran, and I don't know for how long. I've never done very well with boyfriends' mothers," I say. "I used to have to go to Kurt's hockey games with his mom sometimes. Men's moms make me nervous. And I usually don't think they like me."

She draws in a quick breath. "Me neither," she says. "I don't like to spend too much time with Matthew's mom. She's never gotten used to Matthew marrying a person from another culture."

I've met Matthew's mom. I say, "I don't know if she would have ever gotten used to Matthew being with any woman from any culture." His mother adores Matthew. She's critical of Savi, who in turn is not impressed by her, or by the obligatory vacations at the family cabin on Fish Trap Lake.

The only time Savi likes to go to the lake is when Matthew's parents aren't there. Quentin and I went up with them once late last summer right after we'd started going out. We spent a day with Matthew cruising us around the lake on his rainbow-striped catamaran and swimming out in the middle of the lake. It wouldn't have been the same with parents hanging around.

She nods. "I know. And you and I both have issues with our own mothers already. I find it's just easier to be the least amount involved possible with mothers-in-law...or future mothers-in-law."

Savi seems suddenly not so sure I should be moving in with Naveed now that his mother is coming. I have to remind her that she's actually sounding a lot like Melinda sounded when I first told her about Naveed. Since Savi can't stand Melinda, this turns her back around to supporting the relationship, even hoping we get married.

"Well, we aren't engaged yet," I say. "But we've talked about it. I'm pretty sure I would marry him."

"I see," says Savi, the English literature major and the best writer I know. "So he's the right guy. But there is *conflict*."

Mrs. Finklestein sits out by the swimming pool with a big hat and sunglasses and talks to anyone who will talk with her. Except for me. She hasn't talked to me since the night she reported me to the building superintendent. It's probably my last swim at Joppa Lane Apartments, since I'm moving out in a few days.

The sign on the deep end says "NO DIVING" in big stenciled spray paint letters, but I know this is deep enough for a shallow dive. So I do it—hands together forming an arrow out in front of me, I take a deep breath and cut a wide angle through the water. It gives way and opens to let me though deeper and deeper until I touch bottom. With my eyes open under water, I feel it, the painted grainy-textured concrete.

A memory from long ago brings me up to the surface for a breath, so I can swim underwater some more and think about it. Laura learned to dive down and touch the bottom of the swimming pool, in the deep end, at our swim club one year. By the middle of the next year, I still couldn't make it to the bottom without getting scared about running out of breath and high-tailing it back to the surface.

It wasn't so much that I wanted to touch the bottom of the deep end, but I just wanted to be able to tell my mom that I could do it like Laura. So one day I just said I'd done it, even though I hadn't. She didn't seem convinced. I'd wasted my lie.

Later that summer, I finally did touch the bottom. Since I'd already told my mom I'd done it, I couldn't go and brag to her about really doing it this time. There isn't really any point to touching the bottom of the pool anyway. It's just one of those things kids who belong to swim clubs do, a casual rite of passage.

I take another quick breath and then feel my way now with both hands, turning around and going to the deepest side of the pool. I have breath to spare, but not much. Down there at the bottom of the swimming pool at Joppa Lane remembering this moment from my childhood, I remember that my mom said she was going to go running around Lake Calhoun today and she might stop by. The water glides over my skin as I let it buoy me back up to the surface.

There, at the far end of the courtyard, already talking Mrs. Finklestein's ear off, is my mom. She says she's come to clean on top of and under the refrigerator and scrub around the electric burners so I won't lose my deposit. Because she knows *I* won't do that.

Moving Out

Savi sends Matthew over to my apartment with his truck. Matthew and his truck have shown up to help for my last three moves, plus at my parents' house for their big divorce move. It's hot outside—it seems like it's always hot outside whenever I'm moving, and this time I've planned ahead and made lemonade.

Matthew and Naveed move my furniture, including Savi's borrowed red loveseat, while I box up my things and throw them in the truck. I pull my now-forbidden pot pipe out of its secret hiding place, sniffing the pungent resins one last time before tossing it in the dumpster. Even though the neighbor, Mrs. Finklestein, doesn't drive, for some reason she's lurking in the underground garage and sees me.

"You know, your mother is a very nice lady," she says. "You should be a good girl for her. Don't you want to make her proud of you?" She turns away and I go back up to the nearly empty apartment.

I throw away some other incriminating items: photos of me and Melinda hanging out with the Rastafarians in Jamaica, rolling doobies and smoking them while dancing to reggae music with the men who make a living as unofficial tour guides. I think about how we have always said we would go back to Jamaica together someday, like the song from the Jamaican tourism commercial says to the tune of that Christmas/New Year song: "Come back to Jamaica, what's old is what's new."

I save a couple of the snapshots, slipping them into in the middle of a stack of family pictures.

I also throw away at least ten crunchy bouquets of dried roses, picking them off the wall hooks and out of tall water glasses, then dropping them into a garbage bag. Savi shows up to help me do a final cleaning and refill glasses of lemonade. Then she goes with me to turn in my keys, saying sharp things about Melinda every few minutes and then assuring me it's all for the best anyway.

That evening, I find myself at home in Naveed's house in South Minneapolis. The renters saw Matthew and Naveed moving in my things and so when I run into one of them in the shared laundry area downstairs, she says "Welcome" as if I haven't already been there most of the time for the past several months.

I look around and think about how I can make this house my own. How I can put my own stamp of style on it—mark my turf—before Naveed's mother arrives.

It's not like there's a redecorating budget, but I get back in my car and drive to Byerly's to page through magazines like *Metropolitan Home*. *Architectural Digest* is too depressing. As if.

Then right in front of me is this pink, white, and robin's egg blue confection of a magazine: *Martha Stewart Living*. I pick it up for the first time, feeling its promise. It's been around for awhile, but has just come to the magazine rack here at Byerly's. It has a few possibilities that won't cost much more than a can of paint and some stencils.

Martha's advice is to first assess what you like about your space, and to make those things the *design foundation*.

What Naveed does have is one ugly fake Persian carpet and a lot of Persian block print fabric and wall hangings. It's mostly stuff his sister, Firoozeh, sent him from Tehran's bazaar, and it's sort of interesting to me.

Martha suggests that I can *pull the eye up* from the ugly carpet. My marbled silk pillows and a can of gold spray paint I can use on some outdated furniture help with that. Still, I realize, after all of my redecorating and rearranging is done, I haven't done much to put my own mark on this place. It still looks like his style, even though the walls are now Benjamin Moore's "Venus Moonglow" and my books are on the shelves. It still looks very Iranian, and even though I'm becoming obsessed now with all things Iranian, I don't want to be like Melinda and match my style to my boyfriend's country of origin.

So I go back to the magazine rack at Byerly's. Metropolitan Home has an article on decorating with nudes. I remember that I have a stack of drawings from my DRAWING 1001 class in college. Nudes, lots of them, based on the university student models. Only three of the sketches are good enough to frame, even though we drew for two hours, three days a week, for three months. I didn't take that class too seri-ously—it was just for excitement, drawing naked male and female student models that got paid seven dollars an hour. A lot of people hooked up through that class.

Naveed seems impressed by my drawings, but then he goes off to one of the rooms and pulls out his own stack. He took the same class, turns out. All his friends took it too.

We choose three of the best from his portfolio to add to my three.

"Will your mom freak out?" I ask.

He shrugs. "You know, she's not six years old. She's seen nude art." I'm slightly disappointed to hear that she might not be shocked and offended at our drawings of naked people, but I clip a newspaper coupon for Michael's craft store and take the drawings in to be framed.

Coming Soon

I'd blocked it out of my mind, but now it's real. I've only lived with Naveed for one month, and his mother has a plane ticket in hand, with no known return date. I'm afraid, but Naveed is sure everything will be fine.

I go back to his photo album. I looked at pictures of his mom before, but I barely noticed what she looked like. Now I find them and study her. In one photo she's here in the driveway of Naveed's house. It was after her last open-heart surgery, and this carefree photo must have been taken after her recovery. Goli is sitting in the driver's seat of Naveed's blue Honda CRX. She looks a little wind-whipped, like she was out driving with the windows down. Except that she doesn't drive because of her bad heart, and she's just having fun posing as if she was just pulling up into the driveway.

I'm relieved to know that she has fun sometimes—that she has a sense of humor. But I don't know how she really is.

Maybe it is she who drove away the old American girlfriend, or the Iranian almost-fiancée. Maybe those women had a friend just like Melinda, who comforted them by saying, "I'm so sorry—but you know, I was afraid it would end badly."

Shoes

My writing teacher is a peace and environmental activist, a friend and groupie of the author Carol Bly, which is why we're using Bly's text for this class instead of a regular textbook about fiction writing. Our textbook is called *Changing the Bully That Rules the World: Reading and Thinking about Ethics*.

My teacher knows I feel angry about "The Bully" like she does, especially still angry about Desert Storm, a war that seems to have never ended, although I've confessed to her that I'm not an avid war protester. Nor am I a very good environmentalist.

The class actually ended last month, but the teacher had arranged this time for some of us to get together for readings. Some of them are really good and she leans forward, giving encouragement to the writers.

While I read to the class, she chews on her fingernail.

Shoedog

A lotioned, tanned foot slipped into the soft pearl leather pump Megan held open with both hands. When the young customer's exquisite foot was half in, Megan slid her silver shoehorn between her heel and the back of the shoe. Her foot settled into the shoe and arched a bit. She smiled a spoiled smile, her blushed cheeks glowing with pleasure. Looking at Megan sitting on the stool in front of her, she turned open her thigh and inspected the shoe from the inside. She sighed with pleasure at the pretty shoes. "I'll take them," she said, thigh still open and looking Megan full in the face. In one graceful, ponylike movement she slid her pretty foot out of the pump, swung back her long sandy hair, and produced her Visa card from a small pink clutch. Megan accepted her teasing blue-green gaze with a thump-thump to the shiny Stuart Weitzman shoebox.

My class is seduced by my writing, except for the teacher, who takes her fingernail out of her mouth and asks, "Now how can you use that wonderful talent you have to tell us what we know you really care about? How can you juxtapose this spoiled girl in our materialistic American society with your concerns about how U.S. sanctions are killing six thousand Iraqi children per month?"

This kind of question is the reason I registered for a writing class taught by this highly regarded teacher, so I could deepen the political and moral meaning in my writing.

But at the moment all I can say to her is, "It's really, at this point in the story… just about the shoes."

Stillwater

I don't have much time before Naveed's mom is here, so I try to do things to prepare for her arrival in between working at the insurance company and applying for better jobs. I want to impress Goli, so I study Persian. I knew a little bit from working at the Dinky Kebab, but mainly just the words that were on the menu and a couple of swears.

I don't have a textbook, so I'm learning the language by bugging Naveed to translate everything. One Saturday we're riding in the car, just taking a drive to Stillwater.

I ask for the Persian word for everything I see out the window along the way and write it on the blue lines of my spiral notebook. "What about cow?" I ask.

"Gav," he says.

"Gawv?" I ask.

"No, *Gaav*," he moos. We get out of the car on the main street of Stillwater, strolling leisurely, buying old-fashioned fudge, and checking out the antique stores. We take a short paddleboat ride and make out in our seats when nobody is looking.

I learn another handful of new words on the drive home, and every day after that. By themselves, some of the words are ugly sounding. But when people speak the language, the words all weave together like a colorful silk shawl with silver bells sewn on. It's prettier than French. Not more romantic, but more musical.

I imagine I will be able to speak Persian well enough by the time Goli arrives. And her coming is really an opportunity for me to learn a language because Goli's English is not good—I should have Persian nearly mastered in a few months.

"What does your name mean?" I ask.

"Shushtar is a place in southwestern Iran, so Shushtari just means 'from Shushtar,'" he says. But he doesn't know what Shushtar is supposed to mean.

"No, I mean your first name," I say. "What's the meaning of *Naveed*?"

"I don't know," he says.

"Valerie means strong," I say. "And it's also the name of an herb. And Kjos means 'bay' in Norwegian, not 'fart.' I hope you tell your mom that." He says he's already warned her about my last name.

One of the things Naveed has told me about his mother is that she walks slowly. I need to be sure not to walk fast with her because she might have heart failure or something.

They didn't know she had rheumatic fever when she was six, so nobody did anything. They just thought she was sick for a long time and made her stay in bed until she felt better. She was always weak after that. Finally a doctor figured out what had happened and found the damage to her heart. After that, she wasn't allowed to do much outside of the home, but that didn't stop her parents from expecting Goli to help raise all the younger kids, as long as she was home anyway.

Naveed tells me more about her, only because I insist. Her name is Goli Kashani, because Iranian women keep their own last names when they marry, which is also why the neighbors Milad Zand and Yasmin Noury don't have the same last name. Kashani means that they're "from Kashan," where her family has been harvesting wild roses and whipping them into various products for hundreds of years. Naveed grew up helping during the rose harvest. All the family members were given sacs to tie around their necks and sent out before dawn to gather the pink blooms—the *gol Mohammadi*—with the morning dew still on the petals and the fragrance at its peak. They would bring them straight to the family's factory, where most of the roses were simmered and distilled into rosewater, perfume, and soaps. Other roses were cooked into jams or dried for culinary use.

Goli was the oldest child of five. All the kids went to school, and she helped them all with their homework. Her father's mother lived with them and also helped raise the kids. She said girls shouldn't go to college, so Goli didn't go. Her younger sisters were allowed to go, though. One of them got her business degree and took over the family business, living a life permeated by the scent of roses while Goli was teaching sewing classes and raising the children of the man who would eventually take a second wife. Now the sister reinvests profits and funds family vacations to the island of Kish while Goli spends her share of the family money on doctor bills.

"How do you say *sister*?" I ask.

"*kHa-har*," he says. I'm not good at saying that *kh* sound, so I repeat it as 'ha-har,' like somebody laughing mockingly. I think that my own sisters would like that word.

Goli Joon

We go to pick up Goli at the airport, but she doesn't get off the plane. There's a message for us. She got off the plane when it stopped in Detroit, mistaking "Michigan" for "Minnesota."

Her daughter in Iran, Firoozeh, had written her destination on an index card and tied it around her neck just so that this kind of thing wouldn't happen. At least the emergency info she'd written on the backside came in handy.

We wait for her to arrive on the next plane, and I get more nervous as we wait.

Finally, she steps off the plane and kisses Naveed three times on each cheek, holding him by his jaw with both of her little hands and crying with joy. When she stops crying, I see where Naveed gets his dancing smile.

Goli looks sharp in a black silk blouse, cut low as if to show off the pink trackmarks of her two open-heart surgeries. She wears a gold necklace and earrings beset with intense Persian turquoise. Her black hair is perfectly coiffed in an updated Jackie Kennedy Onassis style. She's tiny, and she smells like she's just applied rose perfume.

Her two suitcases are the largest pieces of luggage I've ever seen, more like steamer trunks than suitcases, and I can't believe KLM has allowed these on their flight.

I try to say, "Hello, how are you?" in Persian, addressing her as *Goli*, but apparently I can't even pronounce her name correctly. I'm stressing the wrong syllable, saying it like she's a hockey goalie. She can't understand what it is I'm trying to say and Naveed translates my Persian into the real thing.

She tells me I can call her "Maman" as we walk to the car, but I decide to call her Goli Joon, which Naveed suggests because it means "Goli dear." Joon means life or soul or spirit, but it's just like saying "dear." It's respectful and affectionate without presuming that she's going to be my mother-in-law anytime soon—although I'm honored she offered "Maman." It makes me feel like she's accepting me already.

It's a good thing we got a close parking spot—she's walking very slowly, and Naveed and I are pushing the unwieldy cart with the giant suitcases.

Naveed opens the front car door for his mom, and waves me to the back seat of the CRX before he wedges the biggest suitcases into the hatchback trunk. Then he piles all of the smaller pieces of luggage in back next to me. The road hums under me while I sit silent, listening for a word or two I can decipher as they catch up in the language I don't understand.

On the way home from the airport, Naveed decides to stop at Byerly's for "a few things," which for us usually means pastries and deli meat. He tells us he will only be a minute and we should wait in the car. I'm nervous, but try to see it as another chance to try out my Persian language skills.

I begin confidently, with a few questions to which I already know the answers, like "How many children do you have?" and "How old are your grandchildren?"

But my Persian is apparently so deformed and defective that she can't understand a word of what I am saying. Her attempt at English is equally incomprehensible. We play charades for a few minutes in a last-ditch effort to communicate, but our charades don't match up either. So we stop talking. And we wait.

Goli Joon is not trying to hide her hopes that Naveed will soon return to the car and save us from this failed social interaction. She sighs and gesticulates what seems to mean, *What in the hell is he doing in there?* Finally, we both breathe an audible sigh of relief. Naveed has returned to the car, with three bags of fruit.

Goli Joon needs to rest, but first things first. I learn quickly that she's a bonafide fruitaholic. She eats a banana, a tangerine, and some cantaloupe splashed with rosewater as she tells Naveed about her mishap with getting off the plane in Michigan. Then they move on to talk about other things for at least an hour before she runs out of steam and goes into her room to sleep until dinnertime.

She seems pleased with her dining/bedroom, which I've worked hard to help Naveed transform from how plain it used to be to a lovely guestroom. My first preference was to kick out the renters downstairs and have Goli Joon live down there, but Naveed thought that would seem rude, and that she would have a hard time with the stairs, and that she would freeze down there. He said she gets cold easily. He also would have lost out on the rental income.

For dinner, Naveed and I have worked together to make an herb stew called *ghormeh sabzi*. The word *ghormeh* sounds a lot like gourmet and I don't know if it means that, but this dish is eaten by everyone in Iran whether they're into gourmet food or not. It's the kebabs that they're known for, but ghormeh sabzi is the true national dish. There's rice and a little chopped salad too, and Goli Joon digs in.

She says something, and then Naveed translates for me:
The flight attendants on Iran Air serve kebabs and rice, but
Firoozeh got her the KLM ticket and those flight attendants
don't serve good food.

I'm getting tired from the long day and all of the not-
understanding. I mumble, "As if the flight attendants do
the cooking." Naveed ignores me, and we go to bed and fall
asleep.

The next morning Goli Joon gets up late and makes herself
at home in the kitchen. This is her son's house, and so it is
her house. Naveed has already explained that to me. When
he did, I reconsidered my move, but I didn't have another
good option, so I decided I could see how things went at
least. I still have Melinda's voice, haunting me, taunting, *I was
afraid it would end badly.*

We have already eaten breakfast, and she doesn't want what
I offer. She drinks tea, warms pita bread, and puts chunks of
feta cheese on her plate along with some fig jam she brought
from home. The idea of feta cheese in the morning grosses
me out, especially feta with jam. But this, with copious fruit
and rosewater, will be her usual breakfast.

Naveed and I had some ideas of things to do with Goli
Joon today, but she's still tired. So it's a day of sitting in the
living room together, with her cassette tapes of female Iranian
singers from long ago on the stereo. I go to look at the cassette covers—one is very famous; her name is Googoosh and
I already know who she is. The other I don't know—she's
named Marzieh. I will find out soon that Goli Joon worships
Marzieh, who is still alive but lives in Paris now.

After several hours of talking and listening to the music
while eating nuts, seeds, and rosewater-sprinkled fruit, Goli
Joon needs some fresh air. She goes outside and walks slowly

but determinedly around the house a couple of times, as if the perimeter of the house is a walking track. When she comes in, she tells Naveed that Yasmin Noury was outside with her youngest daughter, Parvaneh.

Naveed waves away the information. He turns down the melon she offers him, and teasingly calls her "Gol-ab Joon," which means Rosewater Dear, because she puts rosewater on so many things.

Goli Joon has brought a professionally produced video of a cousin's wedding in Tehran to show Naveed. We're taken as viewers from the preparations of the bride and the home to a joy ride with the groom, then to the elaborate in-home ceremony. Then we're back in the car on a joy ride to a botanical garden where the bride and groom release some doves. Then we're drooling over a feast like nothing I've ever seen, and finally at a party where the women are dressed to kill in silky, spaghetti-strapped French and Italian gowns. One of Naveed's cousins in the video is the most ravishing beauty I've ever seen, and her blood-red evening gown against her golden skin and long, black, glossy curls enchants me. Just four or five older matriarchs cover their heads with scarves and wear Chanel-like suits. No chadors here. There's no scene like this in *Not without My Daughter.*

An hour later, Yasmin Noury rings the doorbell and presents Goli Joon with a small yellow cake, frosted with cream scented with rosewater that I can smell from six feet away. I think, *She's gonna love that cake!*

Goli Joon expresses her gratitude profusely, and invites her in. Yasmin says no, and Goli Joon repeats the invitation. The woman declines for a second time, and Goli Joon thanks her and says goodbye. I know by now that Goli would have asked a third time if she really wanted her to come in because that is the custom. Yasmin backs away, saying niceties, while Goli Joon keeps replying with more pretty-sounding things until Yasmin has backed into her own yard.

Goli Joon closes the heavy door, walks straight to the kitchen sink, shoves the whole cake down into the disposal and runs it. She takes some brown seeds out of a jar and burns them on an aluminum brazier, pours the seeds—smoking like miniature pieces of charcoal—onto a giant copper spoon, and waves the spoon around the foyer where the woman stood.

Later, I will learn that the seeds are from the wild rue plant, *esphand*, ancient Zoroastrian ingredient for smoking out the evil eye. But right now, all I know is that I would have liked to have eaten some of that cake.

Melinda's Letters

I thought Melinda and I might never talk again, but she's already written me two letters. The letters were forwarded to Naveed's place from our old apartment—I hadn't been on speaking terms with her to tell her I moved. I could just not answer, and she might never know where I am again. I could end our friendship as easily as forfeiting a game by not showing up. That's called a *bye* in soccer, which I know because Courtney played Wayzata rec sports. I could give Melinda a bye.

The first letter was from Santa Fe. I wasn't tempted at all to respond. The second is from Manhattan, where she's already been sent on assignment by the tech firm. Melinda is no more technologically savvy than I am, but she has gumption, that's for sure. She's a trainer, she says. She only has to learn enough to be able to teach others, and for that she just has to follow the software manuals. It's not like programming the software or anything.

The first letter describes her new place in Santa Fe, an adobe townhouse that she swears doesn't look like what I think of when I think of a townhouse. She will send pictures, she says. It's white adobe, she writes, with a Spanish door that's the bright island-blue she knows is my favorite color.

The second forwarded letter includes the photos of her door and other architectural details of her Santa Fe townhouse. It also describes the restaurants in Manhattan, in course-by-course detail of the meals that she gets to charge to her Platinum Visa card, which gets paid by the company.

I'm not sure I'm going to write back. But then she writes "P.S. I know you probably don't have an email account yet, but if you ever get one email me at Melinda.Kirsch@BurtonBusiness.com." Her email address is also printed on her business card, enclosed with the letter.

As if I couldn't possibly have an email account. I've had one almost since I started temping at the insurance company. I probably got it the day she moved, maybe before she moved. I got mine before she got hers! Now I will have to email her to prove I have one.

I email her from work the next day. After a few icebreaker exchanges we start trading advice about what cool things we've found on the World Wide Web. I tell her about recipes.group and she tells me about cooking.group, which she says is much better.

We email each other for a lot of the day, even though she says she's so busy preparing to lead her first training by herself in Manhattan the next morning, and I have a stack of fraud status reports to enter into the national database.

Salt

I know I'm not as good of a cook as Melinda or Ty, but my lasagna is always a hit. I think I'll trot that out tonight and impress Goli Joon.

She doesn't seem to know what I'm making. I've seen lasagna appear regularly at Iranian parties, so I don't understand how she couldn't have ever eaten it. But this gives me an opportunity to show off, to be the one to introduce lasagna to her and open her up to a whole new world. I labor over it all afternoon, and serve it with buttery garlic bread and a salad.

I serve her a piece, using the spatula, but I need her help to cut away the strings of cheese connecting her piece to the whole dish of lasagna. She can't do it, and it just gets stringier and stringier until I finally set her piece on her plate and then cut the strings. Then she gets annoyed because the same thing happens when she tries to separate a single bite from the rectangle on her plate.

After finally, with much effort, eating barely half of her lasagna, some salad, and a bite of bread, Goli Joon says she's full and tired. She goes to her room after nodding to me and saying, "Thank you, Valerie Joon." It feels nice to have Joon put after my name too. We're all Joon in this house. We're all Dear.

A couple of hours later a commotion wakes us. Naveed jumps out of bed so fast that the waterbed waves send me crashing into the headboard. The black onyx panther on the shelf almost falls on my head. Goli Joon has a stomachache and she feels dizzy. Her ears are ringing.

Naveed runs back to her room, exclaiming, "Maman thinks it was that lasagna! She can't have salt!"

"I didn't use any salt!" I swear. It had been hard, but I'd resisted using any salt at all, knowing about her problem.

"Then that stringy cheese must have had too much salt! And it was too heavy for her," he insists. He steps into his bunny slippers and runs back to her room.

I get up to go see her too. She moans and groans, and every time she stands up she falls back down into her bed, holding her hands over her ears to stop the ringing. She can't stand to look at me—when she looks in my direction she begins to heave.

She thinks she's going to die, and Naveed is looking at me with frightened eyes as if to ask, "What were you thinking?"

On the one hand, I'm worried that I made her eat something that could have killed her. On the other hand I think she's being overly dramatic. I mean, isn't the feta cheese she had for breakfast saltier than those Italian cheeses?

If she's like this much longer, Naveed will take her to the ER, but she eventually calms down and goes back to sleep. I can't fall back to sleep so easily, though. She's been here for merely a week and already I'm crying in bed. Naveed puts a hand on my back. "I'm sorry," he says. "It wasn't your fault. You made a great meal."

"I hope you're going to help eat the leftovers."

"Happy to help."

I stop crying and wipe my eyes on the fishing resort T-shirt Naveed has been wearing to bed lately. It got a big grease stain on it, so he can't wear it out of the house, but he didn't want to throw it away.

"How long do you think she will stay?" I say, even though by now I know it isn't nice to ask. Naveed doesn't answer, but keeps his hand on my back until I fall asleep.

The Welcoming

Naveed's friends come out of the woodwork—more friends than I knew he had—to pay formal visits to his mother. It turns out that many of them live close to here, on either side of the Minneapolis-Edina border. Some immigrant groups congregate in the cheapest, most urban neighborhoods, but Iranians who come here are usually a little richer. Or a lot richer. The Iranians in the Twin Cities metro area, it turns out, mostly live here in the nicer part of South Minneapolis and spread over the border into Edina. Edina is the other place in Minnesota, besides Wayzata, mentioned in *The Official Preppy Handbook*.

The friends who come to visit are chemical and geological engineers and an orthopedic surgeon with his dentist wife. They say just a polite word or two to me, taking care not to mention if they recognize me as their former waitress at the Dinky Kebab, as they hand Goli Joon flower bouquets and fill up whole evenings chatting with her. Paying visits to elders is a part of their culture of civility and traditional respect, plus I think they really like doing it.

I serve the fall stews Goli Joon has cooked and insisted they stay to eat. I refill teacups and keep the sugar cube bowl looking like a treacherous mountain, just as Niloofar taught me at the Dinky Kebab.

We watch the videos Goli Joon brought, again, and see the videos the friends have brought from their Iran trips. This year, four of Naveed's friends went back for the first time. Others will soon go too. Suddenly, everybody is ready to go back and see how things have changed. Everybody, from Iranian-American memoirists to the people we know. Even Jamsheed and Kaveh, who just a year ago said they would never spend a red cent in an Iran run by mullahs. Everybody who can afford to go is going. Except for Naveed. He could scrape together the money, but he isn't moving on it. Maybe he will never go.

For now, we settle in before the VCR with these neighbor-friends (except for the Zand/Nourys, who are still not part of our circle). In the years ahead, I will watch hundreds of hours of filmed trips to Iran, expertly edited as if celluloid strips of Iranian life can be sewn together like clothing and packed into a suitcase for wearing again somewhere else.

An American wife of one man tells me how she had to officially convert to Islam, get married again by a mullah here, and take a Muslim name even though she doesn't plan to use it. She did all that just to get the paperwork needed to get into Iran with her husband. She shows me her Iranian passport, asking me if we're going to go to Iran, and if we get married am I also going to become "Iranian by marriage." It's something I've never thought of, that a Lutheran girl from a picturesque lakeside suburb of Minneapolis could gain a whole new nationality by simply reciting the *shahada* and signing some papers.

Provisions

Our kitchen is an earthy brown cave. Goli Joon is our clan's gatherer. In preparation for coming to America, she gathered all of the ingredients she uses in bulk and stuffed them into a king-sized white pillowcase, which took up half of one of her huge suitcases. She's brought out her treasures little by little to show them to me and start cooking.

Many of these ingredients I saw in the market section of the Dinky Kebab, so I'm not as horrified as I could be about the shriveled-up brown limes. This petrified citrus fruit from Oman is as dry and light as a ping-pong ball, so it can be stored for ages. Dried limes are dropped whole into autumn-winter stews.

Goli Joon shows me how she grinds the dried limes for some dishes instead of putting them in whole. She cuts them open, and removes the seeds before grinding them and putting the powder in a glass jar.

The pistachio nuts are way better than the California kind, but I've had these before too. They're tastier inside and out, the shells glossed with lime, salt, and saffron. Sometimes a shell doesn't have that split open part that Naveed says is called its smile, and those we crack open with a kitchen mallet.

Almost everything Goli Joon has pulled from that pillowcase is dried—a shriveled fraction of its former self, whether flower, herb, fruit, nut, or bean. I try to imagine what the bounty would look like fresh, especially the wild Mohammadi roses from her family's acreage, and the deep purple flowers called *zaboonay gav*. I know that word, I think—*gav*. I remember Naveed teaching me that word when we went to Stillwater before Goli Joon came. It means cow, and I know zaboon too; it means tongue. So the flower is called cow's tongue. I'm starting to understand things here and there.

Cow's tongue flowers make a mood-improving tea. I'm going to need that tea later. But right now I'm enjoying this time with Goli Joon, discovering strange new things, like the ghostly white angelica seeds she calls *golpar*. I don't know yet what those are for. They seem mysterious, truly like little angels.

I watch Goli Joon tuck her ingredients into every drawer and shelf and cabinet in our dark kitchen. She finds just the right jar—my antique Ball canning jar that I bought at a garage sale—for saffron rock candy. The jar looks like it has been waiting its whole life to hold these crystal rock formations colored golden by fire-colored saffron stamens. These saffron rock candies, along with cardamom candies, will flavor our afternoon teas.

I watch Goli Joon start every one of her recipes, which she's known by heart for decades, by chopping and sautéing onions. Or grating onions for some things. She never uses a food processor, not even my mini-chopper—just a knife or a grater. She always starts with the onions, and she ends by crushing a dried rosebud over many a dish. When she grates the onions, she always has a good cry. And when she crushes the tiny rose, she whispers a prayer of thanks.

Stillwater Redux

We bring Goli Joon everywhere with us. She came on our trip to Stillwater to see the fall colors. She's been here before during fall, but she still seemed impressed.

I'm still impressed with the colors year after year too. I love to go on the paddleboat ride on the St. Croix and see the autumn colors on both banks of the river. It's the pinks and reds I can't get over, while Goli Joon went crazy over all the colors. She thought the paddleboat ride would be too chilly though, so we didn't go.

Now that the weather is cooling down, Goli Joon is making lots of *khoresht*. Khoresht pretty much means stew. She needs apples for her apple khoresht.

We take her to an apple orchard an hour away after she complains that the apples we buy at the store taste old; she needs *fresh* apples, and she's sure the grocery store is just clearing out last year's apples to make way for the bumper crop at the orchards now.

At first she says she doesn't want to go, and that we can just go pick apples without her, but Persian manners require we beg her three times to come with us. She relents on the third try. It starts raining when we get there, so she stays in the orchard's store, drinking hot cider and perusing the shelves of apple chutney and apple butter while Naveed and I get drenched picking the apples she wanted.

Goli Joon comes with us to all stores—the grocery store, Target, Southdale Mall. We invite her to all the gatherings at my mom's house, and naturally she's always present when my family gathers over here.

As the weather gets cold, we stay inside together more often. Naveed and Goli Joon have taught me a new card came, called *Geesh-knees*. That's the Persian word for cilantro, which is what they call clubs. Now when I look at the club card, I see it. It does look like cilantro. I've never liked playing cards before, but it's fun when somebody gets to shout out, *"Geesh-knees!"*

And the apple khoresht, *khoreshte-seeb*, is just the right amount sour and hot, sweet and brothy over rice. But it still isn't just perfect to her. The apples are sweet and tart enough, and fresh enough, but she complains that they don't taste the same as the ones in Iran. They don't taste enough like apples.

Crevice

My parents' divorce had been in the air and spoken in jest so much that they didn't think they had to reveal it when it became official. I mean, we had heard, "If your father hasn't left me by then…" and, "if we make it another year" so many times that we were supposed to just know.

But, "Your father is really done this time" sounded more concrete.

I told Mom I wanted to hear it officially, from the both of them together. They didn't get together to deliver the news, but Dad came out on the deck, where I was reading with the sun in my eyes. He said, "I hear you want to hear it officially. We are going to get the divorce." He actually said *the* divorce, not *a* divorce, acknowledging the prediction that has been floating in front of us for all these years. This is going to be *the* divorce, like *the* T.V. we had been visiting for months at the local Sears before we bought it to replace our T.V. that got struck by lightning.

I didn't think it bothered me that much. I mean, it was their life. Not that I thought my mom had so much of a life. Even when I was in college I wasn't mature enough to think of my mother as a separate person because she existed for us kids for so long. We had inklings of a life beyond us, like when she took up running and left the house to jog with a male neighbor every morning. But for so long, we'd thought she existed to run the family errands, and watch our ballet lessons. She existed to help us with our sequined costumes and the make-up we got to wear at the recitals, as far as I knew.

I was starting my last year of college by the time of the divorce, but Courtney was just starting high school and I worried about her. She started cutting the skin on her arms, and she started smoking pot too, which I really couldn't lecture her about.

Anyway, it was just a phase for Courtney. She learned to cope with it in record time with an eight-pack of counseling sessions our mom bought for her. Now she wants to be a child psychologist.

Laura and I didn't get offered any counseling sessions. Laura was already out of college, and I guess my mom figured I wasn't living at home full-time either any more. (I'd only been there the day of the announcement to do my laundry for free.) Our role was to be supportive, not to care about the divorce for our own selfish sadness.

I remember Kurt didn't think he cared about his parents' divorce either. Then one night we tripped out on psychedelic mushrooms. I was sleeping over with him at his dad's house while his dad was away at sex-addiction treatment, which he was finally submitting to after his problem of visiting prostitutes had broken up his marriage with Kurt's mom. The mushrooms hit Kurt in a different way that time than they had before. I had to hold him while he cried through the night like a little boy.

The time of my parents' divorce was when the crevice appeared between my mom's perfectly shaped auburn eyebrows. And although I'm twenty-two years younger than Mom, it was about the time when mine appeared too.

Paradoxes

It sinks in that my boyfriend's mother is, for all practical purposes, living with us rather than visiting. And that I'm not really the woman of the house as long as she's here.

I love the meals she turns out in the kitchen, but I don't like how she's moved my olive oil to the rim of the countertop around the stove, and taken out Naveed's ugly place mats I had put away. I bury the place mats in the linen closet and move the olive oil back to its proper corner, which Martha Stewart insists should be away from light and the heat of the stove.

Goli Joon clicks her tongue about this Martha Stewart person. One day, I decorate the tops of the kitchen cabinets with antique baskets and other rustic-looking things. I balance an old iron skillet up there, copying Martha's kitchen décor in a recent magazine spread.

Goli Joon clicks her tongue at me. "Dirt to Martha Stewart's head," she says. "That skillet could fall on us."

Goli Joon also has half of the main refrigerator shelf constantly spoken for with her vats of homemade plain yogurt. I think of it as a sort of revolving science experiment. Every week, she boils milk in an old aluminum pot. When the milk has cooled just enough not to kill the yogurt culture, she stirs in a dollop of the yogurt leftover from her last batch. It sits out for a bit so its acidophilus micro-organisms can multiply and transform all of the milk into yogurt. Then it finishes culturing in the refrigerator, where the pot takes up half a shelf. The pot of plain yogurt comes out of the refrigerator for every meal. I don't know why it should taste any better than store-bought yogurt, because it all started out months ago with a gallon of Kemps milk and a dollop of Old Home yogurt from Byerly's.

Goli Joon has crocheted button tops onto country-style dishtowels she bought at JC Penney the last time we took her to the Southdale Mall. The crocheting is so that she can button the dishtowels onto drawer handles. There's a dishtowel buttoned onto almost every drawer, some with apples on them, some with gingerbread men, and some with roosters. They don't go with my Martha Stewart decorating ideas at all.

I know those are just picky things, but they add up. And, now we have to be proper with her living here. For example, I have to wear a bra in the house if I don't want to feel self-conscious. We have to keep the T.V. volume very low after nine at night when she goes to bed. And yet we have to keep the T.V. on in our bedroom so Goli Joon doesn't hear the movement of the waterbed mattress sloshing from shore to shore in its black lacquer frame.

When I'm around her I try to smile a lot. My cheeks hurt sometimes from smiling. My Persian language is a joke and

I've lost the will to work on it. I've only learned the food words. I like the food, so I speak the food.

I need to talk to someone though, because to be completely honest, I wish Goli Joon would go home. Maybe somebody can tell me how to make her go. A woman, but I don't know who would understand. I momentarily think of Yasmin Noury across the street, but although she always returns my hellos and waves back to me, I don't think we're going to get chummy.

Not Savi—she already advised me months ago about not getting too close to a potential mother-in-law. I don't want to hear an I-told-you-so. So I've been telling Savi things are going pretty well.

All I get is praise from Savi for living with her. "Your place in heaven is assured. You're a real saint." This reaction doesn't make me want to tell her that I don't know if I can do it. Savi saying that I'm a saint insinuates that Goli Joon is difficult to live with, which isn't technically true. If things like dishtowels buttoned onto drawer handles bother me so much, I'm probably the difficult one.

Even though I want her to go home, sometimes I get defensive about Goli Joon. "I get a lot out of her being here," I tell Savi. "She cooks for us, and does so many nice things. She folds our laundry. So, I'm not a saint—Goli Joon is the saint."

Really, I hate it when she folds my laundry, her papery hands folding my private things that are too small to need folding, and serving them up to me in a stack.

Melinda just thinks I'm insane, now that I've told her all about it over email, including how Naveed spends a couple of days a month taking his mom to all of her doctor appointments, and many more hours with all the shopping. Last week, I got a letter from her. A long letter, even though we've been emailing. I think it was her last ditch effort to show me that she was serious about wanting to convince me to move out as soon as possible. On the stationery, which had a Hopi Indian design border, she wrote:

> I just have a feeling there's some-
> body else out there for you, and you're
> preventing yourself from finding true
> happiness. If you're living with him
> because you can't afford a place, maybe
> your dad or Kurt could lend you some
> rent money until you get a better job.
> Or you could call Quentin.

I'd told Melinda about Quentin asking me to go to Paris with him, and she thought I was crazy for not going. She's brought that up a few times now. Even though she didn't think Quentin was right for me, she says that in retrospect I could have probably had five or six nice trips with him if I'd taken him back.

As if she couldn't resist including some bragging points with her letter, she enclosed a few more photos of her adobe townhome and the Navajo-style fireplace she had forgotten to tell me about when she told me about her fabulous blue door and the Santa Fe vistas and spiritual vibe.

Melinda is very absorbed in her new job, Santa Fe *culture*, her expense account, and Roger, who is apparently making a boatload of money at his job in the arts. That last part sounds unlikely, I know, but people seem to be giving Melinda and Roger money when it doesn't make sense. I mean, Melinda must spend one or two hours emailing me from her tech job every day, and she's not even a techie. So now Roger is raking it in working in the arts and he's not an artist. I didn't ask how.

Clearly, Melinda isn't going to be a good listener, but I try—over email—to explain it all to her anyway. She writes back that the worst sign about Naveed is that he doesn't care as much about what I want as he does about what his mother wants. I type, delete, and retype my reply several times before sending.

The thing I cannot explain to Melinda is that an Iranian man who isn't willing to take care of his mother is not a good man at all, regardless of what his girlfriend wants. Anyone who can grow up in that culture and still turn his mother out of the house to please his girlfriend must be immoral by nature. The paradox then is that the more I love him and want to marry him, the more I hope that he will find somewhere else for her to live; but the more I see how good he is in caring for his mother, the more I love him.

Melinda would say the solution to this is to give up the man who comes from this impossible culture and find someone more like us. Someone who would think letting his mom move in on him and his girlfriend would be the immoral idea in the first place.

Greetings

Naveed brings hot tea—the caffeinated kind—to me early every morning. He leaves the house just after five-thirty each weekday morning, and props me up in bed by putting two pillows behind my back and pulling me up to lean against them. He places the teacup in my hand, helping me to rest it on my chest and take a sip as if I'm a sick child. Then he kisses me on the neck and lips, and he leaves.

But today, Naveed has left even earlier than usual to catch a plane for Kansas City, where his newest parking ramp customer awaits him for a design consultation. My alarm clock sounds, and I crane my head around to see if tea has been delivered. No tea. It's seventeen minutes after six, and no caffeine. I push the snooze button six times, the caffeine withdrawal headache coming on and getting a little worse with each nine-minute snooze.

At seven-thirty, the headache is unbearable. I must go and get tea. I hope there's some made.

I exit the bedroom and hear the tea kettle whistle for just a second then stop just as suddenly. Goli Joon must be in the kitchen, and has just taken the tea kettle off the burner. Goli Joon will now steep the boiling water with two teaspoons of the loose-leaf black tea. While it steeps, she will be simmering the milk, and then removing the skin. Once the milk is properly simmered, its lactose sugar properly concentrated until the milk earns a sweet scent that it did not have when cold, Goli Joon will fill her teacup halfway with it and then add the tea. No need for sugar when the milk is naturally sweetened and condensed on the stove.

Here in the flagstone hallway, I freeze, and I consider going back into the bedroom I share not so secretly with Naveed. But then the kitchen's pocket door rumbles open and Goli Joon, in her zip-up house robe, slowly comes into view.

Because I know how pathetic I look, how unbalanced I feel, I do not want to see Goli Joon. So I will wait. I take a step backward toward the bedroom, and wait for Goli Joon to go back into her room before I go into the kitchen to pour my drink of life. I hope she returns to her room, rather than sitting down at the dining table with her tea and flat bread with feta cheese breakfast that I find so unbreakfast-like.

To my relief, Goli Joon leaves the kitchen's pocket door open, then opens the pocket-door to her dining/bedroom, goes in, and slides it closed. I dart back out of the shadows and into the kitchen, but then suddenly Goli Joon is there behind me.

"Salaam-et koo?" she asks.

My sleepy head takes a few seconds to compute a translation, but when it comes to me I'm taken aback. It means "Where is your greeting?" I feel scolded, too stung to give Goli Joon the *salaam* I now owe her. I quickly pour my tea, shake two Tylenols out of a bottle, and hustle back to my room. She goes back to her room too.

When after a while I decide that I'm going to call in sick and possibly stay in bed for the whole day, I leave the bedroom again just to get the newspaper. I open the front door, grab the *Star Tribune,* and close the door. It slams a little too loudly, and then I tiptoe back into my room. The warm waterbed welcomes me in, and I drink tea with the newspaper, reading only the *Taste* and *Variety* sections.

I deserve this sick day, I tell myself, and then I drift back to sleep.

Later, my doorknob jiggles open. I'm under the blankets, but I peek out through a fold, wondering what time it is and if Naveed's trip got cancelled. But it's not Naveed. It's Goli Joon. She's now three or four feet into the bedroom. I'm fully awake now, realizing she must think I left for work when I got the newspaper. She makes it to the black lacquer dresser, scans the top of it, and then carefully slides open a top drawer. My underwear drawer. She pulls out my Victoria's Secret Miracle Bra, pinches the cushioned part that's strategically placed on the outside of each breast to shove them more toward the center, creating miraculous cleavage. My heart is pounding.

I sit up in bed. She freezes, drops the bra back into the drawer, and cries, "Valerie Joon!" as she spins in my direction.

"I'm putting away the laundry," she tells me in Persian, a quick excuse. She carries no laundry with her, but looks at her hands as if she might be able to conjure some. She picks up the bra again, folds it, and pats it back down in the drawer, as if she'd just washed it and put it away.

I look at her with my mouth open for several seconds, and then I slowly ease back into my sick-day position. And I decide not to let this become a scene, not to ask her why she's snooping in our room and in my underwear drawer.

"*Salaam*," I say instead. Here is your greeting.

Someone to Talk to

Dropping in at the Dinky Kebab, I see Niloofar piling sugar cubes into the little red bowls on each table. I ask her to sit with me. But before I start talking, I ask one of the Mexican cooks to scoop up some saffron-rosewater-pistachio ice cream for me. While the ice cream softens enough to taste, I ask Niloofar, "How can Iranian women stand this live-in mother-in-law thing?"

Instead of answering me, Niloofar gives me the jug of tart, red sumac powder to refill the sumac shakers for each table. As long as I'm here, she says, I might as well be useful. I start filling all of the jars, and I ask her again how this kind of situation can be normal for Iranians. It doesn't feel normal.

"Your situation isn't normal," she says. "Consider how progressive Goli is. For one thing, she has not made an issue of the fact that you are not Iranian, and that you are not even married."

"Of course, I know Goli Joon isn't my mother-in-law, but it's similar," I answer.

"Extended families have been normal for most of the people of the world throughout all the ages, probably including your own ancestors. But that doesn't mean it's easy," she says. "One of my friends has a live-in mother-in-law *and* father-in-law who come barging into the bedroom anytime they want to talk to their son. And I mean *anytime*. No knocking. And her husband refuses to install a lock on the door for fear of offending his parents." She adds that Goli Joon's quick peek into my underwear drawer doesn't even come close to what her friend's in-laws walk in on.

"I know it could be worse," I say, "but the closeness is just too much for me, and there are things about her that really bug me. Like the way she says 'no.' She says '*nah!*' I used to get in trouble for saying '*nah*' when I was a teenager, and she also juts her chin up in the air and makes a ticking sound with her tongue against the roof of her mouth. It burns me up!"

"Um, Valerie, '*nah*' is the word for 'no' in Farsi," Niloofar says. "Everybody says '*nah*.' It's our language."

"Well, I don't like the way she says it," I insist. "Isn't there a more polite word, '*nakheir*' or something? Because, in America, you know, '*nah*' is very rude."

When I say "in America" like that, I sound like one of those right-wing pundits on AM radio, and Niloofar's beautiful doe eyes almost roll back into her head, but then she aims them right at me.

I avoid the eye contact, swirling my spoon around in my softened saffron-rosewater-pistachio ice cream.

After a moment of silence, and in a litany of diplomatic but firm arguments, Niloofar makes me see that it's just the idiosyncrasies and loss of control that are bothering me. She knows it's hard, but I need to try to be more tolerant. It sounds to her like Goli Joon is very tolerant, especially considering my girlfriend status and that she probably expected her son to marry some Iranian woman chosen for him by the family.

"I'm sure you are profiting from having her there in many ways," she says, appealing to my own selfishness, "so perhaps the problem is really with you and Naveed. Are you sure he's really the right one?"

"Maybe I'm not explaining it very well," I say. "It isn't just a few idiosyncrasies. It's constant. Our freshly picked apples aren't good enough for her. She complains that American fruit doesn't have any taste. Our apples don't taste like apples. I get out the cherry jam in the morning and she says that our cherry jam doesn't have any flavor. I made that jam with cherries from Bayfield, Wisconsin! The jam has the perfect balance of sweet and sour, the hint of almond, the aroma of Lake Superior air."

"They smell like air?" she asks, seemingly taking Goli Joon's side. "But do they taste like cherries? It's hard to beat Iranian cherries for flavor."

I continue, "She makes Naveed take her to JC Penney all the time, and then take her back so she can return everything she buys! She returns *everything*. She even tries to return things from garage sales. Just last week we had to take her to a house and ring the doorbell to see if she could return a serving dish."

I tell Niloofar that it bothers me that I don't know how long Goli Joon plans to stay, and that I think it's a few months, but I don't really know. She gulps and looks away from me. "What?" I ask. "What is it?"

"If she doesn't have a non-exchangeable return ticket and date already arranged," she says, "I'd be really surprised if she doesn't stay for at least nine or ten months." I just stare at those incredible doe eyes, and Niloofar pats me on the arm, breaking into a smile.

"You'll learn how to cook," she says. "And she can take care of your babies when you have them. All of my friends who have their mothers-in-law living with them save tens of thousands of dollars on daycare."

That does give me pause, even though we aren't even married, and aren't close to having children. Tens of thousands of dollars in free daycare—even if only someday—that's something.

"You'll be fine," Niloofar says, interrupting the calculations in my head: two children perhaps, five years of full-time daycare… "I'm here for you any time. You know I'm always here."

"But are you sure I can trust you?" I ask, remembering. "You didn't even tell me the horrible meaning of my last name in Farsi."

She covers a giggle, as if to say that it had just been too good of a little joke around the restaurant to ruin. "We accepted you for who you are, embarrassing name and all," she says. "And so has Naveed's kind mother. You can become more accepting too. Even if she goes home tomorrow, expect her to come back and to live here a lot of the time for the rest of her life."

I drop my ice cream spoon onto my napkin and get up to put the sumac shakers on the tables. A plotted chart forms in my mind, comparing on one axis how many months or years Goli Joon might live, and on another axis how many I might be able to last at being accepting, at least of the free daycare. But the two plot lines never meet. I give up this computation, partly because both are unknown quantities, and I'm not good with charts.

I have taken over Naveed's extra bedroom (of course, Goli Joon's room is really the dining room). I don't sleep in there, but I do have my clothes, books, and my own antique iron bed. This room was stuffed with Naveed's things that he'd bought at auctions and had no use for but wouldn't dispose of. I implored him to the point of tears when I'd read about places like this being fire hazards. Then I found a family of mice living in a box of string in there. I wish we could have the basement, but the renters are still down there. Finally, he spent a few days working on the mess. But he hasn't stopped bringing home his "good buys," so the mess is building up again.

Writing in bed is more comfortable than sitting at a desk, and I can't write while sitting on Naveed's wavy waterbed. My room is my favorite space in the house, even with Naveed's piles. My antique iron bed is spray painted gold, something Melinda had helped me do. I remember that day. Melinda and I went through four cans of gold spray paint to get the job done. We got so much on our hair, skin, and clothes that we looked like Oscar award trophies.

Now I stand before my closet, trying to decide between blue and black jeans, and also wondering why I'm getting dressed so early when it's the weekend. But of course it's because I want to be presentable for Goli Joon, even on weekend mornings. Otherwise, I might not have even woken up this early.

I wonder how I ended up in this kind of living arrangement, which does not marry well with my personality as an introvert who has never liked to spend time with boyfriends' mothers. I could have moved in with my mom, and maybe I would have if not for her weird boyfriends and Bruce. Is this situation something that I subconsciously willed upon myself? To move in with *someone else's* mom?

Adolescence

My mom has had flirtations for as long as I can remember, and it used to be almost impossible to believe some of them were not affairs. But now I understand that, for the most part, she just needed people who would listen to her.

When I was twelve she went back to college to become a nurse. For three whole years she studied with a Russian student named Pavel. That name became the most heard word in our house. Pavel would listen to Mom talk for hours on end, and in return, my mom would listen to his advice even though she never listened to anyone else's. She would come home from nursing school and say to me, "Pavel recommended this book about emotionally and behaviorally disturbed children," or to my father, "Pavel said the *experience*

of helping others is better than working for money," or to me
again, "Pavel says I'm stupid if I don't think that short marble
pipe I found in your purse is for smoking marijuana."

My mom found my pot pipe in the zipper pocket of my
purse one Saturday when I was thirteen. It was my first purse,
and I thought the zipper pocket was some kind of double-
top-secret compartment nobody would find. I denied that it
was for pot, explaining that I had been smoking cigarettes in
it. So she made me show her. I pulled out the pack of Merits
that was also in the zipper pocket, broke one open and piled
the tobacco in the bowl of the pipe. I smoked it. I was used
to filters, and the cigarette tobacco filtered only through the
pot resin made me dizzy. But Mom believed me, at least until
Pavel set her straight again.

I don't know why my dad put up with all this talk of Pavel.
The guy never even met anyone else in our family, but from
the tidbits Mom told him, he felt able to diagnose all of our
problems. Maybe he could. He was the one who got Mom to
finally submit to alcoholism treatment at Hazelden.

I don't like drinking very much because of those memories
of how Mom acted when she was drunk. And I always associ-
ate how her hair went from auburn red to pure white with her
drinking. Nowadays, I appreciate a good glass of wine or two
with dinner, but that's usually about all. The only time I used
to like drinking was when Melinda and I went out dancing.
Prince was out at the Minneapolis clubs every weekend, and
we liked to get a glimpse of him. Melinda fantasized that he
would admire her dancing and ask her to be in his band—the
new Sheila E. I had to be drunk to dance, even though I had
twelve years of dancing lessons.

When my mom went back to school and started working or
drinking in all her spare time, I rarely saw her. I was thirteen

when she started working the late shift. The hospital ward where she worked had the sickest of babies, those with the rarest and least understood disorders. There were three-year-olds who looked younger than one, and others who looked like old men. Dad couldn't get how she could stand it, but she loved those kids and would talk about them all the time to anyone who would listen. She showed pictures of those sick and dying babies to her friends.

Mom blamed herself for the day I drank until I ended up in the hospital. She guilted herself that maybe being in the hospital was the only way I could get her attention. It wasn't because of her, though. She was wrong.

A girl had written "Valerie Kjos is a slut" in big, purple marker on the bathroom wall at school and started a rumor about me. I came home that day with a plan to get drunk. I didn't know how much I'd have to drink to feel it, so I just kept filling up my red juice glass with gin from the cupboard until the room started to spin.

Dad found me in a pool of vomit, face down, luckily, so I didn't choke on it. I'd peed in my Guess jeans. I woke up in the hospital without any headache, thanks to whatever medicine and glucose they were feeding me intravenously.

"I'm still mad about that," Mom said last time we talked about that day. She suffered hangovers each time she over-did it (which was *every time* she did it). Then her middle child goes and drinks herself nearly to death and wakes up feeling great. And gets a therapeutic massage from a muscular male nurse's assistant.

At least once I became a known bad-ass at school, I dropped the whole airhead Suzanne Somers routine, the one in which I wore my *Sun-In* streaked hair in fountain ponytails out the sides of my head and acted like Chrissy Snow on Three's

Company. "Airhead" had been a compliment, because it went along with "pretty."

Mom knows all of this about me, but I shouldn't take it for granted that I really know my mom. There must be things about Eugenia Randolph that I don't know. Like, for example, why did she drink so much in the first place?

Little Things

Naveed says that Goli Joon told him I'm "pleasant-faced," and she likes how I'm always smiling. I have not told Naveed about Goli Joon snooping in our room, and maybe she's being extra flattering since I have not betrayed her by sharing her secret.

But being liked—if it's truly that—goes a long way with me, and I make a note to myself to keep smiling. Over the next weeks, my cheek muscles will build up from so much smiling, and a smile will become my permanent expression just like my Grandma Kjos. Maybe she smiled a lot because she was a Minnesotan. Or maybe it was because she'd had electroshock therapy in the 1940s.

Goli Joon has many different expressions, one being a little Mona Lisa smile she uses anytime she seems to pity me for my ignorance. Like when I say that Marzieh can't sing. Or that I've never heard of the female poets Simin Behbahani and Forough Farrokhzad. That subtle smile comes with a little click made by touching her tongue to the back of her front teeth.

"Those women are lionesses, but American women think they're the only clever ones," she says with a click. "They hardly even know about Googoosh. So sad."

When she's less pitying and truly put off, she juts her chin up in the air and clucks her tongue. I think it's way less refined than my Grandma Viv's way of indicating disagreement, which is a movie-star-like and elegant little raising of one penciled-in eyebrow.

But I follow Niloofar's advice and learn to appreciate these little tisks, clicks, and clucks of hers most of the time. I like it that she isn't as refined as she appears in her coiffed hair and her elegant gold and turquoise jewelry. And I like how Goli Joon smells of fruit and rosewater instead of department store perfumes like my mom and Grandma. I like to tease her sometimes like Naveed does and call her Gol-ab Joon—Rosewater Dear—instead of Goli Joon.

We call her Roseheart now too, whenever she's acting scrappy with us, because we just watched the Mel Gibson movie *Braveheart* at home with her on DVD.

And she's always cutting up fruit for me and forcing me to eat it between meals instead of Butterfingers and Cheetos, which she says are the cause of my acne. Gummy bears are also to blame, she says, because of the food coloring. When I eat gummy bears, she looks at me like I'm crazy. She calls them *lasteek*, as in elastic, or maybe plastic—I'm not sure. She says a bit of rosewater on some fruit will satisfy my sweet tooth.

I feel healthier eating all this fruit, and I do have fewer pimples. So now I feel guilty when I eat Butterfingers, Cheetos, or gummies, and I do it in my own room with the door closed. I store them in my nightstand drawer next to my gold spray painted bed.

Goli Joon bugs me sometimes, but we have some things in common that make the other clashes more bearable. Unlike my mom—a runner—Goli Joon will never bemoan that she hasn't "worked out." Neither of us likes to exercise too much, although Goli Joon can walk, albeit slowly, all the way to Byerly's to pick up a bag of onions if we aren't around to drive her. I like people who don't feel bad about just doing the normal activities of life and then sitting in contemplation, reading poetry, and listening to music for the rest of the day.

I'm even guilty of some of the things that bug me about her. For example, I've returned things at Dayton's after I've worn them. Yesterday Naveed took Goli Joon to Dayton's because she wanted to return the winter coat she bought there the last time she was here, which was years ago.

She expected that Dayton's would take it back and she could get a different one. There was nothing wrong with that coat—except that it was about four years out of style. Of course they took it back. When I sold shoes at Dayton's during college I once accepted a return for a pair of white go-go boots from 1970. There was nothing in the policy against it. The woman had her receipt.

Hard Candy

Goli Joon's English may not be improving, but I'm learning how to understand her better. I know that I can find her in the kitchen when she yells, "I'm in the chicken!"

I'm not trying to make fun of people who are learning English. It's hard for anybody to learn another language, but you have to admit sometimes the mistakes are funny. Just the other evening at dinner, I accidentally asked Goli Joon if she could please pass the salty penises.

Goli Joon tried to let it go, but she couldn't. Her laughter built, and pretty soon she and Naveed were both slapping the table while I sat there bewildered. They finally calmed down, but Naveed wouldn't tell me until after dinner when we were alone.

I had been asking for the pickles, which in Farsi are referred to as salty cucumbers. The word for cucumber is *khiar*, but I have such a hard time with their sounds so I had said *keer*. I had not known the word for penis was so close to the word for cucumber.

Normally, we communicate by plugging in a Persian word and an English word, then by some charades, until we understand each other or give up until Naveed comes home. I'm learning tons of food words and cooking verbs like fry and boil, chop, and grate.

There's a half-hour between the time I get home and Naveed gets home. Sometimes I run errands in this time, but usually I just go home. I find Goli Joon peeking out the window when I drive up. With a swirl of the curtains, she moves away from the window. By the time I come in through the front door she's on the couch watching reruns of *The Love Connection* and pretending she was never peeking out.

She loves to watch *The Love Connection* and is titillated by the parts she understands. "He said they took a shower together," she says one day of a new contestant.

I say, "No, they never get that raunchy on this show. You must have misunderstood." Goli Joon jerks her chin up in the air at me and clucks her tongue to the roof of her mouth. I hear the woman giggling and confessing to Chuck Woolery that the guy was telling the truth—they did take a shower on their first date.

Goli Joon says "see?" with her gleeful eyes. She's both thrilled and disgusted, and says in Persian, "Dirt to her head!" about the free-loving woman.

Whenever I hear Goli Joon using this expression, I think of people throwing dirt at a woman, but Naveed explains that it probably means something about dirt being shoveled into her grave. Goli Joon shuffles off to the kitchen to check on our dinner. This has been the most exciting moment of her day, I realize.

We know Goli Joon noses around in our bedroom and in the extra bedroom where I keep my stuff, but Naveed defends her right to do this because she's just bored, he says. While we're at work, Goli Joon's winter days consist of cooking; folding our laundry; coloring her hair with L'Oreal; reading unapproved biographies of the former Shah's wife, Queen Farah, and their children; and reading poetry that I will some-day learn was more subversive than I'd imagined.

Oh, and watching T.V., of course. Goli Joon understands the T.V. news just enough to misunderstand and worry. Every time there's a storm warning she thinks it's for our area and she cries and worries about Naveed being on the road. Every time a car accident is reported she thinks it's Naveed who was hit and is dead. This is part of why she's always watching out the window when I drive up. She's sick with worry, and waiting for her oldest son to come home.

If he's really late, or if she's worried because the news has reported an earthquake in Iran or a plane crash during a time when her brothers or other children might be travel-ing, she will hit herself again and again. With one hand, she will hit her other arm, and then alternate hands to hit the opposite arm. The more worried, the harder she hits herself. I ask Naveed if something is wrong with her because of all this self-hitting, but he says not to worry—it's a Shiite thing.

When I come home, it isn't enough to stop the worry, but at least it's someone to tell the day's news. Goli Joon doesn't know that I check the news on AP wires on my computer about five times a day at my new job at Agricultural Education Consultants Inc. I don't have as much free time to surf the web and email Melinda as I did at the insurance company temp job, but I do stay up on current events throughout the day.

I just act like I have been in a bubble all day and let her think she's telling me the world's events for the first time. On slow news days, she tells me about today's rerun episode of *The Love Connection,* or *The Oprah Winfrey Show.* This storytelling ritual gives her some relief from her constant worrying about Naveed's perpetual lateness.

Goli Joon plans her cooking, snooping, reading, and hair coloring around *The Oprah Winfrey Show.* She asks about going to the show, and when we see a magazine at the checkout line at the grocery store featuring a story about Oprah, she buys it with change from her little coin purse. She can't read it, but she likes to look at the pictures of Oprah. I call the Oprah hotline for tickets to the show in Chicago, but I never get through.

"Oprah got thin again," she says in Persian. "Will she get married now?" Then next time, "Bueyy! Oprah is fat again—so fat!" And months later, "Oprah is too thin now, she went too far." And each time, "Is she married yet?"

The O.J. Simpson trial is also on, but Goli Joon tires quickly of this case that has far too much that she doesn't understand in between the courtroom shenanigans. She's voyeuristic enough to want to watch, but the forensics are too time-consuming. So she just asks me every day when I come home, "O.J guilty?"

While we wait for Naveed to get home we try small talk and Goli Joon tries to push some pre-dinner fruit on me.

Lately, a woman at work has been setting out those little Halloween-sized candy bars every day. I eat so many that I'm not ready for dinner at the early hour Goli Joon serves it, much less fruit before dinner. This colleague's husband is a dentist and I suspect she's trying to drum up business for him by giving us all cavities.

But this woman proclaims her innocence by explaining how candy bars aren't so bad for your teeth—it's the hard candies that cause the problems, because you suck on them for so long.

Naveed's Father

Cards have started coming from Naveed's father, who writes in English. Since I have so often told the lie that his father died of throat cancer, these cards are like mail from the grave, written by a ghost. But Naveed's father is very much alive, and living with Naveed's brother in southern Iran so that Darab can make sure he takes his medicine regularly.

Naveed thinks his intention is that I will read the cards and be charmed by the beautiful way he writes of his love for Naveed, thus I will sway Naveed (in womanly fashion) to reconnect with his father.

Goli Joon was arranged to marry Mahmood when she was twenty-four. Mahmood was five years older and the son of a family business connection. He was not sick when they married, but after four or five years, he began to show the signs of paranoid schizophrenia. Those first years together before his sickness took over were good, and they had one girl and two boys. Naveed was the first boy, and that almost is as if to say he was the first child. But he was the second. First was Firoozeh, then Naveed, then Darab.

They were married for twelve years when Mahmood married a second wife. He tried to have the best of both worlds for awhile, but when his second wife got pregnant, he left Goli with their three children.

I have only told my mom and sisters. I can never refer to the half-sibling Naveed does not know. I'm sworn to secrecy. Goli Joon doesn't like how Iranians gossip, and asks me never to tell people about this until she is dead. Even to her best friends, she says that Mahmood died. Nobody knows that he had a child with his second wife, who died recently, and that he's now living in Iran with Darab and Darab's wife and children.

Darab makes sure Mahmood takes his medications to control the schizophrenia. When he doesn't take his medications, chaos ensues. Darab has taken this responsibility to care for this father who was hardly a father to him after he left.

After Mahmood left, Goli Joon was lucky to be allowed to move herself and her children in with her parents. They weren't any more thrilled with the idea than parents here in the U.S. whose kids boomerang back home with kids in tow. But Goli Joon put herself back in school and learned how to run a sewing business with three kids to take care of and no husband.

Naveed doesn't return any pleasantries to his father through the mail, although when Mahmood includes a P.S. asking for a certain type of American eye drops, and a certain brand of American vitamins, Naveed will run out to purchase a generous supply and ship them with insurance.

Cooking with Goli Joon

Goli Joon is not all old-school. She sometimes deviates from her usual feta, pita, and jam breakfast to our Frosted Flakes. She puts the whole box on the table in front of her, and I get a kick out of seeing her eating with Tony the Tiger. I want her to stick her finger in the air and say, "Theyyy'rrre...GREAT!" and let me take a picture. But she isn't game for that.

Goli Joon and I are prehistoric cave women from different clans, developing a simple babel together. We gesture and stumble over simple concepts, like melting. I charade a big pile of something, sinking and spreading out all over the place. "Melll...ttt...ing!" I cry, as I spread out on the kitchen floor like the Wicked Witch of the West in *The Wizard of Oz.*

Naveed plays soccer or basketball with the neighbor, Milad Zand, most Sundays, now that they're friends again. Sometimes I meet my sisters at a bakery and coffee shop in Wayzata, or I go somewhere myself or with Savi, but I feel guilty when I go somewhere and don't invite Goli Joon. So, then I get into a habit of going shopping with her on these days. We come home and I watch Goli Joon cook. I ask her to teach me how to make the rice like she makes it.

"Rice good?" I ask her in Persian, turning my head. She's just six inches behind me. I want her approval of my latest attempt at making the basmati rice that I have got to get as perfect in flavor and texture as hers. I grew up making the Uncle Ben's boil-in-the-bag rice, and Persian rice is quite a bit more complicated. If you've grown up making it, you probably don't realize all the little steps there are that you just do without even thinking. There are tricks, and between Goli Joon and my former job at the Dinky Kebab, I should have them down pat by now.

"Good," she answers, with a lilt at the end of the word and a ducking of the head. She *almost* clucks her tongue. *Good, but not even near perfect,* she means. Basmati only really tastes like basmati when it's cooked right, and then it's so good you can eat it with just some butter and sumac and never want to stop. When it's not quite right, it's only grain.

There are many dishes to go with the rice (or with bread), but only eight or ten that we make often. They're simple enough, and being apprenticed rather than relying on a written recipe, I learn to make them quickly by heart. There are stews, patties, pilafs, stuffed vegetables, quiches, and dips. There's a citrus-y tang from limes, and some heat because their family likes to add chili peppers to many of the dishes.

They're not to be varied too much. You may substitute black-eyed peas for the red beans in the herb stew, or you may choose dried grape powder instead of lime for the eggplant stew, or if you have any, fresh unripened sour grapes. One may choose cubed lamb over cubed beef for any of the stews, but Naveed and Goli Joon don't like our lamb here. They say Iranian lamb is different, and better. The lambs in Iran have a tail like a pillow, full of fat that tastes good enough to cook with. They say our lambs' tails are shriveled up and curled like pig tails.

One day, they will find lamb with that nice fat pillow tail, but it'll require a two-hour drive to a farm each time we want to buy one. Naveed and the farmer will cut its throat and clean it at the farm. Goli and I will have to spend hours in the kitchen hacking the whole animal into pieces ourselves, and then she'll spend more hours cleaning the kitchen with bleach.

One of my favorite stews is the pumpkin one. I watch Goli Joon make it—cutting up big cubes of orange pumpkin and sautéing them with a Persian spice mixture that is sort of like curry powder except that it also includes dried rose petals and a different mix of spices. I learn the name of the stew, *khoresht-e kadoo tanbali,* meaning stew of the lazy squash. The "lazy squash" is what they call the pumpkin.

All in all, Goli Joon sticks with the method, ingredients, proportions, and culinary techniques that she's used for her whole life. She chops and chops until her tendons are sore, and grates onions until her eyes nearly melt out of their sockets.

It's only in the presentation where she may get creative, and Goli Joon delights in her calligraphic artistry with garnishes, producing a different design with each preparation.

Christmas

It was nice of my mom, Laura, and Courtney to get Christmas presents for Goli Joon. They have accepted that she goes where we go and like having her here at my mom's for Christmas. Logically, it doesn't make sense since we don't invite Ty's parents or get them gifts. And speaking of logic, Goli Joon is a Muslim, and while they think Jesus was an important prophet, Christmas just isn't their thing. But Goli Joon loves a holiday gathering and my mom's Christmases are always good.

Goli Joon has received a beaded picture frame, a blue fleece blanket, and some aromatherapy lotions. She doesn't seem embarrassed that she hasn't brought gifts—after all she's the deserving elder. Opening gifts at my mom's takes a long time, and that's after the leisurely brunch.

After brunch and gifts we do blessed nothing. Courtney wants to lie on the couch with me and massage each other's feet. But I'm kind of embarrassed about doing that with Goli Joon here. And I can't relax while seeing Goli Joon wear her coat because she's cold in this house. She's shivering and it makes me nervous. She did the same thing at our family Thanksgiving, but that holiday isn't an all-day thing at Mom's like Christmas.

Bruce is back living with my mom now, having broken up with the woman he'd been jogging and traveling with. Charlie, thank God, has moved on to deeper pockets. Now, Mom and Bruce are wearing matching Christmas turtlenecks, green jeans, and leather belts. They say they're going to throw a small ham in the oven and boil some potatoes, and we're welcome to stay. At Mom's, staying for dinner is always optional on Christmas. Laura and Ty have already left—his mother is cooking a goose. I've never left before dinner, but finally, after Goli Joon unrolls her new fleece blanket to put over her coat, I say, "Let's go."

We gather all our Christmas booty and head out before the ham has even gone in the oven. In the car driving the short distance home, Goli Joon asks Naveed, "Why did we leave so fast? Her mother went to so much trouble and I was having such a nice time."

When we get home I notice that the greenery Naveed hung above our front door for its festive spirit is turning brown. Naveed won't take the greenery down, no matter how many times I ask him and make fun of his "Christmas brownery." That brown mess will hang above our door until I finally get a ladder myself and take it down on a day in February when we're having Savi and Matthew for dinner. We invited them partly so Matthew and his truck can help Naveed take apart and move Naveed's black lacquer waterbed set to a faraway thrift store I found that will accept the donation. Goodwill won't take waterbeds.

Prayer

The reason it's rude to ask a guest how long they plan to stay is that you would never need to ask if you hoped, as you should, that they never leave. Most guests wouldn't overstay, but mothers are special.

Goli Joon has had two heart valves replaced in the past, and now a third one is leaking. We bring her to her specialist who wants to start seeing her monthly once Naveed can nail down some better health insurance. Naveed starts talking about having her stay here, about her getting residency, and says if she stays forever she might get her own apartment and maybe even some kind of job. But his one friend whose mother got her own apartment and a job is talked about behind his back. "Why would he pack her off to a little apartment and make her work when he and his wife have that big house?" they whisper. The answer, of course, is that his wife is American.

It's hard to live with my boyfriend's non-English-speaking mother in just the upstairs of this house with its single bathroom. Naveed is as happy as can be, but not oblivious to the tension. He translates and mediates the daily misunderstandings. He listens when I vent.

I think of what Niloofar said, that Naveed's mom sounds like she's as good as they come and it's just the idiosyncrasies that bother me. It's the loss of control. I'm lucky to have Naveed, a boyfriend who doesn't watch ESPN while getting stoned and drinking eight bottles of Michelob (like Kurt), and who loves me with his whole body and soul instead of keeping me at arm's length (like Quentin). Having his nice, helpful mom live with us for a while isn't too high a price to pay, is it?

Even the idiosyncrasies are minor. I understand them more now, like that the reason Goli Joon leaves water splashed all over the bathroom is because of the necessary ablutions before her prayers. She must be ritually cleansed before praying. Wiping down the vanity after splashing water up her arms would undo the purification.

Even though she doesn't seem religious, like the women who wear chadors and head scarves, she does pray. I accidentally interrupt her during her prayer time one afternoon. I've come to ask a cooking question, which can wait, but I stay a minute. I like seeing her in her gauzy prayer wrap. It's white cotton and so soft, like the cheese cloth she uses to make the thick type of yogurt that Americans will someday discover only as "Greek."

She's prostrate on the floor and in a state that I wish I could learn to enter. I haven't truly prayed since I was twelve, and it's hard to believe I used to pray and pray like God was listening. When I was twelve, my God had a human ear and I spoke to him in my head. I didn't worship him; he was just someone to talk to. But I never had ritualized prayer like Goli Joon has—I wonder if God is her confidant or her object to worship, or if it's possible that he could be both.

I see how Goli Joon opens her hands when she prays to the above. I try it myself, just for a minute, in the privacy of the extra bedroom that I call my own. It feels not very Minnesotan, but it makes a difference. Praying with my palms up does help me feel more connected to the world, to something higher, and I realize that folding hands or pressing them together just makes me feel more clenched-up and repressed. I still don't really feel God with my palms open to the ceiling—to the heavens, but I can see there's potential for that. Maybe when I'm old like Goli Joon I will try it again.

Domesticity

Our kitchen and hallway floors are dark stone, which looks rich but hurts our feet and is cold in winter. I bear it or wear cozy slippers, but Goli Joon buys some Dr. Scholl's sandals at Target for $14.99.

Although the foot beds are wood, she likes the support and the rubberized sole. She wears them on the stone floor and then kicks them off here and there around the carpeted house.

This is one of her very few habits of disorder. The shoes always trip me up. It's usually I who am sloppy and Goli Joon straightening up after me, but in this one thing we reverse roles and I constantly pair the kicked-off Dr. Scholl's. I point the sandal toes squarely to the foyer corner, with no small amount of satisfaction at proving her domestic imperfection.

Goli Joon still doesn't like my lasagna, or my fish tacos and guacamole. The first time she bites into a "Jucy Lucy" she gives me that "dirt to your head" look. She's offended by these burgers that are the specialty of a couple of rival bars in Minneapolis and that I have learned to replicate. It's an oniony cheeseburger with the cheese on the inside. It squirts out at you, burning your mouth, when you bite. It's not nice to serve your boyfriend's mother attack cheese.

Our stove is the color of the darkest red mineral clay. The oven is the same "Coppertone" color with a 1960s bubble design on the control panel. It's the first gas stove I've ever used, having grown up in 1970s and 80s suburban homes and modern college apartments.

I don't think I even knew about gas before, but I like controlling the flame. The flame here in our little cave scared me at first, but not Goli Joon. She's probably always used a gas stove and she has tricks for controlling the heat. When she wants wider conduction, or just to keep something warm, she places a perforated hard aluminum circle over the flame and puts the pot on that. She brought that thing from Iran—I'd never seen one here. She uses a wok ring around the burner when she needs to raise the pot higher.

The cabinets are oak and the ivory Linoleum counters are flecked with light gold stars—I'd always thought of Linoleum as flooring, but apparently mid-century countertops were Linoleum brand too. Goli Joon wants the lights on at all times of day to supplement the tiny bit of light that filters through the trees into the small window. When she complains about the lack of light, Naveed brings home a ceiling fixture the size and shape of a small, florescent flying saucer. I keep the flying saucer turned off during the day when I'm alone in the kitchen. But I'm never alone in there for long.

We use few gadgets beyond the ancient implement of the sharp knife and a mini-chopper. There's an old Black & Decker food processor pushed to the back of a cabinet, one of Naveed's surplus store purchases that even he can't figure out how to put together. There's the robot-looking bread machine Naveed bought at Bank's.

But for what we actually use, it's mainly the big knife, with its sister the chopping board. We chop and slice and julienne and mince. When we make the herb stew from several big bundles of greens, the chopping board is stained green until Goli Joon bleaches it out.

The herbs have to be very finely chopped. Goli Joon's thin arm goes at it and she can't stop. So she chops extra and freezes them in Ziploc freezer bags. She's a chopping machine. I can do all of the other chopping, but mincing the baskets full of herbs gives me tendonitis.

We have one counter space for chopping, but also a small table. Sometimes Goli Joon sits at the table to trim green beans or peel the waxy outer shell and the skins off the fava beans, while I might kneel on the chair across from her, rolling out pie dough. Eventually, like friends who have known each other a long time, we get comfortable with not keeping up a conversation all of the time while we're working in the kitchen.

When we do talk, our conversation is usually small and shallow partly because of our language barrier. But sometimes I muster up the Persian words and patience to get nosy and ask things—like why she sometimes burns wild rue, and why she doesn't like the woman who lives across the street.

Then she gets annoyed with me and says things in Persian that I don't understand until I give up and stop asking about things that are none of my business.

Persian New Year

Naveed's distant cousin coincidentally lives here in the Twin Cities too. She lives not in the part of South Minneapolis where we live but just outside of it, where within twelve blocks the homes go from ritzy to decent to dangerous to live in. She and her family haven't been here very long, and we only know they're here because her grandma told Goli Joon. The cousin and her husband have two little boys, which they support on her husband's taxi driving job. Maybe someday he can be an engineer again like he was in Iran, but this has to do for now.

Goli Joon, like a queen on her throne, waits for the woman to call. The younger should always call the elder. But Goli Joon is lonely at home and she finally bends the rule to call her a couple of times. She invites her and her family to the dinner party we're planning for *Noh Ruz*, the Persian New Year.

To get ready for Noh Ruz, we get to do some major redecorating. We brush the brown brick fireplace with a wire brush until all the loose sand is out, and then we prime it and paint it white. To take advantage of all the renewal, I work hard to make that extra bedroom more my own.

The wild rue—the esphand—I learn, is not only to counteract the evil eye. It's for cleansing, for a fresh start. To push out all of last year's bad feelings, Goli Joon burns wild rue in every room of the house, insisting too on waving her smoking copper spoon of it over all of our heads.

Then, the three of us—Naveed, Goli Joon, and I—spend three solid days together in our little kitchen preparing the spring New Year's dinner party for his cousin's family and three of Naveed's buddies and their families who live around here and in Edina. Some of them also have elderly live-in parents.

Goli Joon walks me through every step of the cooking, like the whole ocean whitefish that still has its eyes. I let her show me everything, even things she's shown me several times before. I'm calm and happy about spring and the fragrant hyacinths filling our house, so I just nod my head and work as assigned.

Except for when she tries to make me soak everything, even the dried dill weed and the dried barberries for the three kinds of rice we're going to make—I rebel at that. Iranians like to soak everything: dried herbs, rice, dried fruit, chicken. The Mohammadi roses are the only dried things that do not need to be soaked because they're clean and pure, being from the family's own estate in Kashan.

I soak the rice, but not the other things. They say they can have sand and rocks in them, but I haven't had that problem yet. Cleaning dried dill in a bowl of water seems like overkill.

I swear they would soak their salt before sprinkling it if they could—a little too obsessive on the cleanliness thing if you ask me.

"My mom and my Grandma Vivian have always said that everybody has to eat a peck of dirt before they die," I tell Goli Joon.

Naveed translates it for me to her. "But we don't want the guests to die at our house," she answers.

When our guests arrive, we serve eggplant dip, cucumber-yogurt dip garnished with dried rose petals, and stuffed grape leaves. Our guests open pockets of pita bread and stuff them with fresh herbs, bright pink radishes, feta cheese, and walnuts. There are also green onions that Goli Joon cut vertically part-way up from the white part and shocked in cold water so the cut-ends curl up like they've had a perm.

We eat the appetizer spread and socialize before we will present the fish, the three kinds of khoresht, and the three kinds of rice. Goli Joon shows the parents of Naveed's friends Naveed's old photo album, which now has some photos of me stuck behind a plastic sheet on the back pages. I hear her say the words for "God willing" and "marriage" and I know she's talking about him marrying me.

She's saying nice things about me, and—I think—giving me all the credit for the cooking. "Valerie Joon made the dill rice, and even the barberry rice, and she didn't even have any help from me or Naveed Joon at all," she says. I'm a little puzzled about how emphatic she is about not taking any credit for the meal, but I figure she's trying to make me look good to the others.

Finally, Naveed and I go into our little kitchen and move the fish onto a large platter. I take the large pot of dill rice off the stove and start spooning the rice into mounds on other platters. I take a little taste of the dill rice, and right away I feel the gritty crunch of sand.

Hoping it's just the one bite, I take another and it's fine. A third bite is gritty again, but I keep mounding the rice, praying that nobody will notice. Naveed comes back into the kitchen to gather more platters. The barberries have been sautéed in a pan with saffron and butter. It's time to drizzle the fragrant mixture onto one of our two mounds of white rice. Naveed starts drizzling and mixing. It looks like little rubies on a bed of gold and pearls.

Then he takes a taste. "Did you soak the barberries?" he asks right away.

"You know, you can't soak every ingredient in the pantry before you use it."

"There's sand in there," he says. One more bite, and then he winces. "And rocks."

Naveed spoons the barberry mixture into the garbage and we're left with the second mound of white rice. He quickly mixes some saffron powder into water and garnishes the rice with that. Now we just have the gritty dill rice and the plain rice with a little saffron. "The dill rice is okay, right?" he says.

"I think it's okay." I'm doomed.

We bring the food into the living room and set it on the dining table, where everyone comes to dish up their own plates. I watch with horror as all our guests crunch as discreetly as they can on sandy dill rice until finally Goli Joon takes it off the table and throws it in the kitchen garbage. I'm red-faced, but defensive. If we bought our dried dill in little glass Schilling jars at Byerly's instead of big plastic bags at the import market, it would not have dirt in it.

Still, there's plenty of food that does not hurt our guests' teeth. Everyone is stuffed before we even pour the tea and bring out the desserts: saffron-rosewater-pistachio ice cream and baklava, and big bowls of fruit.

Golden Chicks

Nobody has chickens around here. It's illegal. Sure, later it will be legal "urban farming," but right now it's still unheard of. But since I started my new job at Agricultural Education Consultants, I've met lots of people who have chickens. The secretary has been selling chicks to other people in the office this week, and I put in my order for two.

Female chicks, of course. The crowing of a rooster wouldn't be cool in Minneapolis. "Where do your co-workers live?" Naveed asks. Clearly they must live out in the country, or an outer ring suburb.

"We'll keep them out back," I say. "Nobody will know, except for the renters."

Naveed says I've clearly never been around chickens. People will know. But I bring them home anyway and Naveed builds a little coop for them. I name them Nancy and Nala.

Goli Joon calls out one of her rhymes when she sees them. She's always calling out rhymes—she has one for everything. It's just part of the everyday poetry of the Persian language.

> *Joojeh joojeh taliyeh, khoonet kojast? To baghche.*
> Golden chick-chick, where is your home?
> It's in the garden.

We keep a lid on it. None of the neighbors find out about Nancy and Nala. Except for the Iranian neighbors, Milad and Yasmin. Somehow, they know.

Their youngest daughter, Parvaneh, flies over to our house like the butterfly she is named after to see the chicks, and instantly falls in love. She stands there over the coop in a little purple tutu and kisses them again and again until Yasmin Noury comes to get her. She yells at her that she should know better and that she's going to have to disinfect her mouth for kissing the chicks. But Yasmin's eyes are full of laughter and love for Parvaneh as she leads her back home.

Jogger

Since the weather has warmed up a little and the streets aren't icy, there are more joggers running by our house. Watching the female joggers, with their suits that get skimpier with each day that the weather warms, becomes another of Goli Joon's favorite pastimes. "They have no shame! Dirt to their heads—why would their mothers let them go out that way?" she asks, especially about those who are the youngest and in the best shape.

But one bright day, I see Goli Joon peeking through the curtains and she's silent. Her whole body contorts as she cranes her head to follow something or someone that is moving out of sight. "What's out there?" I ask.

Goli Joon jumps out from her hiding spot in the curtains.

"Nothing. It wasn't anything." But fifteen minutes later I come back in the room and she's contorted again. I move into the curtains myself and see him: A man at least sixty years old who is not quite jogging and not quite walking. He's olive-skinned and tall, very tall, and handsome. Even I see the appeal.

"He's pretty," I say in Persian. The word for handsome is different, but I don't know it yet so I just say pretty. This is how I always make do with the language. I look out the window again just as the man finishes up his calisthenics and then walks up to the front steps of the house across the street. Yasmin Noury comes outside to bring the man a glass of water.

"Is he Iranian?" I ask—for I can often tell now, even from a distance. "Is that her father?"

"Who—what are you saying?" Goli Joon asks, her olive face turning as pink as the hyacinths we had not long ago on our Noh Ruz altar. And that's the end of the conversation.

The distant cousin has not called since the Noh Ruz party, even though she should have called to thank Goli Joon the next day, and to invite us—or at least Goli Joon—over for dinner in reciprocation.

"Your cousin wore too much gold jewelry! It's not necessary to wear all of one's gold at the same time," Goli Joon says to Naveed after several days of the phone not ringing for her. "She looked like a fat Mexican lady."

"She shouldn't say things like that," I whisper to Naveed. "It sounds prejudiced."

"I know, but she feels hurt and disrespected," he whispers back. Sometimes I'm glad she doesn't speak enough English for people I know to hear some of the things she says when she feels hurt and disrespected.

I'm still learning the rules called *taarof*, which include particulars about inviting, and serving, and at what point you can accept something that is offered. In general, you have to ask three times to give a person the dignity of refusing your invitation twice before they finally accept or truly decline. But there's so much more to taarof than that.

I'm still learning the manners of initiating every communication with an elder. Maybe this cousin and her generation struggle with the traditions too. After all, she's young.

And the woman across the street from us? Yasmin? She doesn't talk to Goli Joon as much as it seems Persian manners would dictate either.

Landscape Planning

Naveed and I are going to grow a garden. We're obsessed with our garden layout. Plant and seed catalogs are strewn about our bedroom. Our first shipment has just arrived. The soil beds are tilled. It's going to be perfect.

This morning, Goli Joon saw us planning our garden at the dining table and bustled back into her room. She came out with her king-sized white pillowcase of mysterious items, telling us to forget those catalogs. From the pillowcase, she pulled huge brown paper packages. She had seeds of tarragon, cress, fenugreek, thyme, cilantro, parsley, onions and shallots, five types of basil, and a cucumber variety that Naveed tells me tastes sweet like melon.

We only have so much space. Now here she is with enough seeds to fill a park, and pretty heavily on the herbs if you ask me. She's generous and thoughtful to bring these seeds, but I don't appreciate it. Not only am I not thankful, but I'm pissed off.

The thing is, the garden has become a romantic endeavor. It's almost the only thing we have just between the two of us. But I have picked the wrong thing to exclude Goli Joon from because she's been gardening since before I was even born.

After some negotiating, some space is freed up for Goli Joon. Also, my yellow marigolds are sacrificed in the negotiations. Yellow flowers, she tells me, invite sickness into the home. I argue that yellow is the color of pure joy, the color of the sun itself. She argues that yellow, in a flower, is the color of death. I say that's fine, I will give them to my mother, who's always planted yellow marigolds. And her kitchen has always been yellow too.

Naveed is reworking our garden blueprint now, tightening up the spaces for all of our flowers, so that Goli Joon can tend her own section of tilled earth.

Horticultural Science

It's early morning the next day and I'm looking out the window above our new bed. Will today be good planting weather or will it storm again? I look to the sky. The sun is out.

"Hey!," I say out loud, peering closer. Goli Joon is outside in her floral housedress, the one with the eyelet lace-trimmed front pockets. She reaches into one of the pockets and pulls out a brown paper bag, then squats over a garden bed that is supposed to be for old-fashioned perennials—purple cone-flowers, forget-me-nots, and such. Her hand reaches into the bag, and then she flicks her wrist. My eyes follow a gust of tiny herb seeds flying across the freshly tilled soil.

She throws out another handful. A few more flicks of her thin wrist and she has filled up my perennial bed. And moved on to another flower bed. This short, sixty-something-year-old Iranian woman who has invaded my newly minted independent-American-woman-of-the-house life barely pauses before crouching down in the vegetable garden and seeding most of it too.

I wonder, should I make a scene in the yard now or just till her seeds two feet under when she's not looking? I mean, this is our garden! I may be overreacting, but this seems to confirm my fears that Naveed and I will never be just a normal couple. Normal to me means nuclear family, not this extended-family bull.

I don't till her seeds under. But Goli Joon has broken our agreement, so I go outside and quietly replant the yellow marigolds along the walkway to the front door. They look cheerful to me, not like death. At first they look cheerful, anyway, but then I somehow lose my enthusiasm for yellow. I can see that it isn't all sunshine, and thinking of Goli Joon's words about sickness, I remember about the yellow plague and bile and Melinda's scruffy chair that she left behind. That classic story I read in Women's Studies class comes to mind too—*The Yellow Wallpaper*—about the 1800s housewife whose doctor husband confined her for a nervous disorder until she really did go insane staring at the walls all summer long.

Still, the marigolds stand, a testament to my own stubbornness, not to be outdone by Naveed's mother's own desire to do things her way.

The rest of the day, I carom between resentment and anticipation. By dinnertime, we progress to talking about what else we could plant in our negative space and what we will cook with our future homegrown bounty. That discussion leads to an evening trip to the plant nursery, where I witness Goli Joon pinch off a sprig of portulaca rose to bring home and root. I glare at her, half expecting to hear sirens and be hauled to a security office.

"Free sample," she says, a term she knows well in English, as she sticks it in her pocket.

A few days later, Naveed and I do our own planting exactly as we have planned. We plant our seeds and nursery plants just where we said we would, even though that space is already seeded to the hilt.

Naveed and I water morning and night, and who knows how much watering goes on while we're at work. I'm sure the garden will drown when the unexpected flood rains of Gilgamesh pound the earth for the next several days. But I watch for signs of life against all odds. We all watch, getting our faces down to the earth several times a day to see if anything has poked up.

When we see the first sprouts, we know we have a jungle on our hands. The seedlings are coming in so thick that it looks more like a carpet, or a lawn, than a garden bed. The how-to books say to thin out crowded seedlings by decapitation. I stand out there and see how my garden plan is ruined.

One day, while I'm watching my plants get strangled by Goli Joon's vines, I see that middle-aged man leave the house across the street for his daily jog. He begins to do his calisthenics in the middle of the road.

I go back inside, having decided not to pinch the heads off of Goli Joon's plants, but to just complain over and over to Naveed instead. I turn the doorknob and give the door the firm kick it needs to open. Goli Joon walks quickly from the living room—probably from her post at the window—toward the kitchen, slides open the pocket door, and closes it behind her.

Naveed confirms to me, when asked, that the jogger is Yasmin Noury's father who lives with them from time to time. I half-joke that maybe if he and Goli Joon got together, then we and the neighbor couple might actually be able to go out like normal couples sometimes instead of with our third wheels. We often see the three of them, with the children, heading out and I realize I have never seen Milad and Yasmin leave the house all alone. Naveed says, "We can go out as a couple whenever we want to. My mom doesn't need a boyfriend to babysit her."

"But we never do," I say. That night, Naveed comes up with a James Bond movie date plan. We don't do dinner out too because Goli Joon had been making the khoresht since right after breakfast, but at least we go out and eat popcorn out of the same bucket, and I can sit in the front seat of the car.

Duluth

The lupines are in bloom in the roadside ditches and fields around Lake Superior in Duluth, where my mom and Bruce are running in the annual Grandma's Marathon. I've never seen lupines before, except on the photo on a seed packet. I bought some seeds last month and planted them in a garden bed as soon as it was safe to plant, but they never came up at all. It could be because of all Goli Joon's herbs, or maybe I should have started them under lights inside.

There are broad fields of lupines here, hundreds of thousands of them. I wonder aloud if they're native or not; they look like nobody had to do anything special to get them to grow and flower. But Laura and Courtney aren't interested.

Mom and Bruce have a suite at Fitger's, the good hotel that books up almost a year ahead of the marathon. Bruce had it booked long ago since he runs Grandma's every year and practically has a standing reservation. Our mom registered late after treating it like the biggest decision of her life. My sisters and I decided just two weeks ago that we should cheer her on, so we took what we could get—a run-down motel room outside of town. Laura wiped down everything when we arrived and always keeps her slippers on when we're there, which is as little as possible.

I'm not even in the race, but it's the most exercise I've had in years, maybe ever. That's because, in our role as encouraging daughters, we drive from one point on the route to another to cheer. We park the car, then we have to dash to the viewing section in time to be sure we see her go by. Then we have to dash back to the car to do it all over again. That's hard for me not only because I'm out of shape, but also because the locals are holding lots of garage sales to make some cash on all the tourists. I've been spending too much time with Naveed and his mom, so I too now brake for garage sales. Laura and Courtney drag me from them, only once letting me stop to buy somebody's old sweatshirt because even in the middle of June the Lake Superior air chills me.

We only see Bruce at the first cheering stop because he's fast and has passed by the time we get to the others. But we see Mom at all five points along the route just as planned. We wave and holler, "Lookin' good, Eugenia!" and, "You can do it, Mom!" even though by the third point she isn't looking good and we aren't sure she should be doing it.

When we arrive at the finish line, we wait for a long time. Courtney wonders if we missed her crossing, so she dives into the crowd to look for her. She comes back with Bruce, who is wrapped in a big silver reflective sheet that's supposed to keep his muscles warm and prevent cramping.

A woman with a prosthetic lower leg crosses the finish line. I look at Bruce with concern, but he's clapping for the woman. "Shouldn't our mom get in before the lady with the artificial limb?" I ask.

"No worries, that lady's an elite runner. She usually comes in a lot faster. She had a bad day."

"So the lady with the artificial leg who had a bad day is done, but our mom is still out there? Should we go look for her?" I ask. There aren't many people left now, mostly people who look like they ran the marathon on a bet or a dare, and one of them pukes in the middle of the road as soon as she crosses.

But then, finally, as if she'd stopped to freshen up, our mom comes into view and we cheer wildly as she crosses the white line. She waves and smiles nonchalantly just like Grandma Viv, as if she's out shopping for a new dress in downtown Duluth, not like she just ran more than twenty-six miles. Somebody hands her a silver blanket as she crosses the finish line. She wraps it around herself like she *was* in fact just out shopping for a new dress, and this is it, and doesn't it look lovely?

We all give her hugs and congratulate her. She pushes us away because she's sweaty, but we keep hugging her anyway because we're so proud.

"Did you see the lupines?" she asks, and I realize she's in a state of runner's euphoria, an earned high that did not come without intense effort. *My mom ran Grandma's Marathon,* I imagine telling my friends and my colleagues at Agricultural Education Consultants. Of course they will be impressed.

I walk with her and then I hold her up from behind while Bruce helps her stretch her legs out in front. I'll never be a runner, and maybe Mom and I don't have a lot in common. But I notice she asked me, and only me, about the lupines. I nod enthusiastically. "Of course, how could anybody miss them?"

Behind Our House

Our kitchen's back door leads outside to four steps and a concrete patio used by the basement renters. Naveed is thinking of kicking them out and letting us finally have the basement, but right now we need the money. This morning, the young women sit on the steps and smoke cigarettes. The chickens are bigger now. Nala squawks at the girls, as if complaining about the cigarette smoke. Goli Joon, safe in her dark cave, peeks out the small window, craning her head sideways so she can see and hear the renters. "How bare they dress! They are almost naked," she whispers to me.

Goli Joon cannot normally understand English very well, but she tries with all her might to make out what the girls are saying. Each morsel of these conversations not meant for her ears is delicious to her and she doesn't care that I know she's snooping. "Shhh," she whispers. "The blonde-haired one is talking. She said she is going to sleep with her boyfriend tonight."

Goli Joon revels in the warm weather and spends a lot of time out in the garden. But she still likes to spy from inside. Naveed claims not to have seen Goli Joon spying on the renters, and he totally denies my mention of her quiet but obvious interest in the man who jogs and stretches in the road in front of our house. I ask her in private if she's met him, but she looks at me as if I'm completely out of my mind. For one thing, she's—at least technically—married. But even without that, having any sort of romance at this point must be unfathomable to her, because—as far as I know—it's been twenty-five years. Still, it seems as if there's some interest.

As much as I pretend like I don't understand why my mom needs a man in her life so desperately, I'm the same and I cannot understand how Goli Joon could go twenty-five years without one. I mention this thought to my mom because I tell her everything when she will listen, even things that are none of my business. She says, "You shouldn't assume Goli Joon doesn't have the same feelings as any normal woman."

I know what she means is that I shouldn't assume that a respectable Muslim woman doesn't have the same desires as any other women.

"I wonder if she's ever, you know, been with anybody else in all this time," I say.

"I would," my mom says, always seeing other people's situation through the thought of what she would do. "I wouldn't just sit around."

Fruition

In July and August, thickets of herb foliage complement the flowers and vegetables springing up among them. But even in June, the radishes are ready. Goli Joon pulls them up from the earth. They're as bright pinky red as the tight shirt Melinda used to wear out dancing at the Minneapolis nightclubs, hoping Prince or somebody would notice her.

There's a rhyme. There's always a rhyme.

> *Torobeche, familet ki ast? Subziche digeh.*
> Little radish, who is your family?
> The other little vegetables.

Goli Joon pulls weeds every day, and the landscape is transformed into something out of a storybook, except for the ugly chicken wire Naveed has surrounded the vegetables with to keep out the rabbits, which he chases away from our yard early every morning. Eventually, he builds a giant frame for the biggest section of garden and extends the chicken wire all the way over it, letting our two illegal chickens range freely in there.

The cucumbers Goli Joon seeded are sweeter than any I've ever had. I realize that cucumbers are more like melons than the gourds they're really related to. Give them a hard rind and they would be melons. Goli Joon picks and serves platters of our raw herbs, which we shove in our mouths between bites of other summer food. It feels so healthy. My skin clears up by August.

In September, the basil and thyme produce a million tiny iridescent florets. You wouldn't believe how they look at night, under the moon. Our nighttime garden is a perfect reflection of the starlit sky.

Uncles

Goli Joon's tongue clicks against the back of her teeth as she stands at the living room window. I glance outside, where her two brothers smoke at the end of the driveway. Uncle Hami flicks his cigarette butt out onto our curb. She clicks again, and then she clucks her tongue too. It's not the first time I've heard her do the click-cluck today—they are her *little* brothers, even if they're nearly senior citizens, and she's just being a concerned eldest sibling.

I had worried when I heard Naveed's uncles were coming for a "visit," but Naveed assured me that these men have busy lives. They're *not* planning to move in with us for the season.

Uncle Hami is a geological engineer who lives in Dallas and travels all over the world inspecting the insides of the earth for mining and petroleum companies. Uncle Omid lives in Iran on family property on the Niahvarin mountainside near Goli Joon's condo that she lives in when she's there but not at the ancestral estate in Kashan. Omid has a business, and a much younger girlfriend, to get back to.

We've spent the last few weeks preparing for the visit. I've noticed the house looks better and better with each holiday or visitor. We framed some old black and white photos to hang on the wall next to our drawings of nudes. Naveed has done the back-breaking work of building raised garden beds and filling them with flowers. We've cleaned, and organized, and Naveed has even moved some of his packrat stuff into the small laundry room downstairs that we share with the renters. It's hard to get in and out of there with a laundry basket now, and the renters complain.

Goli Joon gave me a piece of hot pink, gold-embroidered sari silk that her grandfather gave her upon his return from one of his Indian business trips so many decades ago. She'd been hanging onto it for years and said we should do something with it. I made it into a little lampshade for my ninety-nine dollar floor lamp that I bought at the Bombay Company. A lot happens when visitors are coming.

One of Naveed's family's oldest friends knew that Uncle Omid and Uncle Hami were coming—they had told only one friend, but word travels fast around here. The friend and his wife are having a dinner party at their house twelve blocks west in Edina. Their house is very rich looking, but especially so because of all the antique gilded gold furniture. This is the look Melinda and I had been going for during our gold spray paint phase, if ever so pathetically. This home is filled with real gold gilt, silk Persian carpets and millions of antique dishes and collectible figurines.

"*Hurta-purta*," Goli Joon whispers to me behind the hostess's back, the rhymey Persian term for useless knickknacks.

I hear lots of advice from everyone at the party, like if a good woman believes in her man she will ensure success for the man, and thus they will be happy. Like how if she always makes sure her husband packs everything he needs for a business trip then he will have a successful trip and that will be good for them both. I know this philosophy from women's study class: It's Betty Friedan's *The Feminine Mystique*. Yet these women have careers. Maybe they're just a special breed of superwomen who can do even more than all the other superwomen.

And since they know Naveed is good and believe I'm a woman with a heart of gold, certainly Naveed will become very successful. Certainly, he will get out of his "stalled" career designing parking ramps. I laugh at the "stalled" part, thinking it's a parking-stall pun, but nobody else is laughing. Goli Joon drinks tea off in a corner with another older woman, holding her chin high as she drinks it. She won't argue with anybody, but in her book, her son has done great even though he's not the owner of the company.

I'm relieved at the party when the talk turns to politics and off of Naveed's career. One of the women talks politics too and I'd like to hear what she has to say, but the hostess takes me aside to make small talk, like asking me where I like to go shopping. She's probably trying to be polite by taking me aside to speak with me in English. I half-listen to her and half-listen to the political discussion going on in Persian. I know these Iranians all despise the conservative mullahs. None of them are very religious, except a few who go to the Sufi mosque in town. Naveed is quiet. He doesn't participate in that conversation very much. He doesn't like politics.

Goli Joon tells me, Naveed, and her brothers on the ride home that those old friends, as successful as they are, don't have any class. "For one thing," she says. "The woman put so much rosewater in her basmati rice."

"But Goli Joon, I was sure you must have loved that," I say. "Maybe her rosewater comes from your family's business."

But no, she tells me, "Low-quality rosewater—the kind for pouring to cleanse a headstone at a grave. And the rice wasn't steamed right. You can't pour rosewater over everything and expect it to cover up bad cooking."

She and I are in the backseat together, with her youngest brother on the other side of her and her other brother in the front passenger seat next to Naveed. High on too much tea and saffron, I make her give me a high-five. She and I bond for a minute over defending our parking-ramp engineer, the subject of too much advice at the party. Who knows what those so-called friends would have said if Naveed had realized his true dream job, forest ranger in a forest with trout streams.

When we get home late at night, Naveed goes outside to check his leaf pile where he's composting and collects worms for fishing. He likes to check it at night, with a flashlight. That's when the worms are most active.

The next day is spent outside, from the time our tall *Indian Summer* sunflowers face the rising sun to the east until they have turned their giant gold-orange heads west to say good-night. All three meals are taken in our garden chairs, not far from the chicken coop. More than once the uncles mention that the fatter hen, Nancy, would make good chicken kebab.

Come evening, after the sunflowers have hung their heads in repose, Naveed drives Omid and Hami to the airport for their flights.

Always after having lots of company, it feels like less of a burden to have just Goli Joon. And perhaps she thinks of it as less of a burden to care for only me and Naveed. We're full from so much dining, so for the following days we eat only what we can gather straight from the garden. We're too tired to go to the grocery store, so when we do start to feel hungry again, we joke that we really could cook our good-for-nothing hens. If only they would at least lay some eggs.

Nancy and Nala have learned to fly short distances, and to take dirt baths in the garden. They've been acting strange lately and sitting a lot. I wonder if they're just hot and tired, or if they're going to start laying soon.

They've become very beautiful, but very different, and we won't be entirely sure that Nala is a hen until she starts laying. For one thing, her comb is getting so big. And for another, she acts very butch, always strutting around and trying to control poor, sweet Nancy.

Nancy is your typical fat hen. She's tan and white and looks straight out of a nursery rhyme. Nala is black and white speckled, tall and lean, with a beady hardness to her eyes. Naveed feeds them corn cobs all of the time. Their crowns are always yellow and sticky because the pieces of kernels fly up and get stuck there when they peck at them, but they don't care.

"What a life," Goli Joon says of them. "What must it be like to have no worries?"

Pomegranates

Now that Melinda knows I've been cooking a lot too, she emails me recipes and sends me big packets of food articles. I can spot them from fifteen feet away when I walk into the house and see them on the dining table. Melinda's round, flourish-y handwriting stands out among the other pieces of mail. And I think, maybe the reason I'm cooking more now, and starting to develop a style of my own, is that I'm away from her. Her moving has taken that dominant influence off of me. Not that I don't have other influences now. When her packets and recipes arrive, I flip through them and then throw them in the recycling basket. *No Melinda,* I think, *I am not going to make your roasted fennel salmon bisque or your hazelnut cannolis. I'm not going to make your Italian wedding soup or your Cajun turkey.* Well, maybe the Cajun turkey. I pull that one out of the basket.

Suddenly, pomegranates are all the rage, and Martha Stewart shows how to juice them on her show. This is a new concept for me, since I usually see Naveed eating them over the sink. He cuts them into sections of their ruby juice-filled beads, puts a section in his mouth, sucks out the juice, and spits out the fiber. Bottled pomegranate syrup goes in khoreshts, and meatball sauces. But the food world has decided to put the pomegranate on a pedestal. Before long, we're making our own juice from fresh pomegranates, and serving it on everything from ice cream to salad. The seeds bejewel our pomegranate-walnut *fesenjoon* sauce now when we have company. Goli Joon says pomegranate juice cleans your blood.

Lazy Squash

There are so many characters in the book I'm reading, called *Moo,* by Jane Smiley. I can hardly keep them straight, but I'm glad the author has included them all. It's more real.

There are so many people in all of our lives, and it must be really hard for writers to cull out so many characters when they write more focused novels. I'm learning that lesson with *Shoedog.* I can't fit in all the weirdoes who worked with me in Women's Shoes at Dayton's in downtown Minneapolis, so I'm focusing on fictionalizing a few of them, especially Megan. She's a little bit like me, except a major invention being that Megan secretly had a co-worker's baby and gave it up for adoption. I've been watching *All My Children* with some of the other women at work over lunch, and that kind of thing happens all the time on that show.

Moo takes place on an agricultural college campus in the Midwest, which has a lot in common with where I work now at Agricultural Education Consultants, so it's given me an idea for another novel.

Putting aside *Shoedog* for a little while will let it marinate and get better, I tell myself, because this is the kind of thing that writers say. And I start my new novel, about a dysfunctional farm family, incorporating some of my new obscure knowledge from work, like Best Practices for Managing Soybean Nematodes.

I go to make milky tea and bring it back to my quiet room to read and write. But instead of reading and writing peacefully, I'm disturbed by Goli Joon waking up and fussing as soon as she enters the kitchen. Apparently, last night I must have put a big dirty pot in the dishwasher instead of rinsing it out first or washing it by hand.

Goli Joon is loudly muttering, *"Kheili tanbaleh!"*

I know that this means, *She is very lazy,* and that she's talking about me. Goli Joon wouldn't think I would know a word like *tanbaleh.* But she forgets—I do know it—because the word for pumpkin—*kadoo tanbali*—means the lazy squash. I've learned to make lazy squash khoresht from watching Goli Joon.

How can she think I wouldn't comprehend that word? Does she even care if I do? I should recognize my fault of being like the laziest of all the squashes, refusing even to roll unless given a hard push. Only finding its use at Halloween, scaring people with sober triangle eyes and an angry mouth.

Our little bond we've been forming falls away, and I pull out my journal and write furiously—like an angry letter to myself, I write how:

- it's so horrible to live with my boyfriend's mother
- I know that I'm lazy, or depressed, or depressing
- I hate being guilted about it

But, of course, something in Goli Joon's criticism reminds me of when I lived with Melinda and she complained about me too. It's me. I'm messy and lazy and I still don't squeeze the water out of the sponge or wipe down the counters. What is wrong with me?

When Naveed pokes his head in, he sees me crying, tears smearing the ink in my journal. He comes over and sits next to me on my gold spray painted iron bed, which wobbles because it isn't really strong enough for two adults. He puts his arm around me, and I ask him if he also hates me because I'm lazy.

"No, but you know, you do take a lot of shortcuts," he says.

"Like what?"

"You leave crumbs and the dripped cheese in the toaster oven whenever you make your cheese bread. It flames up for the next person who uses it. It could start a fire. Why don't you put some foil under the bread to catch the cheese?" His mom must have been complaining about that too.

"Because then the bottom of the bread wouldn't get toasty," I say. "But do you and your mom hate me because of that?"

"You wonder if we like you less for not cleaning the toaster oven?" he asks. And then I remember all of Naveed's piles of pack-rat stuff taking over the house and feel a little better.

"Why do you still always find it impossible to believe that I love you? You're the most beautiful woman in the world to me," he says. "Just don't burn down the house."

"Okay," I say, "And you with all your pack-rat piles, you don't burn down the house either." We agree. We will both do what we can to avoid burning down the house.

After that day, Naveed affectionately calls me his kadoo tanbali, his pumpkin—his lazy squash, just like he calls his mom Roseheart or Gol-ab instead of Goli sometimes for all of her rosewater. And although I know it's because I'm lazy, I like it. Because nobody has ever called me pumpkin.

Kitty Cat

Just in time for me to be saved from some horrible crime borne of my own frustration and impatience with living with Naveed's mother, she goes to Montreal for three weeks because Naveed's brother Darab is visiting there. He's left their father in the care of a nurse and his wife's parents who also live with them. Maybe Darab needed a break from all of these elderly parents, but instead he got his mother. Naveed would never say it, but I think he needed a break too because he asked Darab to invite her.

Oddly, I miss Goli Joon in a way while she's gone. Like when I happen to catch a good Oprah show or eat some really sweet fruit that might prove to be as good as the fruit in Iran and I just want to see if she agrees. Or when I'm cold and wearing my fleece stocking cap that she sewed for me to wear around the house. She sewed one for Naveed too, and even one for Courtney.

The yard is full of weeds when Goli Joon is not there to pull them. I look around at all the weeds and think, if Goli Joon were here this would be all herbs.

While she's gone, we take in a stray kitten. I know Goli Joon doesn't like cats, and I know that Naveed knows this too, so I'm not sure why either of us agreed to take the kitty.

When she returns, she seems insulted that we have done so and she starts complaining more about all kinds of things. She seems more easily aggravated since returning from her trip.

One day, Naveed drops me and Goli Joon off at Minnesota Fabrics and says he'll pick us up in forty-five minutes, and then doesn't come back for two hours. He's at Home Depot and doesn't look at his watch. Goli Joon, after almost two hours, waits at the glass door for him, and begins crying. I try to get her to look at the pattern books with me, but she thinks Naveed has been killed in an accident. She begins hitting herself, right in front of the other customers, who then stare at both of us. When he still hasn't come back after another half hour of this embarrassment, I feel like hitting myself too. Instead, I pinch the skin between my index finger and my thumb, which is much more discreet.

When Naveed finally pulls up in his CRX, I climb in back and Goli Joon collapses into the front passenger seat. She cries to him that he doesn't care about her, and that he doesn't want her to live with us, because otherwise why did we get a cat and why would he forget her at the fabric store? She cries that she knows I don't want her there either.

Naveed just lets her vent, and tries to explain that Home Depot is like another dimension to him. He wasn't wearing his watch and they didn't have any clocks in there. Of course we want her to stay with us for as long as she will honor us with her company. And, he adds in the rush of the moment, we will kick out the renters so the cat can stay downstairs.

Agricultural Science

My mass communications degree, my PR work for the Gypsy human rights guy, and my productivity as Editorial Assistant have paid off. I have already been promoted to Production Editor at Agricultural Education Consultants.

I somehow almost fit in at this job, where I write in bullet points all day long. Now that there's the internet, my bullet point writing skills are in high demand. Nobody wants to read anymore, but only to *scan for information,* my boss says. Also, it's a good fit because all the women here and two guys watch *All My Children* in the employee lounge at lunchtime. Along with my promotion, I'm now eligible for the company's tuition reimbursement program, so I start looking at the university's course catalog. After all those tuition checks, my dad won't believe I get to take classes at the company's expense instead of his.

My tuition benefit doesn't guarantee me getting into the class I want, however. I end up in one class about chaos theory after I didn't get into the writing class. There's talk of paradigm shifts, and fractals, and when one student strays off of topic he likes to discuss helixes. I don't know what he's talking about.

One week into chaos theory, a spot opens up in a novel-writing class and I switch. The class is in the evening after work and sometimes I can barely hold on, but I do. I'd hoped to finish *Shoedog* in this class, but that part of my life—when I sold shoes at Dayton's—seems so long ago now. I have farm stuff on the brain in my new job, so I admit to myself that *Shoedog* isn't just marinating, and maybe it's time to ditch it. For the class, I'll work on my other novel, the one about the dysfunctional farm family.

At work, I'm producing textbooks for the technical colleges that teach agriculture. The content liaisons get all their research information from the university, and just rewrite it all so the students can apply it to the jobs they hope to get after they finish their programs. The editors have various content beats, just like at a newspaper. I'm on the manure beat right now.

Now that I'm on the manure beat, I lecture my family about how critical manure really is to everybody, since we all rely on farmers for our food. Now that I don't work on PR for the Romani human rights guy anymore, I'm looking for a new group to defend against prejudice. Farmers are like my new Gypsies.

Maybe it's not as exotic, but I get good story ideas learning about things like hog barns that explode from the methane gas in the manure. My new novel has an exploding hog barn, but it will turn out that it was only rigged to look like an accident.

The ag science liaisons talk about things that have zero, or different meaning to me. Like the "drought of 1988" which has gone down in history as one of the worst drought years ever. I remember that year because nobody could score any weed. The next year, Kurt got a T-shirt that said, "I survived the drought of '88." I never realized that shirt might not have been made just for the stoners, that farmers might have made that T-shirt.

Even though Wayzata was within ten miles of many farms, I don't remember knowing any farm kids. Even kids who lived west of Wayzata in nearby Plymouth and Hamel (which were not on Lake Minnetonka) were considered hicks. Playing with them was taking a risk on popularity. Ironic, really, since so much of the money in Wayzata flows from the family that owns the largest privately held agricultural business in the world. I never knew anything about farm life at all until I dated Quentin. He was a stockbroker in Wayzata, but he had grown up on a soybean farm in Mankato.

Quentin had taken me on a luxury vacation to Florida in the short time we were together. His penthouse condominium looked out over the Kennedy compound in West

Palm Beach. One night, at dinner, he told me all about when he dropped out of agricultural college to learn finance. His family refused to talk to him the rest of that year because he was "going to hell in a handcart." That was probably the only really meaningful conversation we ever had.

Suicide Sisters

Lately, even though we email almost daily, Melinda has started calling and leaving me long voicemails on my work phone. My system cuts off after four minutes, so sometimes I arrive in the morning to the message "You have four voicemails" and every one of them is Melinda telling me some drunken story in installments that my system plays back to me last-one-first so I have to listen to the end before I can hear the beginning.

Listening backwards, she sounds calm at first and progressively more excitable, which leaves me feeling upset, but the real order of the messages is that she's upset at first and calms down after talking for several minutes. I wish she didn't leave me these messages at work. It's hard to edit publications about manure and other topics, like "Soybean rust—when will it hit Minnesota fields, and how will you respond?" when I feel all agitated after her disturbing calls. But she doesn't want to call me when I'm at home at night with Naveed.

Finally, I learn that things aren't going so well with Roger, who may be in trouble for how he has handled grant funds at the arts organization. Apparently, you're not supposed to take a vacation to Cabo San Lucas with that money. She sounds unstable. She asks in one message, "Do you ever think, you know, about not wanting to live anymore...for it to all be over?"

I think, *Yeah, when I get to work and have to get through sixteen minutes of your drunken messages.* But I call and check on her and she acts like she'd just been kidding. I make her promise to tell me if she ever thinks about it again.

At the end of the last one of her messages in order, she says, "I love you," and asks me when I can come see her in Santa Fe. She's been ending our conversations and her messages with "I love you" for a few months, and I say it back even though it's awkward for me. I only say that to Naveed, and I say it back to my mom and my sisters if they say it first. And, Melinda does not have to tell me. I know. No matter how many times she's taken me for granted or screwed me over, I never believe she will do it again. She talks at length about how important it is, she's realized, to cherish the people in your life.

I've known that she really does love me since eighth grade, the time I'd ended up in the hospital after drinking alone and my dad had found me face down in my vomit. My parents had called my friend Anne, who told them I drank because a girl had started a rumor about me. Then when Anne got off the phone with my father, she called two people. By that evening, a new rumor had it that I had committed suicide. Everybody was saying I was dead.

The girl who had written "Valerie Kjos is a slut" in marker and started the rumor? That was Melinda. We barely knew each other. But when she heard I had killed myself, she locked herself in her parents' bathroom and opened their medicine cabinet. She ran a bath, took the half bottle left of her mother's asthma medicine and a full bottle of aspirin. She wrote a note to my family, saying she was sorry. She wrote that she'd been jealous of me because I was so pretty and that she'd just wanted to get my attention. Then she'd gotten into the tub.

While I was being released a couple of days later, I saw Melinda, her parents at each side of her gurney as she was being moved from the ICU to the psych floor I'd been on after I had left the ICU. She was awake and rolled her head to the side, saw me standing up with my mother as my father had gone to get the car.

"That's Valerie," she'd told her mother—they'd all learned by then that I had not died. Her parents were grateful that she had not become my Romeo and died for me. She'd been saved by the stomach pump.

My mother touched my arm. "Who is this?" We all looked at each other.

"Melinda," I'd said.

Melinda's mother gave us icy stares, but my mom looked at her empathetically, because even though she knew Melinda had started the rumor about me, she knew that Melinda's mother was just another mother whose child nearly died.

Because of what had happened, lots of girls sort of held me in awe—or at least were a little bit afraid of me, and they gave me respect. And yet nobody ever asked me to do anything with them, so when my spring birthday came around the only person I could think of to celebrate it with was Melinda. She wasn't so much obsessed with me anymore, but she wasn't saying bad things about me to get my attention either. I guess we'd become friends. The "suicide sisters" thing had stuck, so we just went with it and hung out together at lunch, passed notes at detention, that kind of thing.

Mom agreed that I could have thirty dollars to take a friend out to dinner at the Chi Chi's in Minnetonka. It was the most popular place to be on a Friday night in 1983, unless you happened to be of the crowd that frequented Lord Fletcher's on the lake. But as I've mentioned, we weren't lakeshore families.

Mom and I went to pick up Melinda, my mom promising Melinda's mom she would stay nearby and then have Melinda home by ten-thirty. You might predict that my then-drinking mom got bombed on margaritas in the Chi Chi's bar. But she wasn't that kind of an alcoholic. That would have been too fun, and she had studying to do for nursing school. She just dropped us off and went home to study and drink.

Melinda and I ate a basket of the free tortilla chips with hot salsa, and Melinda ordered the loaded nachos as well, and the steak and shrimp fajitas. Even though thirty dollars was enough for dinner in the 80s, the steak and shrimp fajitas was the most expensive item on the menu. I ordered another basket of the free tortilla chips and a taco plate. Melinda asked the waitress to bring us margaritas, on the off chance that she was even stupider than she looked in her long fake mariachi dress. She was. I didn't have much interest in drinking alcohol after my little incident, but I drank mine anyway and decided it was better than the gin in my parents' liquor cabinet.

I was keeping our total added up in my head, so when Melinda suggested we get the fried ice cream for dessert, I managed to negotiate with her that we could split one if she helped out with the tip. But the waitress accidentally brought two, so we each got our own anyway. By the time we stood up to leave, we thought we had never felt so full in our lives.

"Hey, should we go behind the building and puke?" I asked as we walked out the door and saw my mom wasn't there yet.

I'd just read a novel about a girl with anorexia and bulimia, and even though I thought the symptoms were disgusting, I'd become curious. I told Melinda that if we threw up, none of that fried, cheesy, salty Mexican food would count. Her eyes betrayed her concern, but she said "Sure!" as if I'd just asked her to go with me to the fair.

She was not skinny, and all of the popular girls were skinny. And I was skinny. We walked around to the dark side of the building and stuck our fingers down our throats, leaning into the shrubs down around the foundation. My long fingernail poked my throat and I couldn't make anything come out. Melinda experienced a lava flow, managing not to splatter herself as she covered the Chi Chi's foundation. It took her a minute to catch her breath and wipe her mouth with a dried leaf.

"Lucky!" I said.

"Why didn't you puke?" she asked.

I just shrugged. "It's okay, I guess. I can afford to eat a lot."

"Yeah, you got lucky with the genes," she said. "Weight is mostly what it is because of genetics." We walked around to the front, expecting to see my mom's car. It was Melinda's mom, though, who sat in her Buick Regal at the curb, looking at me with fury and suspicion in her eyes.

"What were you doing behind the restaurant? If I catch you girls smoking, drinking, or doing anything with boys, I will shave your heads—both of you."

I noticed Melinda furtively smell her own breath for the margarita then look offended when the puke smell went up her nose instead.

What happened to my mom, I wanted to ask, but I was too shocked at the head-shaving threat to talk. I'd hardly even met her. Melinda told her mother we were just walking off dinner. Then Melinda asked about my mom.

"Eugenia, it seems, did not stick around here as she had promised me," she said. "Instead, Valerie, your mother is at home too drunk to drive." Then she sighed, and brought it down a notch. "I am very sorry for you, though. It's not your fault, but this is a problem."

She didn't tell me how she'd found out that she would need to do the pickup. She was as quiet as a rock the next ten minutes that it took to get to my house, but she did wait for me to get into the house before she pulled out of the driveway. I was confused. I couldn't tell if Melinda would be allowed to see me again or not. Then I remembered how she said she'd shave our heads if she ever caught us doing anything bad, and I decided that meant we could still hang out together.

Mom was asleep in bed, propped up against her pillows neatly and properly dressed in an ivory satin nightgown and her cerulean blue bathrobe. She was never a sloppy drunk; in fact, she looked beautiful and studious with her textbook open at her side. Her hair was still auburn then, and it flamed a brighter red against the blue robe.

The next day at school, Melinda made a couple of friends telling them about the puking trick on how to eat without gaining weight. She even gave them the title of the novel I'd told her about, even though she had not read it herself. (Laura had given me the book—all the tenth-grade girls had read it.) A few girls approached me that day to ask if I had the book and if they could borrow it, and soon Melinda and I both had new friends.

Within weeks, all the popular girls in our grade had read the book. I had more friends than I even wanted, because just like now, I was already an introvert who dreaded having too many plans for the weekend.

Orientalism

Savi had given me her copy of *The Dance of Anger* book when she realized that I was more conflicted about Goli Joon than I'd tried to let on. She's the one who said I should admit that I actually love Goli Joon, but that I'm angry at her at the same time for moving in with me and Naveed. Only through dealing with my anger, she says, can I become at peace. Even though Savi and I have been friends since college, sometimes I think she doesn't know me that well. I mean, I know she doesn't, because I haven't let her get to know me. She doesn't even know about all of the drugs I've done. I sort of keep my friendship with Savi and my mental/criminal history with Melinda and Kurt separate. So she can judge me all she wants, but she doesn't really know the half of it.

She does see through me sometimes, though. Like how she'd seen through my ruse of always defending Goli Joon and bragging about how much I'm learning from her—about cooking, the musical greats like Googoosh and Marzieh, Persian feminist poetry, and such.

"You're just exotifying her, and if that's what you need to be happy about her living with you, fine, but you will eventually have to realize that behind all of those spices and sitar songs, she's not a temporary visitor from a far-off land of make-believe."

This is all coming from another book Savi has given me: *Orientalism,* by Edward Said. I haven't finished it, but apparently it's all about how my interest in Eastern stuff is a relic of white imperialism, and how I judge everything else in relation to my hegemonic norms.

"I'm not exotifying her," I argue. "She's not some foreign 'other' to me you know—I see her every morning in her velour zip-up robe and Dr. Scholl's shoes. I see her partial dentures sitting in a cup in our bathroom every morning. She's not exactly Sheherazade from Arabian Nights."

I realize that I totally exotify her, of course. How can I not? She's from a land of wild Mohammadi roses. She grew up hip-deep in a rose petal harvest. If that is not exotic, what is it? But I don't mean disrespect by my awe. I learn from her. One reason I don't complain about her in front of other people, even Savi, is because of something I've absorbed from her culture. A Persian saying goes, "If you spit straight up, it lands in your face." This means that when you talk shit about the people in your own family, you're talking shit about yourself. Goli Joon is my own family now. No matter how else I feel about her, I know this is true.

Savi may be projecting some too. She gets offended sometimes when people treat her like an exotic bird in a cage. Although, not always. It depends, I think, on if she's being admired or treated like a second-class citizen. She's very beautiful with her shiny black hair and big brown eyes, so of course she does have that Eastern allure, but I know one woman in Matthew's neighborhood assumed she was the housekeeper when she first moved in with him. All in all, I don't feel that bad about thinking of Savi as slightly exotic and imagining that being her friend makes me a little more interesting. I'll admit it—being her bridesmaid and standing next to her in her wedding sari felt special. When she married Matthew, I'd secretly hoped maybe she'd have her bridesmaids wear saris too, but in retrospect I know I would have looked like a fool.

Also, going to Savi's Caribbean dance parties and her Hindu Diwali dinners is something unusual to tell people about at work when they ask what I did on the weekend. It's not all that shallow. Savi brings something else—some sort of happy spirit—to my life. Sometimes she even gets me to dance.

"Goli Joon thinks Rice Krispie bars seem exotic," I tell Savi. "See, everything is relative."

Professional Help

Goli Joon is having oral surgery. She's had partial dentures on the bottom already, but she needs more teeth pulled so she can have full bottom dentures and a bridge on the top. She's very confident, but she has to have it done at the hospital because it's riskier for her than for most people due to her blood-thinning medications. She had to go into the hospital two days early to start weaning off one medicine and she's going on another one temporarily.

The health policy Naveed got her doesn't cover oral, so she's hoping the result of all this is going to be worth a chunk of her bank account.

She hands Naveed her gold and turquoise jewelry in a small plastic bag, then gets wheeled away while Naveed and I croon after her. She waves a fist in the air. "I've survived heart surgery!" she yells with bravado.

"Aye! Fight, Roseheart!" he calls after her. "To battle, Roseheart!"

Goli Joon bleeds out. They have to stop the surgery before they can remove all the teeth. They'll have to try again later, and the whole ordeal is all very tiresome for her.

Still, she gets up to cook our meals and then she mashes up some of the rice and khoresht for herself with a mortar and pestle until her mouth recovers slowly over a few months. "Dirt to her head!" she says about the oral surgeon.

She doesn't smile for weeks. She barely clucks, she just frowns a lot. She can't even spy out the windows anymore at Yasmin Noury's father or the other joggers.

She won't go anywhere with us, and I even beg her sometimes to come along, "We could go to the mall and buy all new underwear, and then we could go again to return it tomorrow!" She just clucks and tisks at me, but I see a thin smile break through at my teasing.

Even though neither Naveed nor I have good feelings about the world of professional psychology, Naveed learns about an Iranian woman who is a psychologist.

"Does she offer an Iranian discount?" I ask, joking, but Naveed says that in fact she sees almost exclusively Iranians, and yes they do get a very good rate. It's only twenty-five dollars a visit.

Here I always thought Iranians were sort of stoic like Norwegians and wouldn't get professional help, but those with enough money do—like those who lost loved ones during the Iran-Iraq war. Or those who were tortured by the shah's SAVAK, or during the Islamic Revolution. Or those who just lost all their money when the shah fell from power and are still traumatized by that. The psychologist is a middle-aged woman with the purple henna-dyed eyebrows. She makes house calls, but we have to leave the house when she comes. This is the best thing ever to happen because Goli Joon gets company while we go on a date without her.

Besides seeing the psychologist, Goli Joon gets cheered up by watching T.V., but she isn't watching *The Oprah Winfrey Show* anymore. Oprah has changed to a less voyeuristic perspective. She's truly helping people now, and has become an inspiration to all.

Also, the reruns of *The Love Connection* have gone off the air, much to Goli Joon's dismay. She switches to *The Jerry Springer Show*. We put an old T.V. Naveed had into her bedroom. I'm embarrassed one evening when I walk by her closed door and hear her all by herself, yelling, "Jerry! Jerry!" along with the studio audience before the show begins. But at least her post-oral-surgery depression is lifting, I think.

I'm not sure about my own.

Reluctantly, I'm reading the *Dance of Anger* book Savi gave me. There's a chapter on mothers. The advice would help me with Goli Joon, except that it's impossible to use the advice because it's all about communication. We cannot communicate deeply across languages, so we act passive aggressively toward each other. I was nicer for awhile after Goli Joon's oral surgery. But as soon as she started feeling better, she started making more little digs, and then I reverted to my passive-aggression.

Sometimes I get a sick little joy out of coming home to a big dinner she's prepared for us and refusing it. While the two of them dine on khoresht, salads, and fancy yogurt dips with rose petals and curled green onions, I fry two eggs in butter, sprinkle them with Cajun spice, and eat them in a pita bread pocket.

"That's the kind of fast meal some women eat when they need to run quickly from one job to the next," says Goli Joon slyly one such evening as I down my egg sandwich while still standing at the stove.

I get this faster than she expects me to. She's insinuating something like the Sicilian *spaghetti alla puttanesca*— whore's pasta, because of its quick sauce.

Naveed gets it right away too and shoots her a warning look. I just shrug. "We women all need to eat."

When I act like this for more than a day or two, Goli Joon will issue a silent challenge by making a dinner that I can't resist, like her "potato chops," which are potato patties stuffed with spicy meat, fried, and served with garlicky dill yogurt sauce. I don't know exactly how to make those myself because she's kept the exact spice mixture a secret. Also, I don't know how to make them stick together in the pan. I have to eat them when served. But even the magical potato chops might not melt my icy feelings that have reformed lately.

"You sure do love my potato chops!" she'll say.

"They're okay," I'll answer, and she'll drop another one onto my plate just to rub in her victory even more.

Naveed tries to help us by translating, but I don't think he's a very good translator. I can tell he isn't translating everything I say, which is probably smart since what I'm basically saying is, "I'm angry at you, even though you haven't done anything wrong."

Like all of the books I find about mothers-in-law on the internet, *The Dance of Anger* urges communication. But communicating across cultures, across generations, and filtered through Naveed—it's a booby trap, a mine field. It's impossible to communicate without miscommunicating. And maybe better not to.

Rendezvous

We're flying back from Turkey, where we went to meet up with Naveed's sister, Firoozeh. It's a bad flight. You're supposed to think of turbulence as bumps on a road, but the bumps scare me anyway. I'm not afraid of flying—I would love to be able to fly like a bird. I'm afraid of riding in an airplane. Or like my southern granddad always said, I'd be fine with riding in an airplane if I could drag one leg on the ground.

Sometimes in my dreams we're flying, and sometimes we're crash-landing. Sometimes I'm just at the airport and the service desk won't help me, or I'm at home packing even though my flight is leaving in five minutes. In the dream I had before we left, half my body hung out of the plane through a hole in the floor, and I held my arms out against the floor to keep from falling out all the way.

Naveed had been worried about Firoozeh for a few months. She was depressed, he said. *Join the club*, I thought. She wouldn't tell him that exactly, but he knew from his conversations with her. And she'd asked him to send her selenium, because she couldn't get it in Iran. He looked it up and read that it was a natural remedy for depression. They had not seen each other for eighteen years. Naveed never wanted badly enough to visit Iran, and his sister hasn't been able to get a visa for the U.S. After so many years apart, Naveed decided he had to see her. They decided to rendezvous in Turkey, and that I might as well go along.

Goli Joon came too, of course, and since we were on a tight budget, we all shared a hotel room. It's a good thing we didn't waste money on two rooms, because Naveed and his sister stayed up talking every night. During the days, we visited the Topkapi Palace in Istanbul, the Blue Mosque, and a nearby island in the Bosphorus Straits.

I thought Naveed might want to take the long bus ride across Turkey to a place that looked out across the border to Iran. Just so he could lay his eyes on his childhood home. That idea made him laugh, as if he hadn't even thought of it. But then he said, "Who would spend twenty-five hours on a bus to get to the middle of nowhere?" which made me think he'd thought of it enough to check the route.

We brought Firoozeh to the American embassy to get permission to bring her to the United States for our "upcoming wedding." We aren't really engaged yet, but we think we will be, so we didn't feel bad about the exaggeration. Then the woman behind the desk asked what month. We paused and then I blurted out, "May!" while Naveed said, "June." There was a silence, and then I said, "May or June—we haven't set the date."

The woman said the answer would probably be no, but we could fill out the paperwork if we liked, as if for sport. So we did that. We spent most of a day in a café drinking Turkish coffee and tea, and even I helped with some of the forms because there were so many. Since it's about the same number of forms, we went ahead and filled out the ones for residency as well as the visitor's visa—not that Firoozeh thinks she wants to move to the U.S., but just in case.

To take a break from filling out forms with Naveed's family, I went to a payphone to call my mom, using a phone card. Mom was taking care of the chickens and our cat at her house.

She told me this would be the last time she would baby-sit our animals. The previous night she couldn't find the chickens, even though we had set up a fence for them in her backyard. The cat ran away twice. She had to walk around her neighborhood last night calling after all three. Her neighbors thought she was crazy, and she felt lucky none of them reported her when she told them she was caring for chickens in this suburb that does not permit farm animals. Minneapolis doesn't permit them either, of course. When she got home from searching for them, she looked up and saw Nancy and Nala roosting in a tree.

I'd come back from making my phone call and found Naveed out in front of the American embassy taking photos of the entrance to the parking ramp. This is typical for him—we've taken a couple of trips together now and he takes pictures of parking ramps everywhere. That's the kind of engineer-nerd he is.

But it's not a good idea here. A group of armed guards brought him back. They questioned and researched him for more than an hour to confirm his non-criminal interest in parking ramps. I thought Goli Joon would die from fear, or from walloping herself for most of the hour. She wouldn't stop kissing his cheeks when he got out.

When we left Istanbul a week later, Goli Joon took a different flight. She went back to Iran with Firoozeh and will stay there for awhile.

Whenever we're in an airport, we push Goli Joon in a wheelchair. Because of her heart, she walks too slowly for any place bigger than Southdale Mall, so it's easier to just push her. But being in the chair, she looked older. She started bawling about leaving Naveed, and about how her children being apart from each other is so unfair. Firoozeh wiped her mother's nose with a wad of tissues. I think the only reason Naveed and Firoozeh didn't cry when they said goodbye to each other is that their mother did all the crying for them.

Naveed hardly speaks the whole trip home. I say something about how lucky he was to be able to see his sister, but he steels himself against the tears that are right behind his eyes and doesn't answer me. As soon as we get home, Naveed checks on the paperwork, trying to hurry along the bureaucratic process for his sister to be allowed to come to the United States.

Goli Joon is still visiting Iran. I'm not sure how she went from "visiting" us to "visiting" Iran. Even though I promised myself I would be nicer about her staying with us, I have to admit how happy I am right now while she's gone.

I feel free again, with the kitchen, bathroom, and my man to myself. I run around the house bra-less, my breasts jutting out freely through my thin T-shirts. Salty, stringy lasagna and fish tacos with guacamole grace our table again. I have the bathroom to myself—no denture cup. No pre-prayer water splashed all over the vanity.

Melinda visits Minnesota without Roger, due to his legal problems over the grant funding. I have her over for dinner, and while Naveed thinks she's obnoxious, we still have a fun dinner together. She's impressed with my new cooking skills, albeit dismayed that I'm not yet using real *Parmigiano-Reggiano* instead of regular parmesan cheese. How could I? I've never heard of it until now.

We get invited to Laura and Ty's house and to Savi and Matthew's. We reciprocate and have them all over to our house, celebrating gregariously. Savi rolls her eyes when she sees the shiny, velvety cushions I made for my house after being inspired by the ones in the harem rooms of Topkapi Palace, but I can tell she's impressed that I sewed so many.

When Savi asks if I'm happy that Goli Joon is away, I deny it.

"Well, I will admit that I'm much more excited to invite you over when I don't feel obligated to invite Goli too," Savi says, out of earshot of Naveed. Laura agrees with her on that. They both express that they know I must be feeling so relieved right now. Savi pours me the Caribbean rum that she brought as a hostess gift, even though I thought she knew that I don't drink much because it often makes me sick. "It's a special occasion," she says. "Have a drink to celebrate your independence."

So I do drink rum, and then we open the bottle of wine that Laura and Ty gave us and drink it too. And for once, I wake up the next morning and feel just fine.

Engagements

The breakfast in front of me is served on a Christian Dior plate, purchased for pennies on the dollar at the Minneapolis discount store called Bank's. Nobody would know. The plated meal looks like a Gourmet magazine cover. Perfect pancakes are topped with whipped cream, dark berries, and chopped pistachios. On the side, tangerine wedges merrily encircle something not entirely unexpected. It looks like a pomegranate seed, but it sits on a ring of gold.

Princess Diana had a sapphire when she married Prince Charles, so not everyone needs a diamond. I will have a ruby, for passion, something Diana and Charles did not have. Now Diana does have passion with her Egyptian boyfriend Dodi Al-Fayed.

There are some drawbacks if I say yes to Naveed's marriage proposal, but I know I will. I tell him I need a few days to think about it, as if I might say no. Still, I take this decision seriously and write down the pros and cons in bullet points, as is my habit.

The cons:

- loss of my expectation for a regular nuclear family
- our parents' failed marriages lower our chances
- Naveed is a pack-rat, [which will later be known as a *hoarder*]

Here are the pro bullet points, but it really just comes down to the last one:

- Naveed is a very good man
- the cool stuff I learn from Goli Joon, and potential free daycare
- Naveed is my greatest lover of all time, and we're still on fire

Bachelorette

Of course I say yes to Naveed, yes to getting married to the man I love. But I still spend the next weeks ruminating about my bullet points, especially reflecting on my parents' marriage.

I used to like telling my friends about how my parents got together. Then my mom started saying things like, "if we make it to our twenty-fifth anniversary," or, "if your father hasn't left me in disgust by then." She started saying these things when I was in junior high school and her drinking was out of control. But then she went to treatment and she was doing great. My dad wasn't happy with a sober wife either.

When people asked me why my parents got divorced, I approached it from the optimist's perspective. "The question is," I would say, "How did they stay together for nearly twenty-five years?"

They had nothing in common. They dated for two weeks (knew each other for six weeks) before they ran away to Las Vegas to marry. My mom wore a twelve-dollar white knit dress from the store across the street from the pop-up chapel. My dad wore one of his Control Data suits. My dad's parents were up here in Minnesota, and they knew my mom was southern and Baptist, but they were just glad he wasn't marrying a Catholic.

I'm not still devastated by their divorce, but wary of the prospect that I could end up getting divorced too, that in Melinda's words, "it could end badly."

When I tell Melinda about my engagement, though, she seems happy for me. "It's not what I'd want to do, but it seems to be working for you," she says.

Then she invites me to Santa Fe for a bachelorette trip with just her. She says she'll treat for everything and I won't have to spend any money other than my plane ticket, so I go. But I do end up treating for one of our outings, a little tourist gig they have going in outer Santa Fe, called the Psychedelic Peyote Tour. That, along with the spa treatments Melinda treats us to while we're still on our first-ever peyote high, are worth every cent I spent getting here.

Although I'd scoffed at Melinda for writing it to me in her first letter from her new home, it's true that Santa Fe does have a special vibration. And I love her adobe townhome and its blue door.

Return

I'm outside working in the yard with the neighbor girl, Parvaneh, hanging around me when Naveed drives up with Goli Joon. I hadn't gone to the airport, which was probably rude, but I'm busy hiring a flower girl. Parvaneh, somehow, has found out about our engagement.

"Somebody has to throw the rose petals when you walk down the aisle," she says, gesturing a gentle toss of petals from an imaginary basket. "Then you step on them and it makes your shoes smell good."

I'm not sure Naveed even planned to invite the Nourys to our wedding, but not inviting them makes no sense to me. And I can't resist Parvaneh for anything when she demonstrates to me how she's been practicing her flower girl walk—step/ step-together/step—to audition for the job.

By the time Goli Joon and Naveed unwedge that monster-sized suitcase out from the trunk of the car, Parvaneh has landed the job as the best flower girl ever, and we already have plans to go shopping at Dayton's for her dress.

Goli Joon brought lots of things from Iran again. She brought *pashmak,* which is the original cotton candy, pistachios, and cherry jam. The jam is her own, homemade, which she's brought back in a big plastic jar that does not conform to the USDA's food safety guidelines on food preservation, which I have learned at my job. Goli Joon has brought it, I think, just to say, *This is how cherry jam should taste.*

Again, the items come out little by little. There's a separate pillowcase for the goods from the family rose business: rose perfume oil and soaps to last for years, and the new product that Goli's sister has come up with to rejuvenate profits. It's a capsule that "harnesses the ancient medicinal power of wild roses to increase metabolism and reduce bloating."

"If it works, then wouldn't drinking plain rosewater and eating rose petals do the same thing?" I ask. Goli Joon juts her chin up in the air and clicks her tongue, but she also smiles and doesn't bother to defend her sister's entrepreneurial invention.

We told her we're engaged over the phone when she was still in Iran, and I know there's also gold jewelry for me in one of the other pillowcases.

Naveed is so happy to have his mom here again that he takes her out to Southdale Mall almost every evening for a week. I go once, but the other nights I stay home and write or just stare into space.

One night, they come home with Goli Joon's new mother-of-the-groom dress and it's charcoal gray. The wedding will be in August and she's picked scratchy gray wool, probably because it was on the eighty percent off rack at Dayton's from last winter. I'm too sensitive and totally offended. Why gray? Why not put some money into a dress for her son's wedding? She's pushed for us to get married, but is she now remorseful?

I also know she will be too hot and won't stop complaining. I can see her now, complaining about Minnesota again—so cold most of the year and then so hot and humid that you nearly melt. In between my ears this conversation rages on and I'm saying, *Well, you wouldn't be so hot if you weren't wearing a dark wool suit!* I get so worked up perseverating over this conversation in my head that I finally have to insist that Naveed take her back to Dayton's. I want him to get her in something pastel and summery, something not marked down eighty percent, and I remind Naveed that she's probably going to return it after she wears it anyway.

Our wedding is at a big public garden on Lake Minnetonka, just to the east of Quentin's home. My bridesmaids, my beautiful little flower girl, and my ring bearer—Savi's boy—are hidden away because the bride should not be seen yet.

We're in a white gazebo overlooking the lake when I briefly imagine that Quentin is going to have heard of the wedding and drive his speedboat up to the garden's shoreline. He'll make off with me like a masked man on a horse in some Harlequin Romance novel, even though now it has been more than two years since I last heard from him. I imagine Parvaneh doing her little flower girl steps over to the people seated in their garden chairs to tell them I have gone.

Everybody looks good. Naveed's beautiful and successful cousins from his father's side come, rebelliously wearing black designer gowns for a summer garden wedding. They make all the other women look frumpy in their flowery garden frocks.

Seeing their sultry Persian beauty, I remember the time I dyed my hair brunette in college when I worked at Dayton's. A man who worked there with me noticed and said, "There's a place in a man's heart no blonde can go." I know he was only being kind by applying this truth to me—my brunette dye job couldn't really get me into that place. But Naveed's stunning cousins are all the way in that place. Every man there gawks at their beauty.

Grandma Vivian is staying at my mom's, and Goli Joon has copied her dramatic drawn-in eyebrows. Melinda admires my grandma, how she knows how to hold her wine glass daintily by the stem instead of holding it by the bowl of the glass like the rest of us ogres.

Savi is my maid of honor, much to Melinda's disappointment, but she's sure that I chose Savi only because Savi lives here. I hadn't even asked Melinda to be a bridesmaid at all when she started asking me what her dress would look like. Then she insisted that I not make my bridesmaids wear those *hideous* satin shoes dyed to match, which I did anyway, mainly because she asked me not to.

Melinda feels she has done her gracious best by being a regular bridesmaid, but she makes sure everybody knows that she's known me longer, and better, than Savi. Laura and Courtney are bridesmaids too.

My father looks handsome when he comes to the gazebo ready to walk me down the brick path aisle to give me away to Naveed. As soon as Parvaneh, in her pink dress, starts her step/step-together/step along the path in front of us, and tosses out the first rose petals, my father starts to cry. But he quickly wipes his tears, and our march is on.

My mom does a reading, the one I'd chosen about how a man leaves his mother and cleaves to his wife. There's an awkward feeling in the air as she reads it, because everybody knows that we have cleaving going on in different directions in our house. My mom reads it beautifully though, and it's a wonderful concept, that leaving and cleaving.

After our reception at a Persian restaurant that is fancier than the Dinky Kebab, we carry out a few little Persian wedding traditions, like having some cones of sugar rubbed together over a cloth above our heads to sweeten our lives together. Also, the bride is supposed to make cookies to serve at the wedding, so I did that and everybody is impressed because I made five kinds of Persian cookies and I'm not even Iranian.

I'd also read about this charming tradition in which some colorful threads and a needle are placed by the cookies. It's supposed to symbolize the sewing shut of the mother-in-law's mouth. But when one of Naveed's cousins comments to Goli Joon about it, she says she's never heard of this symbolism and she exclaims to God that she has done nothing to deserve such disrespect.

"It's right there in my *New Food of Life* book of Persian recipes and cultural information," I tell Naveed, but he says he doesn't know what I was thinking.

"Don't talk to me about it," I say. "It's your tradition. *My* mom thought it was cute."

The rest of the reception goes better, except that it takes an hour and a half to serve all the kebabs. When our limo drops us off at home, Naveed carries me over the threshold in my wedding gown. His mom has forgotten about how I have symbolically attempted to sew her mouth shut and ululates like a joyful human noisemaker. Naveed's cousins have been staying here for the last three days while I spent my last days "single" at Laura and Ty's. One cousin's husband gives us the Islamic blessing to supplement our Lutheran ceremony.

My wedding gold is twenty, twenty-two, and twenty-four karat gold. There are pieces that are chunky, pieces that are dainty and filigreed, and pieces with palm trees and griffins etched into the gold. Some of my new gold bends because it's soft, unlike the strong but impure gold alloys that we have in the United States. A few weeks later I will show Naveed and Goli Joon a crunched bangle and a bauble that has become loosened from the gold. Goli Joon will cluck and say it's better than the "fake" (fourteen karat) gold we have here, and hers never bends. She's been wearing her Persian turquoise necklace and earrings for forty years and the turquoise has never fallen out. I'm probably not taking good care of my jewelry.

But today, everything is perfect for me. I didn't know we would have another party after the reception, and nobody has invited my family and friends, but that's fine with me. I can tell them later how I was showered with gold jewelry, and how we ate and danced until it was time for us to go to the hotel room we've reserved for our wedding night, which Savi surprised us by filling with fresh flowers.

I know that one person's wedding day is always the day of another person's death. It's always this way, I tell myself when Princess Diana dies on our wedding night, with her boyfriend Dodi Al-Fayed.

Other things happened on our wedding night too—I learn later from Naveed (and not from Melinda) that his best man spent the night with Melinda and that she was "wild in bed." His best man had bite marks.

Fishing Opener

I always imagined that my first year of being married would be so memorable, but the time goes so fast and I won't end up remembering very much of it. We work a lot and life gets busy. Not much seems different from the past couple of years, except that now my name is Valerie Shushtari. I have finally shed the name that has an embarrassing meaning in Persian for another name that hardly anyone knows how to pronounce. I don't change my name to his to be old fashioned, and Naveed doesn't ask me to because it isn't even a Persian tradition. I change it because Shushtari sounds cool, and I'm ready for a change.

I guess the late 90s are pretty good. Naveed still surprises me with things he knows how to do, like carve a radish into a rose, weld pipes, and repair my broken jewelry. He's always buying me flashlights and safety gadgets like pepper spray. The tea delivered to me in bed each morning is another steady example of his thoughtfulness.

But, I don't know, I just thought we'd be a little more romantic one year in. Naveed hasn't been himself. I asked him if he was seeing somebody else once. He pulled me into his lap and said never, that I would always be his and he would always be only mine, but that he's stressed out at work. He doesn't feel like himself either.

Lately, he's had to start doing the sales proposals and "relationship management" more than the engineering work he was built to do. If not engineering, he would have been a forest ranger, or a professional fisherman, not a "relationship builder." He spends hours at night at the dining table, working on the proposals, and thinks the people he's pitching to are jerks.

When he's not working or taking his mom to the doctor, he also needs time with the guys, like lunch at the Dinky Kebab with his Iranian buddies or fishing with American friends.

I might spend weekends reading in bed, or baking pies in the kitchen with Goli Joon. Naveed has become friends with Matthew, and now they even spend more time together than I do with Savi. I think this might be because Naveed likes to fish but doesn't have a boat, and Matthew likes to eat fish and his sailing catamaran is great for fishing. Meanwhile, Savi is always running in a hundred different directions with her kids, volunteering, and covering stories—not to mention with all of her Caribbean community stuff that doesn't involve me.

Also, Matthew needs help fixing the catamaran, and Naveed likes fixing things. Because of all his collecting, Naveed has every tool known to man, large or small, power or hand. He has not only every tool, but every kind of glue, every kind of string or rope or line or cord, every wheel, every winch, jack, or pulley. If he can ever find any of them in the garage. He lets Matthew come over and dig through the stuff, and he finds a few things he needs to get the old boat in shape for the fishing opener.

So, once it's all fixed, Naveed goes up to Fish Trap Lake with Matthew and his parents, while Savi has stayed home with her kids. I'm spending the weekend reading in bed, trying to motivate myself to write but not actually writing, and watching T.V. in the living room with Goli Joon.

So this...this is my marriage. And yet, even though it's not what I expected, I'm not really complaining. Not about the marriage itself. Maybe, though, about my life, thinking it would be a little brighter—and have a more special vibration—if I could take a bong hit just once in a while.

Blue Dress

Goli Joon has been at home all day watching the news while Naveed and I were both having long days at work. The change of scenery, in going out for dinner, does us all good. I have two glasses of garnet-colored wine before our kebabs arrive.

We've starting eating at the Dinky Kebab now that I don't really feel ashamed anymore about dating my customer. We've been married for a whole year, so I imagine I've proven that it wasn't just me being a slut.

Finally, I'm getting more into wine, and drinking hardly even makes me feel sick anymore. The Dinky Kebab got a beer and wine license and they carry one label that's made by some Iranians in California. It's meant to taste like the wines of ancient Shiraz.

Because of this marketing and the Persian wine label, I'm able to convince Goli Joon to take a sip, even though it's against her religion and illegal in the Islamic Republic of Iran. She claims she never drank wine. I know this isn't exactly true. Long ago, the Kashani rose estate had wine grapes. By *long ago*, I mean like 5400 B.C., but also only fifty years ago when she was a kid. Naveed is sure she drank the wine, but only her sister drinks it now. Naveed says Goli's sister grows just enough grapes to make wine in secret to drink as "ancient Persian medicine."

At first, she makes a sour face. "What it says on that label is clearly just lies because real Persian wine couldn't possibly taste this bad," she says.

"It's a good thing you don't like it, because you shouldn't drink more than a sip without asking your doctor first," says Naveed. But when Naveed isn't looking, she drinks the rest of my glass except for the last sip, swallowing it down like lemonade on a hot day.

After a few minutes, Goli Joon leans in toward Naveed over her chicken kebab, which a waitress I do not know has just delivered. "Tell me why the man wants the blue dress."

I look around and notice that I don't know any of these new waitresses. Naveed shrugs. Goli Joon leans diagonally across to me. "Ken Starr. Why does he want Monica Lewinsky's dress?"

"I don't know. What are they saying on the news?" I take my last sip of wine.

Goli Joon strains to try to think what she can remember from today's news. "I understand half only."

While I've been reading about President Clinton and his intern-mistress on my computer at work, Goli Joon has been watching the news about it on T.V. constantly. She's quite excited about the whole thing. Each day, there's another juicy tidbit in the news about it and Goli Joon desperately wants to know the whole story. This business about the blue dress is a piece Goli Joon doesn't understand. She asks Naveed again.

"Maybe President Clinton bought it for her," he says, "and that proves they had an affair."

"No," she says. "On the news they say Monica Lewinsky bought it herself at The Gap."

"She wore it on their first date," I say, taking a sip from Naveed's glass of wine, which he is drinking too slowly, "in the Oval Office."

I'm laughing inside. I'm kind of enjoying the conversation. It's much better than what we usually talk about.

"But why does Ken Starr want to test it?"

"To prove that it's the same one she bought at The Gap," Naveed says, even though he knows that doesn't make any sense.

Goli Joon gets louder. The wine is having its effect. "Why do they have to test Monica Lewinsky dress?" she shouts. I see Niloofar coming from across the room, with the pot of amber-colored tea. "I do not understand why you do not tell me."

"Maybe Ken Starr's a creepy perv," I say, but she looks at me blankly, not understanding these words.

"Maybe Ken Starr wants to try on the dress himself," Naveed adds, not being able to stop himself from enjoying this a little bit too.

I sprinkle salt and sumac powder on my kebab and cut it with a fork and knife, then I hold up a piece of it that I'm about to eat. I'm going to tell her. I don't know the Persian word for sperm though, but I could take a guess.

"Why Ken Starr wants the dress?" she yells in English. People glance over at her, then look away.

"They have to test the dress for President Clinton's seeds," I yell back in Farsi. Good Farsi, apparently. It's taken me until this moment to get it right.

Stainless steel cutlery drops at the table behind us. Conversation stops. Goli Joon shrieks, draws in a loud breath, and holds it. My linguistic guess of seeds for sperm was spot on.

Niloofar turns on her heel and heads to the other side of the room with her teapot, then looks back at me shaking her head. Goli Joon is both offended and delighted, her eyes full of life. "Dirt to her head!" she says.

"President Clinton is the one who is married," I say. "Dirt to *his* head!"

She slaps the table three times and takes a sip of Naveed's wine. "Yes, dirt to his head! Dirt to his head!"

The other customers at the restaurant are looking at us, but then they try to go back to their food. Niloofar goes back to pouring tea. Naveed doesn't take us back to the Dinky Kebab for the rest of the year.

Three Bedrooms Upstairs

It didn't hit me that I could be pregnant, even when I was puking my guts out until two-thirty yesterday. I had called in sick, then slept and threw up all day.

It seemed like flu, but when Goli Joon started looking at me funny the idea occurred to me. I went out and bought a pregnancy test during her afternoon nap, but waited to take it until this morning. I didn't even have to wait the full three minutes because it turned purple right away. Fortunately, today is Saturday and I don't have to go to work.

As I bound outside to show Naveed the purple pee stick, he announces that our chickens have finally laid eggs. We'd given up on eggs a long time ago, thinking our chickens must be infertile and still unsure about the sex of Nala. He holds them up; one egg is green and one is brown, so he thinks they each happened to lay at the same time. He's busy cleaning out their coop, but finally he sees me holding up the stick and dancing around him.

He hugs me, but I think he's scared. When he tells his mom, she tells him not to let me lift heavy things because my back has to stay good and strong. And that (for all her love of the female Persian greats) she's wishing for a boy.

Now that we're going to be a family, I want to move to another house because I want us to have a place that wasn't Naveed's before, so that I will feel like it's "our" house. Also, lots of families move out of South Minneapolis and over to the Edina side or to another suburb because South Minneapolis has more and more crime lately.

"But this house is perfect for us," Naveed says. "Everybody wants a house like this, with three bedrooms on the upper floor. And this part of town doesn't have that much crime."

"Well, technically..." I say, "two bedrooms plus a dining room with a pocket door."

"Plus a basement," he says, "with more bedrooms."

"Which none of us want to sleep in," I answer.

"Still," he argues, "three functioning bedrooms upstairs."

I know, I think... *three bedrooms for the couple and two kids, the perfect family.* Not three bedrooms up for the couple, a baby—I will lose my extra upstairs bedroom, and a mother-in-law.

So we start looking at houses with three bedrooms upstairs and one decent guest bedroom on a main floor instead of in a basement, since Goli Joon refuses to live in a basement. It's my dream to have my little family in a space of our own, and I picture an upstairs that is like a little nest in a tree for my nuclear family, with Goli Joon staying down below. But the nice houses that fit the bill, the few we can afford, are not in Edina but further out in the direction of the airport.

Goli Joon goes with us to look at one house, but she panics when she hears the planes overhead. "Voy!" Goli Joon exclaims. "That airplane is very loud. Look, the whole house is shaking—this house is under the path for airplanes, very bad."

"It's not that bad," I say.

"It reminds me of the war," she says of the times when Iran was under attack by the U.S.-backed Sadaam Hussein and her family was in harm's way. "Of course I was grateful that Naveed was safe and sound over in America, but I will never forget the fear of bombs dropping on the houses all around us."

We do not move. We remodel—we bump out our bedroom and the extra bedroom because they're both so small. The remodeling generates an amazing disaster, and having the house opened up as summer turns to fall and fall turns to winter means lots of insects are able to get inside and settle there for the winter. Our house becomes home to thousands of what look like ladybugs to me—the newly invasive Asian ladybeetle. We vacuum them up every day, but they fly around all the time, walking across Jerry Seinfeld's face while we watch T.V., and having parties on our warm, south-facing living room window.

We get started with this remodeling project almost as soon as we know I'm pregnant, but each phase seems to take a hundred years. Hiring a contractor is a ridiculous idea to Naveed, and we can't afford it anyway. My dad can't get this, and he thinks Naveed is just being eccentric. "Why don't you just write out a check?" he asks him when he comes to our house for Thanksgiving.

Soon, the stress of remodeling gets to me because I'm helping and it seems like we never get to do anything else. I want to go to the coffee shop with Savi and work on my farm-family novel, which is almost done, while she works on something she's writing. But if I do, Naveed will go out with his buddies too, and we have so much work to do before the baby comes.

Naveed has been in the wiring phase forever. I hadn't even thought of wiring as a phase. I thought it would be done in one day over a month ago when Naveed's electrician friend came over to help do it.

"I don't get what you are doing that is taking so long," I say. "There's still no flooring other than the plywood and there are tools and stuff everywhere. When are we going to get to the floor? I thought by now I would be painting, but you're stuck on the electrical. Maybe we should hire a contractor."

My instinct is to feather my baby's nest. I want to paint, stencil, and buy baby furniture. Instead, my next task after wiring will be to stuff pink fiberglass insulation between two by fours.

"I'm doing the best I can," Naveed says. "Electricity isn't something I want to get wrong."

"But we've been snaking these same cords through the studs for two months! Pulling them through, pulling them out again, rerouting and undoing. Anytime it looks like we're almost done, you take it apart again!"

"Look at it this way," Naveed says. "You want to go to Dunn Brothers and work on that shoe book today, right?"

"*Shoedog*," I say. "And no, I'm working on a different novel now. It's about a family that lives on a hog farm."

"But how long have you been working on *Shoedog*? I think you started it right around the time we met. That was years ago. Why haven't you finished that one? I've only been working on this wiring for two months."

"Well, putting wire in a wall isn't art," I say, and I stomp out of the house.

Savi has just called to say that the writer Jamaica Kincaid is speaking and signing books today at a private college an hour away, so we meet at the nearest parking lot between us along Highway 35W and then take my car the rest of the way. When she takes questions, I ask the writer how she manages to write and raise her children. Being pregnant, I'm worried about being able to do anything once the baby comes.

"Nobody asks male authors that, I bet," she says. But she answers me anyway. While her husband has his own music studio out in the woods, she's developed the attitude that her art is a domestic activity, like cooking, and she just fits it in, writing in the kitchen at a built-in desk where her teenager takes over, putting his feet up on her manuscripts. But she does it. It works for her because she accepts her domesticity. I will sustain myself on Kincaid's sage advice for years, thinking of it as some sort of neo-feminist Goddess wisdom. Years later, Savi will tell me that Kincaid has divorced.

Soon, the work that is invisible to people who have never thought about what is inside of a wall, is done. Naveed's friend, a licensed electrician, comes back to inspect and approve, and I cross my fingers that it would pass inspection even if the inspector weren't a personal friend doing it for free. We're finally cleared to put up the wall boards.

Being pregnant, I can't help lift the huge sheets of gypsum, and Naveed can't do it alone. This time, instead of calling his buddies again, Naveed wants to tap my side of the family.

I call my dad. Dad seems happy to be asked to help with the manly work. My sister Courtney is also gung-ho about showing off her carpentry skills she gained in high school when she spent half a year in the vo-tech program.

Courtney arrives first, Courtney the former tomboy who in recent years has blossomed with feminine beauty and acquired pink blouses and gauzy skirts. She surprises me today by wearing tough bootcut jeans and Timberland construction boots. She seems to have acquired a construction worker's tan just for the occasion and is wearing a white wife-beater tank top even though it's winter. I think she wants to impress my dad with her muscular forearms, with her strength in lifting wall board and using the power drill.

Dad arrives with his own special surprise. "I have a little present for you," he says. There is something wrapped in newspaper. I cannot imagine what this will be because Neil isn't a big shopper. I take it from his hands and unwrap it. It takes a moment to remember what this is, and then I raise my hand to my mouth. *"Where did you find it?"* I choke out.

It's the light switchplate from all of the bedrooms of my childhood, a wooden scene that looks Scandinavian, a boy and a girl. The boy is holding out a little carved wooden shoe for the girl. He is perhaps her cobbler, perhaps her prince. It's probably this thing from my childhood that made me love shoes.

The switchplate doesn't exactly fit this newer light switch, so Naveed and my dad work on a retrofit as soon as the big boards are screwed to the wall with a rectangle cut out for the light. The walls aren't prepped and painted yet, but the guys temporarily affix the switchplate to the wall. They can't wait for me to see how my new baby will have the shoe boy and girl switchplate that I had, that my dad kept in a box where he would be able to find it all these years later.

Pregnancy Brain

Rushing on all of my projects at work in time to have an easy project hand-off before my baby's due date, I make a lot of errors.

On a publication meant for agricultural students who may end up working at fruit orchards, I type, "Store harvested apples at approximately 320 degrees F." I try to tell my boss that any reasonable person would know I meant 32, but I have to get the whole thing reprinted and the company has to eat the expense.

On another print order, I type the wrong Pantone color code. The scientist calls my boss when the delivery guy drops off five thousand copies of his manure application guide printed in bubblegum-pink.

But it's another incident that almost gets me fired. I apparently dropped the *o* in a proposal addressed to a county commissioner. Never leave the *o* out of the word *county*.

My boss calls me into his office, smiles at my belly, and tells me that I need to pay more attention to detail if I want to continue working there. I see his smile as feral and his sharp white teeth as dangerous. I promise I will not make such mistakes again as I back out of his office.

When I'm not fretting over my workload and my pregnancy brain, I dream about having a luxurious eight-month maternity leave in front of me, during which I will do my best to maximize my infant's happiness and intelligence by stimulating its mind as much as I can. And when I'm not doing that, I'll be finishing my two novel drafts.

Goldfish, my baby's nursery theme, are arriving daily in the form of my eBay orders of stuffed animals, wall decals and figurines. Savi and Matthew give us a mobile that they made together out of origami goldfish hanging from a birch crossframe.

I'm not picky about whether the decorative items are specifically goldfish, and even an orange clownfish has made its way into the nursery. I can't find any kind of orange fish this year in crib bedding though, I guess because goldfish aren't in style. It's a big year for frogs.

All of these things we need to get ready for the baby cost a lot, even though Savi hosted a baby shower for me and some of my friends from work. Savi had even invited Melinda, probably thinking there was no chance of her flying in for it, but it turned out that Melinda's parents had wanted her to visit too. She came for the weekend, killing two birds with one stone. The wives of Naveed's buddies came too, and my mom and some of her bridge lady friends.

All in all, it ended up being a lot of work for Savi so I pitched in on the cooking. Goli Joon made cookies—the same kinds I'd made for my wedding, with rice flour and chickpea flower, cardamom, rosewater, and orange blossom essence.

Even Melinda brought a cheese plate, giving Savi an opportunity to correct her when Melinda said it was "artesian" cheese.

"It's *artisan,* or *artisanal* rather," Savi told her, "unless it's from a well."

"I said *artisanal,*" Melinda replied, a stone cold lie.

The baby shower brought in a lot of the things from our Babies 'R Us registry and most of what we needed, but we've still been buying more. We've never spent so much money—much on credit, but it seems important to get everything just perfect.

Naveed is also finally buying a dining table that is not literally garbage, like the old one that he had picked up from a curb the night before a garbage day long before I met him. He had said we would buy a new one, but although the purse strings are loosened, there isn't much money in the purse.

He goes for the Scandinavian look, natural cherrywood with clean lines. Contemporary is really in. I think people are so overstimulated by media overload that they need the starkness in their homes. I don't usually like contemporary, but it lets my eye rest inside this house, which is too full of garish things from the Persian bazaar. Some modern Scandinavian design wouldn't hurt. But Naveed cannot pay full price or even sale price for something this expensive. On the internet, he finds out that the set can be had for much less in Canada, and even less than the reduced price because their dollar is so weak right now.

For five days Naveed and three friends go ice fishing in Canada with the excuse of going to pick up our dining set. This is how it is living with Naveed. Everything must be had for less, for the rock-bottom price so low that the salesperson will hate you by the time you walk out the door. And everything must be had with something more, a "free gift," a bonus, or ice-fishing trip, that you squeeze out of the deal.

The baby nursery is finally done, just in need of a coat of seafoam green paint, which I apply. For five days in the house without Naveed, Goli Joon and I arrange the room, buy baby things, and set out toys. I insist on sewing the curtains, without help from Goli Joon. I want to choose the fabric at Minnesota Fabrics, and Goli Joon declines to go with me because she's still so busy cleaning up sheetrock dust.

Going to the fabric store is an easy thing to do with Goli Joon. Whenever I offer to take her somewhere with me alone

I feel smug, like I'm doing her some grand favor by offering her an outing with me. But I have to admit that, even though she's my mother-in-law, there are times when we go to the fabric store when it almost feels like we're friends. I genuinely want her to come with me today and ask three times. After her third "no," I even ask one more time, but she says she's too tired, needing a rest after all the dusting and also wanting to color her hair and read the poetry of Parvin Etesami.

I call Savi to see if she wants me to pick her up. Matthew's catamaran is parked in their backyard for the winter, the rainbow-striped sail full of holes. She'd like to buy Sunbrella sailcloth. For that we have to drive all the way to the ten-acre S.R. Harris fabric warehouse north of Minneapolis, instead of the nearby Minnesota Fabrics. I don't mind though, because I imagine the possibility of finding goldfish fabric at S.R. Harris.

Savi invites me for more shopping after the fabric warehouse, but I'm down about not finding the perfect fabric, and I'm so big with the baby now that walking around the huge store has worn me out. I tell Savi I need to go home and lie down.

Pulling into our street at the same time I do is the neighbor couple and their two kids. The girls get out of the car and start an impromptu snowball fight.

As I kick open the front door, my big pregnant belly and the rolls of curtain fabric preceding me into the house, Goli Joon is sliding the pocket door of her dining/bedroom shut and has vanished behind it before I can greet her. I yell a hello anyway, but she doesn't answer me.

I think she was pretending to be napping because she doesn't want me to know she's been sitting at the window worrying about her son as usual, or about me. Now that I'm pregnant with her grandchild, she worries about me when I'm out driving in the snow and ice.

But something is out of the ordinary in the living room.

The silver teapot of our samovar is out on the fireplace hearth, next to a pile of poetry books. *Hafiz* is written in English on the cover of one of them; the rest of the book is all Persian script.

We usually just use a regular porcelain pot; the samovar is for when we have guests. The matching silver sugar bowl sits next to it, piled high with sugar cubes and saffron rock candy. I slide open the kitchen door and see, in the plastic dish drainer, two freshly handwashed glass teacups. And not only that. I look closer at the tray, and I see a ring of something red, or purple. Is that *wine*?

But dinner is on the stove. It's ghormeh sabzi, the stew that takes so long for Goli to make because she always chops all the herbs by hand. Except…on the other side of the sink, drying on a dishtowel, I spy that old Black & Decker food processor that I never use because it's impossible to put together.

From this, I have to deduce that:

- Goli didn't want to spend all day cooking
- she had something better to do than chopping herbs
- she put together that impossible old food processor, or
- somebody else helped

I peer out the kitchen window that faces the back of the house. It looks cold and lonely out there and I know nobody has used that back door since Naveed took out the garbage before he left for his trip. But I peer closer out the window and see tracks—jogging-shoe footprints—in the snow.

PART III

Millennium Baby

I'm watching the Eiffel Tower fireworks on T.V. from my labor bed in between contractions. There are also Ferris wheels in London. In between contractions, Naveed is laughing in the New Year with the nurses. They're all happy that the whole Y2K computer glitch thing wasn't a problem over in Europe, so it shouldn't be a problem here.

Then, after hours of fruitless labor and no progress, Naveed gets tired and asks for a cot. So much for the birth partner thing. After his little rest, things pick up and he helps deliver our daughter, the first "millennium baby" at Fairview Southdale Hospital. Yep, Southdale. In between visits here, Naveed and Goli Joon can go to the Southdale Mall across the street.

We name our daughter Simeen. It means "of silver," and Goli Joon says it's the name of the first female in Iran to publish a major novel. I confirm that it fits her when I first hold her in the operating room after the doctor pulls her out at twenty-seven minutes after three in the morning.

We don't get through the first day without one of my sisters asking if the name sounds too much like semen, but I let the question roll off me. Enough worrying about names.

Naveed is in love with her already and says, "She is my True North" like this is some kind of sappy dog sledding movie.

In the hospital they have lactation consultants who go around and watch the babies nurse in order to give the mom tips on how to make it easier. The consultant who comes into my room, which is filled with flowers in vases and a four-foot tall Mylar balloon in the shape of a baby bottle, says there are three types of nursers. Simeen is a "gourmande," meaning that she tends to nurse like she's having a six-course French dinner. It's pretty time consuming having a baby like this.

Laura visits us in the hospital every day. She holds Simeen so I can nap when Naveed and his mom take breaks at the mall. She's pregnant now, and can't get enough of my baby, nestling her next to her own baby bump.

We go home and I settle into a long maternity leave—months on end with Simeen and Goli Joon, and an occasional visit from my mom, who comes over sometimes after work in her nurse's smocks patterned with hearts and teddy bears.

And just as Niloofar suggested so long ago, that day I sat down with her at the Dinky Kebab, Naveed and I begin to plan on Goli Joon taking care of the baby when I return to work.

Americans

Simeen's fortieth day on earth means something to Goli Joon. I don't know what—maybe just that she isn't a newborn anymore. Naveed also honors the occasion with his famous mixed-berry pancakes with whipped cream and pulverized pistachios.

Simeen cries a lot and we have to gently walk around bouncing her all the time. I can only calm her by singing and nursing, but for her fortieth day, Goli Joon whispers a prayer in her ear that makes her stop crying. Also, Yasmin Noury rings the doorbell, and when I answer she gives me a gift for the baby, a little stuffed giraffe. I invite her in, three times, but she just comes in far enough to see the baby. She coos at her for just a minute and goes back to her house.

When Goli Joon burns wild rue in the foyer after she leaves, I ask her not to because I don't think the smoke is good for the baby. I put the cute baby giraffe away in my closet, hoping to save it from the garbage can. It seems like Goli Joon thinks that neighbor is a witch. Ever since the day Goli Joon put Yasmin's welcome cake down the disposal, I've wondered what exactly is going on with our family and theirs. The neighbor doesn't seem like a witch to me.

Although sleep is a distant dream, and the ceaseless crying makes me crazy and frustrated, I'm so happy that it seems unnatural, and I determine that it's hormonal and chemical, some lucky inverse of the post-partum depression my *Mayo Book of Pregnancy and Baby's First Year* warned me about.

We begin taking Simeen out of the house, and one of her first outings is to visit her almost same-age new little cousin. Laura gave birth to Bella six days ago. Ty has made a standing rib roast for dinner, and Laura serves her apple pie. I can't believe she's already up baking apple pie so soon after giving birth, but that's Laura. She will be running again by next week, and back to work at the PR firm in just two more weeks, on the hook for twelve hundred dollars a month in daycare.

My mom is over there too, trying to keep up with having two grandbabies to visit and spoil rotten. Simeen falls asleep on her grandma's shoulder and sleeps for the rest of the night.

Simeen has been good at night lately. She had been so hard to get to sleep that we'd had her in our bed every night. I finally followed some advice I read in a magazine. I let her cry herself to sleep in her crib, just checking in at certain timed intervals to let her know I was there but wasn't going to pick her up.

The first two nights she cried for an hour before falling asleep. Goli Joon said, "I'd heard that Americans don't comfort their babies when they cry, but I never believed Valerie would be like that." She went down to the basement and ran water so she wouldn't have to hear. Naveed stood outside the door to the nursery and watched through the crack because he was worried that such intense crying could hurt Simeen.

But once the hard-core let-'em-cry advice works and she snuggles into her crib without a peep, they rejoice because we all get a little more rest.

Life

We've been trying to teach Simeen to say "Baba" forever—like since the day she came home from the hospital, because we want her to call Naveed the Persian word for dad. Well guess what she said today? Dad. She said it this morning and then she said it all day long. "Dad. Dadadadada."

Then suddenly she starts saying Mama, and Na-gee for Naranji, the cat. We always thought the cat's name would be one of Simeen's first words since she loves him so much. She crawls to him to grab his fur, but he usually gets away, which is good because every time Simeen touches Naranji, Goli Joon carts her off to the bathtub. She doesn't like us to let her touch him, and she washes her all over with wet wipes or water every time she manages to pet him.

Goli Joon spends her days crocheting and knitting baby clothes and blankets. My mother also knits an afghan for Simeen. It's a Cinderella theme, and it is so detailed. Mom is not such a prolific knitter, tying herself to us with skeins and skeins of yarn like Goli Joon, but when she does make something it's always a masterpiece.

Both of these women have tried to teach me how to knit, but I just couldn't get it. Like trying to learn how to drive a stick shift on a hill, I found the knots kept coming undone and my rows unraveling as soon as they had climbed to any respectable height.

The first two days of my return to work have been rough for me and I cried even more today than yesterday. I'm tired.

My certainty that I had avoided postpartum depression is fading. I'm still crazy in love with the baby, but I need more sleep. Simeen still nurses late at night and early in the morning. But Goli Joon is in her element, nuzzling and coddling Simeen all day and happy to be in charge of her.

I'm a mess at work. Even now that I've come so far in this organization that I have a skyline view and a door, I still don't have focus, and being a tired mom makes me even more scattered. I'm a business advisor now, because my male boss thinks I have a very solid business sense. (When I tell Melinda this, she says that it is impressive because she remembers me as incapable of paying bills on time even when I had the money.) The other business advisors tell me that continuing to watch *All My Children* in the lounge at lunchtime is career suicide. So I work through lunch at my desk and never take a break at all, except to email with Melinda and glance at the *Star Tribune* online.

When I get home from work, the tireless Goli Joon doesn't always want to give back the baby, so sometimes I just play with her for a little bit and then hand her back so I can work on my novel about the farm family. The main character is a kid in an ag program at the community college. He reads publications like the ones I produce at work. It's sort of a mystery. A barn explodes, and it looks like it was caused by the methane from all the manure, but there's a culprit. Maybe it's one of the farm hands. Maybe it's the Amish neighbor. Maybe it's someone nobody would have even imagined.

Unlike *Shoedog*, which is still sitting on my computer and a printout still sits in a drawer, this ag story writes itself. A first draft is done in two more months. Since I know I need some feedback, I sign up for another class with the tuition benefit offered by my company. Naveed is annoyed that I'm doing something so frivolous when we have a little baby at home. But the class is just once a week for four weeks and, as Laura says, new moms need to get out of the house sometimes and do something for themselves.

Mother Mary

Simeen likes to grab her cousin Bella's face and stick her fingers in Bella's mouth. She tries the same thing with my Grandma Vivian, who is here for Simeen and Bella's double Christening. Simeen loves being with this beautiful Grandma who brought my mom's christening gown for Simeen to wear. Bella is wearing Ty's gown, which looks just like a girl's.

Naveed feels fine about Simeen being a Christian, mainly because he thinks she'll feel more like she belongs in the community. I know this because we have to attend a quick meeting with the pastor right before the ceremony. He asks Naveed if he's a practicing Muslim.

Naveed says no, he doesn't like organized religion. He laughs at our pastor's standard deadpan response, "We aren't really all that organized."

I groan. I've been hearing that one since I was a kid.

Naveed is then slightly taken aback when the pastor says, "I commend you to join the faith."

Even though his English is really great, the word "commend" sounds like "command." I too have to think for a second to remember that commend means ask. They quickly get it sorted out, though, and Naveed is relieved nobody is commanding him to do anything when it comes to religion. Because that sounds all too familiar.

Simeen gets a gold Mother Mary necklace from Goli Joon for her Christening. It looks more Catholic to me than Lutheran. Naveed doesn't want her to wear it for the party because it's valuable, but Goli Joon looks disappointed, so I insist.

Garage Sale

Our first year with our baby is going fast. Spring came and went in a heartbeat, with just one or two Persian New Year parties and we didn't even host one. Summer was over before we even had a chance to plant anything other than Goli Joon's herbs. I wish we could have summer all over again, but we promise ourselves that fall will be better, and we'll take more walks around Lake Calhoun. Where does our time go?

With all of the Iranians in the area, and all of their relatives moving in with them or nearby, I'd always thought of this border area between South Minneapolis and Edina as Little Iran. Since having a baby and going back to work though, we've been so busy and so tired that we've started to lose touch with Iranian-American families—well, actually, with almost everybody. It takes more effort to get together. I don't have any energy.

I have to stop when I'm feeling sorry for myself about being so tired and never getting to sit down. Simeen is a healthy baby, and we take that too much for granted.

Little by little, in undeniable pieces of unwanted information, I find out something terrible. Little Parvaneh, my flower girl, has cancer. I've been pretending it's a miscommunication. Now the Zand/Nourys are trying to raise enough money to pay their bills.

I learn about this by overhearing bits and pieces of Persian going back and forth between Naveed and Goli Joon and putting it together, until one day Parvaneh comes across the street to tell me about her trip to the children's hospital.

"The doctor's are funny, but the medicine made me throw up on my teddy bear," she says.

I see she looks both gaunt and puffy at the same time, with dark circles under her earth-toned eyes.

"Do you have any more flower girl jobs lined up? I would be happy to act as a reference," I say, giving her a hug. She shakes her head and skips away, but her skipping isn't as high as usual and only lasts a few steps before she slows to an overly mature gait.

Naveed says he doesn't want me to think about it. It's unthinkable. And I don't need to worry, he says, because the prognosis is excellent. The girl is going to get cured. It's an *easy* form of leukemia.

One day, I get the idea to have a garage sale at our house to raise money for a foundation funding childhood leukemia research. I also have the ulterior motive of getting rid of some of Naveed's piles of stuff because it's hard to find space for all of the baby's things.

We sell the bread machine, and all the other crap that Naveed bought at Bank's, and a lot of tools and things he has kept around here for years. We collect things from our friends, donations at work. My dad gives twenty-five dollars. Naveed takes care of Simeen while Savi and I staff the sale for three days. Savi rolls her eyes when Naveed has trouble parting with a few things—a broken vice-grip and a couple of college engineering textbooks—and he takes them back inside. She doesn't see him when he puts them back out.

But everybody is there when he sells his 1982 Yamaha motorcycle. We have to hold his hands while the buyer lifts it up into the pickup bed (because it doesn't drive) and hauls it away. But that brings in four hundred dollars, and he didn't ride that motorcycle anymore anyway. He holds Simeen, bundled in her cardigan zip-up sweater even though it's a warm fall day. He sells things he would never have sold, in order to be able to write a check that's supposed to help cure sick children. And I come into the house and breathe a sigh of relief because now there's space for some of other people's things too, and space where I can rest my eyes.

But before long, new things—freebies, clearance finds, dumpster-diving treasures—find their way into the house, and with the cold weather comes a whole new season's worth of junk.

And the little girl's cancer doesn't go away.

Soap

On Christmas Eve, Simeen received a gold cross from my dad. On Christmas morning, she opens lots of toys and clothes from everyone else. And teddy bears. She loves teddy bears. We're at my mom's house, where Simeen has lined up all my mom's collectible Santa bears from Dayton's department store and her new teddy bears on the floor next to each other. She cuddles each one, pressing her face to its face. Then she sees there's a polar bear on the cover of one of my mom's National Geographic magazines. She takes the magazine and puts it on the floor next to the other bears. She kisses all the stuffed bears in a row, and then she presses her face down on the magazine cover to give the polar bear a kiss too.

My mom makes a big brunch while the rest of us lollygag around her house and play cheerfully with the girls. Grandma Viv and Uncle Percy call while we're opening gifts, and I'm annoyed because this isn't the time for Uncle Percy to be complaining to my mom over the phone that Uncle Andy won't talk to him anymore because they had a big stupid fight that involved Andy's fourth wife. Percy is just sick about it, but I say they should talk later because we were having such a good time. After we've all worn ourselves out with the gift getting and giving, we take naps—on the floor, on the couches, on the reclining chair. Even Goli Joon is crashed out on my mom's leather couch with two fleece blankets.

The day after Christmas we've promised to take Goli Joon to Southdale Mall to return most of her gifts. Before we go, all the good cheer from Christmas disappears in an instant.

Now, Goli Joon is downstairs in her room, knocking back and forth frenetically in her glider chair and crying. I must go apologize and make it all better.

A skillet fell from atop our cabinets and hit me on the head. "You yourself put it there like that to copy Martha Stewart! So dangerous!" she yelled in Persian as I lay on the ground half-dazed with a throbbing lump on my head.

I narrowed my eyes at her and said, "Shut up." She watches enough T.V. to know what that means.

She turned to stone, but one tear escaped and coated her single gray eyelash. It was that one eyelash of hers that I always want to put some black mascara on, or tint, because it bothers me that it doesn't match. Or maybe because it makes me think I might get a gray eyelash myself someday. That one tear was just the beginning, but she waited until she got downstairs to open the floodgates to the rest of them.

Now she's begging Naveed to send her home. Even though part of me thinks that's a great idea, I realize her reaction was her way of caring for me without crossing the boundaries that I put up. What did I want her to do? Come running to me with an ice pack and administer tender loving care? I'd have shooed her away. I can't believe I told her to shut up, and right after such a nice Christmas, and when she takes such good care of my baby for me every day. I must be evil.

It's lunchtime in the lounge at work, a week after the skillet fell on my head. During commercials and during the boring filler parts of *All My Children* (which I refused to stop watching) I confess to a co-worker that I think I'm evil. Or a sociopath, at least. She thinks I just need to lighten up and be more *creative* in my coping methods. She says I'm not evil, but I just made a lazy choice in saying "Shut up." Instead, she says I should pretend the whole thing is a soap opera, and let myself see such scenes unfolding as through the set camera. I should experiment with different roles, perhaps start by playing the role of somebody who is actually evil.

Goli Joon is pretty much *acting* normal with me now at home, but I don't know how she's changed inside from these two words I have uttered. Shut. Up. We've been upset with each other before. We've cried before. But this Shut Up has changed something. Something that can't go back.

So I try to be more creative when I'm unhappy. I use my imagination to calculate and manipulate, like we're on the soap opera set. I talk nicely to Goli Joon about the taste of her homemade pickles. Then I turn my head to an imaginary camera and my face turns cold and sinister. The imaginary camera pans to a meat mallet. The studio audience is asking, "What will she do?" I imagine, then, something less vicious— pouring the pickles over her head.

This is Minnesota and I'm a stereotypical reticent Minnesotan. This home is also Iran, where elders must be revered and respected.

I must stay within the boundaries of both of these cultures, but this soap game is a pressure valve. It works better for me than the advice in *The Dance of Anger.* But even though I'm not religious, I attended Sunday school, and I know my co-worker is wrong about this creative game. I know that it could send me straight to hell because bad thoughts are as sinful as bad deeds.

Roseheart

The medications Goli Joon takes for her heart got terribly out of whack, and she's in the ICU at Fairview Southdale Hospital. She cried out in the night, but then she was unresponsive, and that's when Naveed called the ambulance. She said she died and came back—came back because she had to take care of our baby.

Today, her third day in the ICU, she's showing improvement, waving her thin arms around and saying she isn't ready to die. But the cardiologist is not so encouraging. Her congestive heart failure is getting worse, he says.

Naveed argues this point with him, "She keeps up with our baby all day, she cooks, and she's knitting scarves and hats for our whole neighborhood."

The doctor pulls up a computer screen image of Goli Joon's heart and the look on his face is as if he's looking at a photo of the walking dead. The wall of her enlarged heart is as thin as a grape skin. In the pericardium cavity is a mess of leaky and old artificial valves and irregular pumping.

The doctor asks how Goli Joon is doing mentally, if she's been forgetful lately or doing anything unusual. "No," Naveed says. "She doesn't have any problems like that. It's just her heart."

Then the doctor tells Naveed that it's actually a little more than that. When the heart isn't circulating the blood properly, it can trigger small strokes, so small that—he says—nobody should blame themselves for not having noticed. I study Naveed closely for his reaction.

"Did my mother have a stroke?" he asks. I see a giant tear well up in the corner of one of his beautiful brown eyes. He takes a quick breath and the tear doesn't fall. It defies gravity and orbits around the outside of his eyeball, like a teardrop in space, until it disappears somewhere.

Of course he will blame himself for not knowing that his own mother, whom he sees every day, has had a stroke.

"It looks like she's had several, but they were very, very small. Nothing catastrophic to have alerted you she was having one. Just enough to cause some problems with memory and the senses."

Naveed thinks back, trying to remember if there has been anything unusual. She's been perfectly attentive with the baby.

And then, we both think of it at the same time.

Last week, one night, there was sand in her khoresht, so Naveed had asked her if she had forgotten to soak the dried herbs. She got angry and swore that she had been cleaning dried herbs for fifty years. She asked how he could even imagine she had forgotten. We all sat at the table and chewed on the sandy stew together, and Goli Joon had finally blamed it on the fact that Naveed had bought the ingredients from the Arabic store instead of the Persian market at the Dinky Kebab.

As she gains strength, one of the nurses tries to talk with her a little bit. They're good with her here, unlike another hospital where they were quickly exasperated with the language barrier. This nurse asks her if she has a husband, even though it's pretty obvious that if she does he isn't in the picture.

"He died," Goli Joon tells the nurse, with just the right touch of sadness to be appropriate without inviting further questions. Naveed translates this to the nurse in the same tone. He's a top-level conspirator in this eternal lie. Goli Joon keeps her head high, but accepts the sympathy pat the middle-aged woman gives her high up on the arm, above the IV line.

My mom comes to the hospital and brings apricot roses, knowing they're Goli Joon's favorite. When she arrives Goli Joon is reading a Victoria's Secret catalog that was in a stack of reading material her nurse brought her. Goli Joon looks at my mom and gestures to the underwear models. "Bad, very bad, dirt to their heads," she says to my mom in Persian while continuing to flip through.

My mom doesn't understand her; she says she wishes she looked like those models.

Goli Joon can hardly stop tisk-tisking the Victoria's Secret catalogs to thank my mom for the roses. Naveed teases her. "Do you want to take that catalog home when they release you?"

My mom turns to me and says, "She looks pretty good. You know, she just may outlive us all." We don't think so. The doctors are saying that her time is certainly limited without surgery, but open-heart surgery would be as likely to kill her as it would be to make her better.

And the doctors also say that Goli Joon's days of providing daycare for our little girl are over, which seems suddenly obvious. We need to find a daycare center, pronto.

I use Naveed's cell phone to call Melinda in New Mexico, and tell her the end is near for Goli Joon. She tells me they thought that about her grandma two years ago and she's still alive. "She could get better," she says, and I don't know if she means this as encouragement or just a statement of fact.

"I don't think so," I say. "It's amazing she's made it this long. But she can't babysit Simeen anymore."

"Oh my God, I'm so sorry," Melinda says. She's sorrier for me about this than she is about the possibility of us losing Goli Joon. "The one thing you've been banking on all along to make it a little bit worth having her there!"

Well crap, I think. I guess I have said that a few times, as if she's just some sort of childcare commodity I trade in, begrudgingly putting up with her for twelve hundred dollars a month in daycare savings, which has not even lasted long. But it's not like I really meant it.

I hang up and come home with Simeen while Naveed stays with Goli Joon. He calls Darab, Firoozeh, and his aunts and uncles.

My job is now to start calling around for daycare rates. But first, walking into the house, I look straight ahead at the pocket door to Goli Joon's dining-bedroom.

I slide the door open slowly, as if she might surprise me like I surprised her that day when she went to snoop in our bedroom not knowing I was there. On the shelf is Goli Joon's gauzy prayer cloth. I don't dare touch it—it seems sacred. But I sit down, crossing my legs, on her prayer rug.

First, I tell God I'm sorry because my recent indulgence in evil thoughts about Goli Joon might have caused this. I tell God it was just supposed to be like a soap opera, and I felt terrible as soon as I let those thoughts enter my mind. I wonder if I might be a terrible witch, and if I should leave, and if they should burn the wild rue seeds after I'm gone.

For a few minutes, I just sit there and think about Goli Joon, wondering why it has to be so hard for me to live in harmony with her when I really love her. I do. I love her. She's like my other mom—she's my Rosie, my Rosewater Dear.

My Roseheart.

I wonder why I get so upset about little things, like the crocheted kitchen towels. I promise myself and God that I will be better, if only she can get better and come home.

And it occurs to me that I was wrong when long ago I considered it a "loss" to not have the nuclear family I expected. Not wrong, really. It did feel like a loss to me. But, I guess what is dawning on me is that if extended families were the norm for my ancestors until the generation right before mine, that extended family was what was "lost" for this upper-middle-class American culture of my peers. And what I have been given is a chance to recover something priceless.

It feels like a small revelation, something to feel grateful about. Not that I want any more of our parents to move in here.

Buzzing with this feeling of warmth and gratitude, I seat myself cross-legged on the prayer rug, looking more like some school kid on the classroom rug than like a pious woman. But then I turn my palms up, and hold them open to whatever or whoever is above—I will call that God, I guess.

I don't say any prayers really. I just hold my hands open to God and feel the air on my palms until I can't hold them up anymore and I fall prostrate to the floor with them in front of me.

Two days later, Goli Joon gets out of the ICU and we're told she just needs to stay on another floor for a few days of observation.

Goli Joon, in her hospital room, can't stand at her window to watch for Naveed to come home. So she uses the phone. A lot. Half the time our phone rings it's Goli Joon. She calls to ask if I made dinner, what I made, if we are eating yet. Checking up to see if I'm feeding her son and granddaughter or if we're all starving to death in her absence.

Tonight Naveed is on a Mississippi River paddleboat ride for a parking ramp engineers event. I was invited, but rolling down the river with thirty engineers and a handful of spouses didn't appeal to me for a Monday night. I'd rather stay home and watch the CBS Monday night line-up, with my baby cuddled up to me after her first full day at the daycare center that we chose for her, the most expensive one in town, so it hardly even pays for me to work. But it was the only one with caregivers who seemed as kind as Goli Joon. It was the only one that didn't smell like dirty diapers and canned green beans.

The phone is ringing. I'm betting it's Naveed's mom (there's always a fifty percent chance). It's Goli Joon and she's telling me we should all go to our basement because there's a tornado.

Apparently Naveed didn't tell her he's on the Mississippi tonight and I don't want to tell her because she will start crying if she knows he's out on a boat when the end is nigh. So I say he's at work, and that anyway the tornado is two hours away and we're not even under any warning in Hennepin County.

But my Persian language skills fail me. To Goli Joon, a tornado touching down in Mankato is no different than Minneapolis, and I'm reminded of when she got off the plane in Michigan instead of Minnesota. All those M places in the Midwest.

It must be hard for her, not knowing English better. Like whenever she hears the words "war" and "Iran" in close proximity on the news. She knows the word "war" means *jang* to her. *Jang* is a word, and the thought and the memory that strikes fear in her heart. And she hears the word often—in English and in Persian—because the possibility is never too remote. She doesn't always know if it's just political commentary or if George Bush is about to drop a nuclear bomb on Darab and his family.

Tonight when she hears *tornado*, she wants to call Naveed at work, so I say he isn't at the office—that he's working somewhere else. Now she's suspicious and I know she won't sleep until he calls her. I say he will be working late and she shouldn't worry because the tornado is far away. She thinks I'm lying because she can see right on her T.V. that there's a tornado and they are telling people near Mankato to go to their basements.

I can tell she thinks I'm lying by how she keeps asking the same questions over again, rephrasing them slightly to see if my story will change. I learned that trick in a journalism class I took for my mass communications degree and realize it's probably just an old trick that some journalist picked up from the parenting part of his or her life.

Luckily, the other line clicks in and it's Naveed. "I'm off the boat and on my way home," he says.

"Your mom is freaking out. Call her!" I say. I hang up with both of them so they can get in touch.

Just three minutes later my phone is ringing again. It's Goli Joon and she's in a hilarious, happy mood. "Thank you, Valerie Joon," she tells me. "Thank you and thank God the tornado he sent did not eat up Naveed."

I don't know why I get any credit—maybe just for putting them in touch, and because she's so happy. She asks me if I can visit tomorrow and bring her Googoosh and Marzieh music cassettes.

"I will come home from the hospital soon to take care of the baby," she adds. I remind her about what we had to break to her already, that the baby has daycare now, but that she can still watch her for us when we're working on projects at home.

"When I come home, I will teach you the secret to cooking the potato chop, your favorite meal," she says.

"Oh, I think I know the secret. Angelica powder, right?" I say. I've been working on figuring it out, and it came close when I added the powder of the ghostly angelica seeds I found in the old pillowcase Goli still keeps in the pantry.

"Ha ha ha ha! Angelica powder? You mean Golpar? No, no. Well, not only golpar. But you are getting close! I will show you."

"I knew there was angelica."

"Also," she adds. "I want you to take my turquoise jewelry."

"Goli Joon," I say. "Stop. Let's not go overboard here."

"The turquoise is from a cave near the place my mother was born, and I want you to have it and pass it on to Simeen when she is grown."

I can hear the strength coming back to her in her voice. Her mind is made up.

I protest, not because I don't love the jewelry, but because she's talking like she's ready to divest and leave this earth. And anyway, I say, she should give her jewelry to Firoozeh.

She says no, it's for me and Simeen, and she will also give Simeen her silver candelabrum and other things she begins to list. Firoozeh will inherit her condominium on the Niahvarin mountainside, so she may always return to Iran—so she may always come and go as long as governments allow, living between worlds.

She talks for a while longer about what she's going to cook when she can—God willing—be done eating this hospital food. Suddenly I hear her laugh and cry out, "Naveed Joon!" Naveed has decided to pay her a surprise visit, charming his way past the nurses because it's outside of visiting hours.

Snooping is still in my nature. I'm not so different from Goli Joon after all. I'm all alone and Simeen is sleeping when I feel the urge. Not because I want to be nosy. Let's call it curious instead, like Goli Joon and her curiosity about my underwear drawer. The sliding door to Goli Joon's bedroom glides effortlessly. I turn up the light, a circular dimmer switch befitting the room's original dining purpose. Inside the room to the right is the closet, with its shelves meant for dishes. On one shelf is her collection of purchases she plans to distribute to relatives on her next trip home to Iran. Another shelf holds a bin of yarn and knitting needles. On the top shelf is a set of boxes.

My own mother had these same boxes, and she kept them on her top closet shelf as well. They're clear plastic, with colored plastic lids, and they're meant for shoes. My mother stored her old love letters from my father in them, from when they were newly wed and my father yearned for her while away on business.

Goli Joon stores letters in these boxes too, I find, by standing atop the chair that belongs with her sewing table. It's hopeless to read them because I still have not learned to read very much Persian, and the handwriting may even be difficult for the well-trained language learner. Still, I thumb. One envelope calls to me. I look at the clock. Even if Naveed only stays for a few minutes, certainly I have enough time for one envelope.

And then, for one more, and one more after that. There are old photos in some of them, and each photo tells a story.

But what story is this? A photo of Yasmin Noury?

Why does a wallet-sized portrait of Yasmin Noury tumble out of the last old envelope in the box? I stare at it as if any second the woman in the photo will morph into someone else that I don't know, who doesn't live across the street.

I glance over the letter accompanying the picture. Indecipherable. The sound of a car pulling up outside causes my heart to race, and I shove the photo and letter back in the envelope and into my front pocket. I slide the box onto the shelf, and move the chair back in place. But the key is turning in the lock, and the front door has a direct line of sight to Goli Joon's door.

Panicking, I grab the only excuse to be in there I can think of. As Naveed walks in, I turn off the light and walk out of his mother's room with a bundle of yarn and two needles.

"Hi!" I say. "Thought I'd give knitting another try."

Naveed tilts his head, surprised, but comes to give me a kiss. "Put that down," he says, taking the knitting supplies from my arms and casting them aside. "Last night with the house to ourselves. Maman is being released tomorrow."

While Simeen sleeps innocently in her crib, Naveed loves me slowly and completely. But all the while, I'm thinking that I have to hide that letter that's in the front pocket of my pants, which are on the floor at the end of our bed, as soon as he falls asleep.

And I'm biting my tongue, because I need time to think before I ask him, *Why does your mom have a tiny portrait photo of Yasmin Noury?*

Mourning

At the end of this work week, I didn't think I'd end up in Atlanta on Saturday night to be with relatives mourning Uncle Andy's death. But remembering how he used to speed and swerve around on that motorcycle, I shouldn't be surprised. I'd ridden on that motorcycle with him, and somehow that is the only part of this that is real to me now—that the motorcycle is gone. I can't imagine Uncle Andy is gone too.

They said he was coming up on a clover leaf ramp and a car was stalled at the top of it. He was going too fast to slow down or to change lanes, if even there was an open lane. He flew off his bike and kept flying.

He wasn't really talking to any of us for the last year, either because he was so angry after his fourth wife had left him or because he was just fed up with his and my mom's whole family for bugging him about his failed marriages.

It didn't seem fair for him to quit talking to me, his niece, but I guess that's how it goes when people stop talking to somebody. You stop talking to one sibling, and then you have to stop talking to their kids and everybody else connected with them. A rift between two people becomes a rift between families, and people take sides. I don't even really know what it was about.

Andy was thrown from his smashed-up bike and a couple of ribs punctured his lungs. His spleen bled inside him. He asked those who arrived to help him as he gasped for breath. He was taken to the hospital where he died on the operating table at eleven-thirty at night with his separated wife and Grandma Viv there beside him.

I flew out with my mom and Bruce and Courtney. Laura and Ty were closing on a new house, so Laura couldn't come.

While Courtney shares a guest bed at Uncle Percy's with Grandma, I stay at the house of a neighbor woman I don't know. Uncle Percy and his second wife Lorraine have two big dogs I'm allergic to, so I can't stay there. It's late and it has been a hard weekend, so I fall asleep quickly in this stranger's house. I miss my little girl already. She's not a baby anymore.

Grandma was at Percy's when I arrived there, but I hardly saw her before I moved across the street. It was midnight two nights after Grandma's baby boy was killed and yet she was more beautiful than ever.

She's gotten more beautiful every year of her life, but I didn't expect it tonight. She wore a lilac skirt and a taupe silk sweater, house shoes with little kitten heels, perfume, pink lipstick, and full make-up. Her eyes, a brighter teal than ever, brimmed with tears that couldn't fall. Percy said she'd cried a lot already, that she was beside herself.

The second night, my cousin Izzy invites me to stay with her and we wonder why we didn't think of that in the first place. With Izzy, I take my first hit off of a joint in such a long time. And like back then, a rerun of *Cheers* is on. Izzy and her boyfriend, who has provided the pot, and I are staring at the television and not believing how funny it is. It's an episode I've seen a hundred times before.

It's not like the scare anti-drug campaign of years ago, where the guy offering the pot is an evil conspirator lurking around a corner. Izzy's boyfriend is just a tired young guy who says he has to relax from his horrible job. Izzy doesn't frequently smoke pot, but tonight she says we should smoke one for Andy.

Uncle Andy would be pretty mad about this, since he was a straight arrow of a cop, but we smoke one for him anyway.

Translations

Niloofar sits waiting for me at the Dinky Kebab. I called her to ask her for a favor, some help with translation, I said. When I arrive, she has my work cut out for me: filling the sumac shakers. She's emptied and washed them and they all sit on the table next to a half-gallon jug of sumac powder and a funnel.

I pull the letter and photo out of my pocket, looking around to make sure we're alone. The only customers are two elderly men. "What's this say?" I ask.

"Hello, how are you, and nice to see you too," Niloofar asks rhetorically, reminding me of my poor manners. "What am I, the CIA? You want me to translate from Farsi—why can't Naveed do it for you?"

I look at her, sitting pretty in her white shirt and perfect lipstick. I realize that Niloofar keeps her white shirt clean and crisp all the time, while I used to have fried eggplant or butter on mine after the first few minutes of every shift. And regardless of the omnipresence of her perfect lipstick, I have never witnessed her applying it.

She sees the photo, and takes the letter from my hand. She begins to read to herself. "I know about this woman," she says, flicking her finger at the photo. "She's a lawyer. I've read a couple of articles about her—she helps torture victims."

"Really?" I ask. "She lives across the street. I found this letter in Naveed's mom's stuff."

She keeps reading. "You should really ask your husband if you want to have any trust between you. But I'll tell you this: The letter is from your husband's mom's sister. She's trying to arrange a marriage between this woman, Yasmin, and Naveed. It's a letter to sing Yasmin's praises. And there's plenty to praise."

When she says, "and there's plenty to praise" I imagine she's looking at me and thinking, *He could have married her and he married you instead?*

"Anything else you want to tell me?" I ask.

She shrugs. "Nope. Just some advice: Talk to him if you're worried. He should be honest with you. Married people shouldn't keep too many secrets. And you should be honest with him if you have anything you need to come clean about too."

Naveed isn't the forbidden fruit, or the bad boy, or the millionaire. He's just this parking ramp engineer who wants stability and to go fishing and to collect stuff. Who loves me. I don't know though—maybe he wouldn't have wanted me in the first place if he'd really known me.

Except that he says he does want me. But that he's very mad at me, because I promised I would never use drugs again, and I put myself in a very vulnerable situation. Niloofar's advice to come clean and be honest is what convinced me that I should tell him I smoked a joint with my cousin Izzy and her boyfriend in Atlanta.

"Wait a second," I say. "Nothing bad happened. We watched *Cheers*. Oh my God, how dangerous."

"Nothing happened? You broke a promise, and you risked your safety, and now I don't know if I can trust you not to do it again and possibly even risk our daughter's safety."

I roll my eyes. He just doesn't get it, I think. He thinks pot is like meth. I would never make light of drugs like meth or coke or pills, but pot is therapeutic for me and not that dangerous.

"You know," I say, "when pot eventually becomes legal, which it will, you can look back on this day and realize you were doing the equivalent of nagging me for just drinking a beer."

"It's not the substance, it's the addiction," he says. "What if your mom were to drink a beer? You know it wouldn't be *just a beer* then."

I pause at this—at how he has hit a little below the belt by bringing up my mom and her alcoholism. I'm not an alcoholic, so it's not relevant. I return to arguing about the promise.

"Holding me to a promise to never, ever smoke pot again is like how my dad held my mom to the decision not to go to movies anymore since they'd bought a seven hundred dollar T.V. in 1972. They agreed at the time they wouldn't go to movies if they bought the T.V. But Mom didn't think that would mean that he would never take her to a movie for the rest of their lives."

"I'm worried for you," he says. "And for Simeen. I have to hold you to your promise, or maybe you should get some help if you can't stay off of drugs."

"Oh my God. It's not *drugs*, it's just pot," I say.

And then, the thing I've been holding back since the night before my uncle died comes out. "And, I know you are keeping something from me, so you are not perfect either."

"What are you talking about?" he asks.

"You were going to marry Yasmin Noury," I say. After all this time living across the street from her, I still tend to call her by her first and last name. The distance between us requires it. Yasmin by itself would be too casual.

"Oh," he says, looking at me. "So you know. Did Maman tell you?"

"I found her picture in a letter in your mom's closet, and Niloofar at the Dinky Kebab read it to me. But I still don't understand what happened. It sounds like you were to be engaged."

I have no good reason to cry now, but it's stressful, and I'm embarrassed about my snooping. A few tears fall on the letter as I pull it out of my purse.

Naveed invites me to sit on the ivory damask sofa, and I sit, waiting to hear what I hope will be the truth, and what I fear will bring out the horrible jealousy I always have inside of me.

"You know I love you, right?" he asks. "And you know I hardly even know Yasmin."

"I'd never seen you even talk to her that I can remember, until Parvaneh got sick," I say. "Except maybe at our wedding."

"Let me tell you the story," he starts. "My mom's sister knew the family. Everybody knew Yasmin's mother and father were divorced.

"The divorce brought a lot of shame on the family because the mother was so open about it—she was seen as a prostitute because she had an affair with an American businessman after the divorce, and then people started gossiping that she was having affairs with all the foreign men in town."

"Was she?" I ask.

"Probably not. She was just more worldly than the city of Kashan was ready for, and she was bored with marriage and life there. She and Yasmin moved to Tehran, and then later Yasmin moved to California for school. Divorced women didn't normally have custody of their children, but Yasmin's father didn't want to force them apart.

"My mom's sister, the one who runs the business in Kashan, hired Yasmin's father as a salesman when he lost his attorney job after the Revolution. Everybody had been trying to get him to remarry, but he never did. He knew Yasmin would never forgive him—she was always hoping her mother would come to her senses and go back to him."

This fashionable neighbor who lives across the street, coming and going in her professional attire, now coming from and going to medical doctors with her sick daughter, comes into better focus for me.

"Why would you have married her?" I ask. "You didn't even know her. I thought you were too modern to accept an arranged marriage."

"I would have accepted the match. But she married Milad instead," he says. "And that was okay. I was happy for them."

"But, did you love her?" I'm looking at him like he's a stranger. He's always seemed so Americanized. If he would have married her, it seems like he must have wanted her.

"I liked her right away. She had this incredible strength and passion about fighting for justice. I thought the love would grow later. I've seen it happen many times. You have to know some of the happiest marriages I've seen are like that."

Relief—wanting to believe that he didn't want her in that way, that he was not still harboring feelings for her—combine with another realization. "But your mother…"

"Maman was hurt and upset. She thought she had been on the progressive moral high ground, proposing her son to the woman other families didn't want anything to do with. Yasmin was seen as the daughter of a damaged woman, but Maman felt sorry for her. And she was educated. My aunt had helped out and she had been able to go to California and get into law school."

"So your mom thought she was doing Yasmin a favor by setting her up with you?"

"Yeah, you know, she thinks I'm such a good catch because she's my mom." He grabs my hand, and I hold his.

"You are a good catch," I say.

"My mom was also scared that I would be marked by being rejected by Yasmin and I would never be able to get married. She didn't know if she was going to live or die from her heart problem. She wanted to see that I wasn't going to be alone. And she wanted the chance to spoil grandchildren.

"But there were more important things to Yasmin than what kind of a catch I was or wasn't. She flew here from California with another relative, but it was mainly just to satisfy the old ladies who thought she needed a mate. She wasn't looking for a husband, and she knew her mother hadn't been happy in an arranged marriage.

"It seemed like she was open to the idea, though. She liked me. We were getting to know each other. But before we even had our final gathering to drink tea together and decide if we wanted to spend the rest of our lives together, she was introduced to Milad. They fell in love at first sight."

I ask him if that's why he and Milad had a falling out. "It wasn't over Yasmin," he says. "Like I said, I was happy for them. Holy cow! They had such chemistry. But my mom was so upset about Yasmin rejecting me, her son. So my mom said bad things about Yasmin to make it seem like I was the one who rejected her. Milad got angry at my mom, and then Milad and I got into the mix. It got big."

I knew that things happen like that sometimes among families, and of course I'd seen those rifts in my mother's family in Georgia. Someone's pride gets hurt, and that person hurts another person out of their own pain and fear, and then everything falls apart.

"So then what about Yasmin's father, Mr. Noury?" I ask. "What's going on there?"

"It seems like Mr. Noury has been interested in Maman since the first time she was here for heart surgery, but I don't know the details. He comes and goes from Iran, but they'd been here at the same time once before. I'd come home early from work one day and they were drinking tea together in the garden. Yasmin drove up early too, and he pretended like he had been visiting me, not her. I think Yasmin has just never gotten over the divorce and doesn't want him to see any other women. She sees him as too old, anyway."

"Well, yeah. Isn't your mom too old for that too?"

"I don't know. We just don't talk about things like that. And right now, I think that all anyone is really worried about is little Parvaneh."

I'm tired and not ready to absorb all of this. Being reminded of Parvaneh is too much on top of what has already been a heavy conversation.

258 / CATHERINE DEHDASHTI

Only an hour before, I was feeling so harassed about having smoked a joint in Atlanta. I'd wondered if maybe Melinda was right: I had the chance to have the luxury life with Quentin, who wasn't so judgmental. I'd been thinking about how I'd be sitting out at the pool with all the cake eaters if I hadn't married Naveed. And yet now here I am remembering that I'm in love with him and it's only the beginning. It must be only the beginning if I'm still only learning about him.

So we sleep, but I'm not off the hook about the pot. I know Naveed thinks I was one of his do-it-yourself fixer-upper projects, his labor of love, and he doesn't want to see me fall to pieces. But for now he takes my new promise to heart, and I give in to his love for me as he rescues me from all of my exhaustion, touching me and assuring me deep into the night.

Sister-in-law

An official-looking letter arrived from the INS today, addressed to Naveed. I gave it to him and he tore it open. A smile polkaed across his face. Firoozeh is being approved for immigration. She can come in a couple of months. She's very independent, so she will stay with us for just a few days if she can find an apartment. There are plenty of beautiful old apartment buildings close by, reasonably priced. One of them will be perfect.

The Unthinkable

Goli Joon hits herself over the head with a candelabrum. I rush to take it away from her, but don't reach her before she hits herself two more times. Her head bleeds before Naveed takes it away and washes her wound. I make her drink a half a glass of wine—ancient Persian medicine—which is now officially doctor-approved for her. And then I drink a glass too.

Parvaneh Zand—daughter, sister, flower girl, butterfly— has died from her "easy form" of cancer. Goli Joon hardly knew the little girl, but she cries that it might be our fault because we let the little girl kiss our chickens when they were brand new baby chicks and maybe she got the germs from them. And that she never should have let me plant so many yellow flowers in our garden. Now sickness has come to the neighborhood.

Naveed tells her that he knows she knows better than that. He has to practically yell at her to get her out of this state.

"I thought you said it was an easy kind of cancer to cure!" I yell at him, crying and holding Simeen tight.

Naveed takes Simeen from me and nuzzles her. "They were trying to be positive," he says.

Disbelief sets in, but the family follows the Muslim tradition of burying her within twenty-four hours, before anyone can even imagine it's true.

When Parvaneh is buried at Lakeview Cemetery on Lake Calhoun, the harsh reality of the pine casket forces unripe acknowledgement of her passing.

Women wail as genuinely as ever I've heard. Yasmin Noury faints and is almost taken away. But then she revives and tries to jump into the grave. Her other daughter is taken away to the car, looking lost without her baby sister. The men try not to cry, but they do cry. Co-workers and friends who are not Iranian try to comfort them so they will all stop the wailing and crying, but they only get louder.

We cry too, all of us. By the time we leave the cemetery, we're about as wet as Lake Calhoun, with eyes as pink as the rose petals Parvaneh tossed at our wedding.

The next week Naveed goes and buys three Lakeview Cemetery plots for me, himself, and his mother. Because he's realized that's where all the Iranian people get buried. After little Parvaneh was buried, we'd walked around and looked at all the graves in that section of the cemetery. There are rows of headstones with Persian script on them, and some with English-Latin letters but Persian names.

Lakeview is filling up fast with all the old mothers and fathers who have come to live with their grownup children, and even now with some of the early arrivals themselves, those doctors who came in the 50s and 60s, and those few who died far too young. Parvaneh isn't the only Iranian-American child buried here; she's in the company of another little girl and boy, which is sadly comforting.

And I realize, this little section of Lakeview Cemetery— this is the real Little Iran. I know I call our neighborhood that, but it isn't really. There aren't that many of them here in the Twin Cities—only a thousand or two. There's no physical community of Iranians here like in Los Angeles. "Little" places are usually pockets of low-rent for refugees. Then the people rise out of poverty and move out and the next wave of refugees moves in.

Not so with Iranians. They move in sprinkles. Some in this area, some in that. They move to the best place they can afford. Sometimes very nice places.

The only place there are several of them all close together is right here in the cemetery. And this is where I will be buried too, right next to Naveed and Goli Joon, and all of the other Iranians and people who are Iranian by marriage. In this sepulchral Little Iran.

None of the graves in this section of the cemetery are too ostentatious, just flat slabs. Even the graves of the rich doctors are simple. Those who were ostentatious in their homes are simple in their deaths, wrapped unembalmed in a white cloth, placed in a pine box, and buried within twenty-four hours.

Families like it here at Lakeview because it's pretty and well-kept, and the neighborhood is like Shemiran, a beautiful old neighborhood of northern Tehran. One of the guests points this out to the family—that the neighborhood around Lakeview Cemetery is just like Shemiran. *Shemroon* is how they pronounce it in the typical colloquial, like how joon comes from the proper *jan*. This Shemroon-like neighborhood overlooking Lake Calhoun is a good resting place for Parvaneh.

The way they say Shemroon sounds so magical, like the Persian version of Hanalei. For just one moment, the Zand/Nourys seem to pull themselves together.

Sisters! Fight!

It's the morning after my big fight with Laura, on a sister-trip to southern California. Courtney came up with the idea because she thinks she might want to move out here before the next horrible Minnesota winter. I didn't want to leave my baby for four days. Parvaneh's death has scared me so much that I hardly ever want to let Simeen out of my arms.

Contrarily, though, some part of me needed to get away.

Laura and Courtney have gone for a jog. Courtney isn't a runner, but she goes along anyway while I sit in our hotel room wishing I had some pot to smoke. This is California. Aren't there supposed to be marijuana dispensaries on every street corner? You know, places called "Puffin' Stuff" and "Kite-High Kafé"? Not that I would actually go into one. Just dreaming, because being high goes well with crying.

When they come back everything is still so tense from the fight, but we'd planned to drive our rental car to Pasadena to visit the Huntington Gardens. Ty had recommended the Huntington to Laura, and it was also in the *Let's Go* book Melinda had mailed to me when I told her we were going to take this trip. She'd bookmarked it with a Post-it, also marking pages telling me where we could find women-owned restaurants serving achiote pork in banana leaves and art galleries where we could buy signed prints by our favorite artists we've never heard of.

The fight was the first we've had since we were teenagers and could fight comfortably without feeling ashamed about the fact that we don't always get along. Now that we're adults, we're supposed to be reasonable and mature. That's not always easy for me because of how I'm "angry and cynical all of the time," which is how Laura put it.

All I want to say about the fight is that it involved:

- Arnold Schwarzenegger, governor-elect of California, whom we wish well, or wish to fall flat on his face, depending on whose perspective
- me, accidentally slamming Laura's finger in the car door after mentioning said Terminator-elect
- Laura falsely accusing me of crushing her finger on purpose, and me calling her a dumbass for putting her finger in the door hinge (followed by sister-trip to Kaiser Permanente Medical Center of Los Angeles emergency room)
- Courtney getting whiplash trying to pick a side or not pick a side

At the hospital while I was waiting for Laura to come out, I'd gone into the bathroom and seen in the mirror that the crevice between my eyebrows, that gash of a wrinkle that I have inherited from my mother, had branched off with a smaller diagonal wrinkle on each side of it. My crevice is now a little peace sign in the center of my face that will now appear every time I furrow my brow, as if to make fun of me for not being as peaceful as I claim to be.

I came back out and sat five seats apart from Courtney, who was watching the news about some minor celebrity who died after being mauled by his own tiger that he kept as a house pet. I don't own a cell phone yet, so I asked Courtney if I could use hers to call Naveed.

I started crying again, waiting for Naveed to answer the phone. Goli Joon answered. She was watching Simeen while Naveed ran to Byerly's, even though it's against doctor's orders for her to babysit.

"What's wrong? What happened?" she asked in Persian, alarmed at my tearful voice. I had to tell her something, so she wouldn't worry it was something worse.

"*KHa-har...Dava*," I said, meaning *sisters...fight*, in Persian, but she didn't understand me. I always get the word for *fight* mixed up with the word that means *medicine*. That made Goli Joon more alarmed, so I yelled it in English, "Sisters! Fight!"

She understood immediately. Thank God for all of her daytime T.V. and Jerry Springer. "*Khoda nakone*," she said in Persian, a saying asking God not to allow such a thing.

"Sisters are like that. I know!" she said. "Laura is good. Courtney is good. You're good. It will get better."

After we hung up, Laura came out. Amazingly, the finger wasn't broken, according to the L.A. doctors, but I didn't believe it because it looked purple and dead (and because I don't trust doctors who aren't from Minnesota). At least they put a splint on it anyway.

So now, with a day to go before flying home, what would we do to kill the time if not go to Pasadena? My head hurts from crying, and Laura's finger doesn't look better. But Courtney drives us there, and walking around Huntington Gardens, we see blue ponds with koi fish bigger than Minnesota walleyes. The gardens and the fresh Pasadena air calm us, and again we're just three sisters out exploring Southern California, two of us with puffy reddish eyes to take in paintings by Belgian masters, and me with a peace sign wrinkle engraved in my brow because I'm squinting in the sun.

Once we enter the art collections, we find the painting *The Blue Boy*, by Thomas Gainsborough, which Ty had told Laura not to miss. Across from that we notice *Pinkie* by Thomas Lawrence.

The two paintings are always displayed together, even though they're from different artists and time periods. We probably saw them on episodes of *Leave It to Beaver.* We're told they, or maybe just reproductions, were used as props in the home of Ward and June Cleaver and their two boys—prop art for the perfect American family.

Pinkie, Sarah Barrett Moulton, was the English girl of a Jamaican plantation family. There's something about her that disturbs me, and it's not only that I learn she died young and I'm still heavyhearted about Parvaneh and missing Simeen. Maybe it's a little bit because of that, but Laura and Courtney feel it too. She beguiles us, and she upsets us.

We're all taken with Pinkie, and we gaze at her for the longest time.

International Arrivals

Firoozeh landed yesterday. It must be so weird for her to live in Tehran one day and Minnesota the next. The plane landed at twelve-thirty in the afternoon. We sat and waited for her to come through the International Arrivals gate, Goli Joon knitting a rainbow-colored sweater for her grown daughter who will need warmer clothes.

At three-thirty, we still couldn't get any information from immigration/customs about Firoozeh's status. KLM confirmed she had been on the flight, but the customs policy is to release no info. We asked travelers and employees as they came through the opaque custom doors if there were any people left and were told no, unless they were in the "small rooms where they do interrogations."

Naveed's mom put away the knitting and started crying. She harassed the travelers who came through the gates long after Naveed and I had given up on that tactic. Since she still doesn't speak much English, it was fruitless. But she couldn't stop herself from playing charades with the poor, tired travelers.

By four, she was flagellating herself repeatedly. That disturbed other people around us, and I took Simeen away because I didn't want her to see her grandmother hitting herself. We went home. Goli Joon, wailing, said she was going to throw away all the food she had prepared for the welcoming feast and break the dishes on her head.

When Firoozeh called at six, Goli Joon launched into thank-you-heavenly-father prayer mode. She had been interrogated the entire time, with the officers using all the tricks, like, "We know who you are and why you are really here," and threatening to send her back "unless you give us the information we need."

So finally Naveed went back to the airport, and it was a good thing we didn't all go back because her giant suitcases took up most of our new Toyota Sienna. It would never have fit in a regular car, and neither will our newly expanded family, so I guess it's a good thing I finally gave in on the damn minivan.

Firoozeh brought us way too much stuff, including some small Persian carpets, tons of dried foods, gold jewelry sized for a baby, and a big furry nomad vest for me and one for Simeen. The tot-sized version is ultra suede, but mine is real suede and fur and it stinks like they didn't scrape out all the meat from the hide.

Today she should rest and sleep, but it's Naveed's only day off this week so they need to spend the day doing things like apartment searching. Firoozeh will sleep in our basement for now, but she's very independent and wants to have her own place as soon as possible.

While we were at the airport yesterday, I saw someone from long ago.

It was when we were at the end of our rope waiting, while Goli Joon was beating herself and we were all tired and stressed. Only Simeen was having fun, pulling my sweat jacket hood over my head and laughing and acting like a monkey. It was while I was thinking, *What kind of crazy life am I living with this whacked-out family?*

It was then that I saw Quentin.

Quentin, the rich stockbroker boyfriend with the house on Lake Minnetonka, the cleaning ladies, and the vacations to Paris. Quentin, with the Andy Warhol silkscreen of Marilyn Monroe. I *still* miss that Marilyn Monroe.

He was at the baggage carousel next to the custom doors, with his very young-looking girlfriend, and it was for a flight coming from Florida. I realized right away it couldn't have been Dori because Dori would be older now. This woman wasn't older than twenty-four.

We barely caught each other's eyes, and did not even say hello. I remembered when he and I went to Florida. Quentin and the young woman looked like they'd had lots of free-spirited fun, and they looked tanned and relaxed, and free of whacked-out relatives and rambunctious kids. They looked like all they had to do was go back to his house on Lake Minnetonka and have more sex.

It was like looking back in time. I went to the bathroom with Simeen, and walked right by the girlfriend on the way back. She had a hard look, even though she was pretty. She's in it for the free travel—I can tell. Back in our airport seats, I observed them together for just a minute, even as Simeen was pulling my hood over my face. The hood, with its perforated fabric that I could see through, was the perfect disguise.

Quentin and his companion grabbed their baggage from the conveyer belt and left. As Goli Joon paced the width across the forbidding customs doors, slapping herself silly, I let Simeen pull the hood over my face and laugh again and again.

I played along with her, making her laugh all the harder as I yelled, "Hey, where is everybody? Somebody turned off the lights!"

Running

"I just ran a whole fucking mile," I tell Savi. I don't swear around her like this usually—this is more my talking-to-Melinda language, but I deserve this f-bomb. I had forced myself to do something, to get out of bed and try to act more alive.

Savi seems distracted. "Your family will be proud of you."

"Yeah, well. One mile is about a third of Laura's usual cool-down, but still. I didn't even plan to do it. I was just walking around the track. I bent down to tie my shoelaces tighter, and when I stood up I suddenly just took off. *Zoom!*"

Savi stirs her coffee. I had told her that sometimes I think I might have depression, and felt surprised she wasn't giving me advice (and books) like she usually does. "Walking is just as good as running," she counters.

"To be honest, I'm not sure I was running. I thought I was, but everybody passed me—old people, a bow-legged man, even a Somali woman in a long skirt and head scarf." The Somali woman used to walk at the same time I do, but she started jogging last month.

This wakes up Savi. "Why do you assume that the Somali woman would be slower than you?"

"Because of the skirt, as I said," I answer. A lot of people are coming to Minnesota from Somalia lately. "But they're tall, so I guess the long legs make up for it."

"Oh my God," Savi says. "The woman probably survived a war and still you assume you should be superior to her. Do you ever even think about other people's realities?"

Stung, I take a sip of my tea, but I have to try a couple of times before I can swallow it.

"It's not my fault I've never had to survive a war," I say. "Don't you think I could?"

I try to change the conversation to ask Savi about the book she has peeking out of her bag. But a shadow passes over her face. I notice she looks older now; it's as if it's the first time I've really looked at her in five years. "You really don't ever think about other people. Did you even know I suffer from depression too?"

"No," I say, "because you didn't tell me." Now is the moment when I should ask her about that, obviously. But instead, I get up to leave.

The next day, I call Savi and tell her I'm sorry. That maybe we could go walk, or run, and that I want to hear about her depression too, not just tell her about my suspicions about my own mental health.

"Of course you have it too," she says, and again I feel stung by her insinuation that I turn everything back to myself instead of caring about others. She adds that she has a writing project deadline looming, but maybe another time.

I go to the community center with my mom instead. She runs strong laps, achieving a state of flow, so it doesn't look like it's even difficult. There's no sign of her former knee injury. Her right hip gives her trouble now, but she keeps going and passes me more than every ten minutes. I repeat my magic moment from the other day, walking a few laps and then bending down to tighten my shoelaces before taking off.

I wonder how many miles I would have to run to get the runner's high.

Beating Hearts

Goli Joon goes home to Iran, staying in Darab's house. Her long-separated husband lives in the gardener's cottage, around which he grows the tarragon, mint, and basil with which they begin every lunch and dinner. She lives there for three months with all this family, her son and his wife, the grandsons, Darab's wife's parents, and her so-called husband, Mahmood. She survives well enough with her grape-skin heart to assist with dinner every night.

Darab emails Naveed a photo of Goli Joon and Mahmood, Mahmood's arm around Goli Joon as she tosses a salad in the kitchen and smiles like a school girl enjoying the attention.

Naveed shows me the photo, and I say, "There is so much I don't understand."

"Me too," he says. But then he tells me, "It's not what you might be thinking, though. Actually, they have agreed to put the paperwork through to officially end their marriage."

"That's not what it looks like to me," I say, "because they look sort of flirty in this picture."

Naveed looks at the photo and then he blows his nose into a tissue. "It looks to me like forgiveness," he says.

When Goli Joon comes home to us, she looks healthier. Even though we know she's very ill, we begin to take her for granted like before because she seems young again.

One Sunday morning, Naveed's sister is at our house for brunch. Naveed has invited her, and even though I'm tired and feeling very heavy and low, I get up to cook because I feel shame that I have not been a good host to her. Firoozeh's apartment, naturally, is right in the neighborhood. Maybe this is still Little Iran. Firoozeh's arrival has rejuvenated the dinner and tea party circuit. Today we have people coming for afternoon tea, and then later we're all going to have dinner at somebody else's house. Although I might weasel out of it.

I'm in the brightly lit kitchen, making omelets with the bacon, onions, and green peppers. I'm frying the bacon separately to keep it out of Goli Joon's omelet. I keep it out of Firoozeh's too, just because she thinks it's gross—not because she's religious. She's not—she's only "spiritual."

Goli Joon has been looking out the window from her perch on the couch. As I go to tell her that brunch is ready, she gets up and peers through the glass, then begins gesturing wildly to something outside the living room window. "Where is the phone? Call 911," she says. "It's the neighbor!"

I see the old man, Mr. Noury. He's almost in his usual post-jog position out in the road, but he looks like he has been doing his knee bends and arm rotations when his left side fell. He's still standing, but as I watch he slowly moves into a crouched position on the ground.

As usual, the cordless phone is nowhere near its charger, but Goli Joon quickly finds it on our fireplace mantle as Firoozeh and I yell for Naveed. I have not seen Goli Joon move so fast before, fast enough to make me worry about her heart.

Naveed turns the knob of the front door and yanks hard to open it. We run to the man. He smiles up at us, trying to shake his left arm, which seems glued to his side.

"Goli-am ku?" he asks—where is my Goli? Goli Joon leans out the front door with the cordless phone and I run back to her, taking the phone and explaining that we need paramedics, that our neighbor might be having a heart attack.

Naveed motions for me to come and sit with Mr. Noury while he finds Milad Zand. They come back together and help him to our lawn. Yasmin runs out of the house with a bottle of pills and a glass of water. She helps him take two pills, and then she rubs his left arm as if she could make it come back to life and fend off the attack.

Goli Joon is watching from our door, trying to direct Naveed and the neighbors from a distance, which almost makes it look as if she's in control, except that she's hitting herself at the same time. Firoozeh gently takes her mother's hands and makes her stop, and then tries to pull her back into the house.

"Goli mikhaum" the man tells his daughter—*I want Goli.*

Yasmin looks toward the house and sees Goli Joon and Firoozeh there at the door, Goli looking ready to sprint over but hesitating for some reason. Since losing Parvaneh, Yasmin looks twenty years older. She has no effervescence, and yet she doesn't seem weak either. She stares ahead, but when the ambulance arrives and the emergency responder asks who all is coming along with the patient, Milad and Yasmin look at each other.

Yasmin suddenly lifts her chin up and hollers at Naveed, "Call over your maman!" Then she checks her manners and adds, "Please!"

Goli Joon comes over as quickly as she can, not waiting for Naveed to ask. She climbs in, and off they go, red lights twirling atop the boxy emergency room on wheels.

"There's still so much I don't know," I tell Naveed, baffled. I still don't understand how the falling out between the families, caused by Goli Joon's damaged pride over Yasmin's rejection of Naveed, fits with this—I don't know what to call it—*relationship?* between Goli and Mr. Noury.

"I don't even think I want to know," he says. When we go inside he tells me in an unnecessarily quiet voice that the other day he came home and his mother had *six* grocery bags from Byerly's to put away.

She told him she'd walked there, as she often does while we're at work, but he knows she can't carry more than two bags by herself. "There were even Idaho potatoes," he adds, and then shakes his head again, repeating that he doesn't even want to know.

For now, all I really know is I need to cancel our afternoon tea party and dinner plans too.

When Yasmin Noury brings Goli Joon home late at night, Goli acts as if the events of the day were no different than her usual days of cooking or watching T.V. But everything has changed, and when the older man returns to his daughter's home, a new unspoken agreement will have formed among all of us.

There will be times ahead when Naveed and I will bring Simeen to my mom's house and go out to a movie, or even to walk around Lake Calhoun and eat dinner in Uptown.

I suspect that Naveed somehow lets the neighbors know they should plan to go out too. They don't go out to have fun by themselves; they are to be forever mourning for Parvaneh. But they go somewhere with their other daughter, maybe just to buy groceries with her, maybe to go shopping for pretty things for her. Or maybe they go for a visit to pour rosewater on Parvaneh's grave at Lakeview Cemetery like Goli Joon did on the fortieth day after her death.

I imagine this isn't easy for Yasmin Noury, but I don't ask her. We still are not friends, but someday I hope we will be—if she ever has the time, that is. I know she's still working on putting one foot in front of the other after losing Parvaneh, but she's back to work now. I see her leaving the house in the morning in her crisp white blouses and black everything else. She looks tired and angry and sad, and yet I see determination in her eyes as she heads off to another day of getting justice and preventing torture.

I understand now how the falling out happened because of Goli's pride and worry, and also how Yasmin had probably not been ready for her father to move on and love a woman besides her mother. But I still don't know how Mr. Noury and Goli Joon initiated their affair, or when, and they keep everything so very decorous and their reputations as pure as the driven snow on a Minnesota Thanksgiving.

I guess there are some things that are just meant to stay private in their culture, and not all secrets are bad.

Naveed and I ask Goli Joon to come with us when we go out, but we will not ask three times on some evenings. I imagine the same ritual happening across the street. When the elders stay behind, we will only smile and not tease if, when we come home, the good teapot and two glass teacups, or a book of poetry and a purple ring from a glass of wine, are left on the fireplace hearth.

Rejection

I'm expecting my writing teacher to be impressed with what I think is the final draft of my novel, *Hogwash*. I'd signed up for more classes to revise the book and learn about how to get published. I anticipate the teacher—the same one I had years ago when I was writing *Shoedog*—to say I've missed some big opportunities to change the world with my writing by not addressing the politics of environment-destroying agriculture.

Instead, she skips the politics and says it's "entertaining," but that she isn't sure what my main character's motivation is.

I know my main character pretty well, since she's basically me. "She doesn't have any motivation," I say. "That's part of her character."

"It's not *how much* motivation; it's *what* motivates her that I'm wondering," she says. "Anyway, she has a lot more motivation than you give her credit for."

I wonder if that could be true.

Her other main comment is that I still have work to do to develop "a *professional interest*" in my characters.

Even though it's a different novel, there's a father character just like in *Shoedog* who ignores his family and likes to golf a lot. There's also a hoarder.

"You have to let your characters have feelings," she says. "Even people who like to golf a lot have feelings. And people who won't part with old possessions do too."

She says she could give me some writing exercises so I could explore themes of isolation and loss in order to develop this *professional interest* instead of having the narrative voice of a female Ben Stein.

I decide I'm not doing any more work on it, and ask her for recommendations on agents. She gives me some, and gives me the kind of smile my mom and Goli Joon give me when they resign themselves to letting me learn my own lessons. I had been thinking that once I got an agent and we sold the book, I would come to her for a glowing blurb for the back cover. My teacher has Carol Bly's recommendation on the back of her book, and it just seemed right that I would get hers on mine. But now I don't think I'll ask.

I submit the novel to some agents and publishers, and once it's out of my hands, all of my energy collapses. When I'm not at work, drafting proposals for a curriculum on mastitis in dairy cows, I'm home in bed in the dark, letting Simeen watch the *Teletubbies* with Goli Joon and waiting to find out if there is any hope for me at all.

Calhoun

This is the summer of 2001, when all our tomatoes rot, in the garden and on the counter. Goli Joon shares a garden plot down the street at Firoozeh's apartment building now. She lives with us but spends more and more time there, and as happy as that should make me, I feel abandoned, slighted. She had helped me and Naveed get the garden started, then when everything took off she started harvesting produce at Firoozeh's place instead of here. Naveed picks the vegetables, but he doesn't cook more than once or twice a week.

I haven't been cooking at all. Like a writer's block, I have a cooking block. I can't think of anything I want to cook or eat.

Cucumbers and eggplants turn to slime on the kitchen counter. Fruit flies take over. The herbs dry up and turn brown. I feed Simeen things from the refrigerator and we buy take-out food. Every week, we eat pizza, tacos, and gyros sandwiches, and Chinese, Vietnamese, and Thai. We eat pasta salads and chocolate cream pies from Byerly's, and we're grateful when Goli Joon stays at our place to cook or invites us to eat at Firoozeh's.

One night Goli Joon asks Naveed why I haven't been cooking, and when he says I'm just too tired, she asks him if I should see her old psychiatrist. I tell Naveed I'm just really tired, and that I'm in a bad mood because of work. "Join the club," he says, but then he rubs my shoulders until I soften.

My boss took a supervision course while I was on vacation. In place of his previously rude and unappreciative self, I came back to a different person, and when I see how he has changed, I realize that he must have really wanted to change all along. I open my email and instead of his old demands and put-downs, it says, "Thank you for your great work on the manure management proposal! You did a great job of keeping it realistic and positive!"

Two years in this job, and this is my highest accomplishment: pig poop. The proposal was nothing but bullet points, for a curriculum made up of a bunch more bullet points—burned onto a CD-Rom along with some video clips of foaming manure and interactive quiz questions so that we can market it as multimedia.

Suddenly Melinda's long, suicidal voicemails don't seem so absurd.

I'm supposed to feel lucky to have a job, to have the privilege I have. Believe me, I know. Half of my thoughts are about how fortunate I'm supposed to feel. Gratitude, Valerie! Millions of people would love to have a job like mine, a house, and a precious family. I am grateful for all of it. But it doesn't change the bad thoughts chasing bad thoughts in circles in my head, wringing my brain and exhausting me. I'm trying really hard to perk up without going to a psychiatrist, or smoking something to take the edge off, or taking something else to be able to feel the edges of this nebulous, blob-like depression.

Simeen helps, when she laughs, when she reaches out to me and wraps her tiny hands around my neck. The running, although I can still only do one mile, seems to help a little too.

I've heard that recovering alcoholics and coke addicts turn to running, and former potheads turn to yoga. But not me. In five more years I will be the only person I know who does not do yoga—except for Savi, and I will think it's ironic that the only other person I know who doesn't practice Indian yoga is my one and only Hindu friend. But running is okay. I know walking is just as good, but I'm proud that I can run a mile. Sometimes I can walk after the first mile and then run another one.

Maybe I have more motivation than I give myself credit for.

I also try to get my act together by learning to keep a budget and pay my bills on time, and I've even started a Roth IRA for my retirement. Maybe I'm finally growing up, Naveed teases. I tell him I'm trying to prepare for when I'm a successful novelist and the money starts coming in. I'll need to manage it well.

Laura wants to encourage me in all this, so when I tell her I'm going to walk and jog around Lake Calhoun with Simeen in the stroller, she brings Bella and her jogging stroller to meet me. She jogs a full lap around Calhoun first, while Simeen and I stroll with our clunky Graco stroller. I watch her run off, her tight figure after having a baby a sharp contrast to my softening muffin-top belly rising up over the top of my hip-hugger sweatpants. When she comes back around she slows down and I speed up so we're both walking fast. It's a cool-down for her and I'm still warming up.

As we find our pace, I vent to Laura a little bit about Naveed and his hoarding, and how he really needs to quit buying shit now that we're paying twelve hundred dollars a month for the daycare that we used to get for free.

"Ty isn't always easy to live with either," she confides. I think she's just trying to make me feel better. Ty hand-cranks fresh pasta and none of his family members have ever moved into their house.

We keep walking, and the girls begin to babble with each other, pointing at puppies and geese. Eventually, we start talking about our parents. "Dad wishes they never would have gotten the divorce," Laura says.

"Sure, he says that now," I say. "Regrets are so easy. But he had the chance and he didn't pay any attention to her. He wouldn't even take her to a movie."

"Mom didn't divorce him just because he was a stick-in-the-mud. She just married too young. She needed to redo her young adulthood."

"But she didn't do that—not really," I say. "I mean, she found running. She bought that little house. But then she just found other men, and then Bruce."

"You don't have to be so cynical," Laura says. "Buying that house on her own...that was huge for her. The running too. She's run marathons. And now she has Bruce and they like to do the same things."

We stop and sit down at the beach and let the girls out of their strollers so they can play in the sand.

"Mom was nineteen," Laura begins. "She was in college. Dad was working in Atlanta. They met at a parade, and he asked her on a date. Then they had a few more dates."

I don't know why she's telling me this. I know the story up to here, and I know how they eloped to Las Vegas after just weeks.

"Mom had an ex-boyfriend. He would park down the block and watch her comings and goings, and he would threaten her and beg her to see him," she says. I listen. This part sounds only a little bit familiar.

"He would then apologize and convince her that he would stop scaring her. That he'd only been kidding and he wouldn't do it anymore. But when she met Dad, she cut him off.

"One night, Dad dropped Mom off at home. He walked her up to the door and kissed her goodnight. He asked her to see him again the next day, said he wanted to spend the whole day with her. She said she would think about it.

"Lights were on in the house, and her mother's favorite music played on the turntable. Dad waited for her to get inside, and then he started driving back to his apartment. But then something felt wrong. He turned back."

Laura pauses, gives me a minute to fill in the gaps. "Mom's ex-boyfriend had gotten into the house."

I say it as if I've always known, and Laura nods.

"Her parents weren't really home. He'd turned on the lights and put the music on," Laura says. "Then he'd waited in the laundry room. When our Dad drove away, he came out. He said he loved her too much to let her waste her life without him."

"So then dad came back, and he saved her?" I ask. She pauses.

"He scared him off just in time." Laura looks to the left though, like she's not sure. Or like she's not sure what she was supposed to say or not say.

Bella puts a handful of sand in her mouth and Laura jumps up to go wipe it out while I sit there in the sand, just clutching a handful of it and feeling the grains slip out from between my fingers. Laura doesn't have to tell me the rest. A memory comes to me vaguely. I think Mom has tried to tell me about this, but I didn't let her.

"Did they call the police?" I ask, thinking about Uncle Andy. If only he hadn't been just a teenager. If only he'd already been a cop then.

"Yes, but they didn't do anything." Laura has to go back and wipe more sand out of the baby's mouth. "People didn't really want to make a big deal out of things like that back then. They thought it sounded almost romantic, but Dad knew she had to get away."

"So then what?" I ask.

282 / CATHERINE DEHDASHTI

"Mom packed a suitcase and went back with Dad to his apartment. He went to work to ask for a week off and a transfer to Minnesota. They gave it to him, along with a salary advance the same day—he just had to go to accounting and they wrote him a check."

Laura hands the babies a couple of toys from her diaper bag, which starts a fight because they both want the one that can scoop sand. Laura has another scooping toy, and takes it out so they each have one.

I'd always heard our dad say our mom had been the valedictorian of her high school class. She could have become a doctor. But she didn't want to go back to college after leaving Atlanta, and Laura had been born a year later.

We already knew the part in between Atlanta and Minnesota—the part where they get married at a little chapel in Las Vegas and Mom wears a dress she buys for twelve dollars at the shop across the street. That's the only story we knew before and we always thought it was so romantic, especially because in the wedding portrait the chapel staff took of them, our auburn-haired mother looks as beautiful and glamorous as a movie star in that cheap dress, leaning into our blonde father.

There's a place in a man's heart no blonde can go. I think about his second wife, Wanda. She didn't get there. Dad and Wanda have separated, and Dad's living at his cabin.

I ask Laura how she knows all of this, and she says our mom and Neil have both talked to her about it. They wanted me to understand how miraculous it was that their marriage had lasted almost twenty-five years, instead of thinking of it as so terrible that they had gotten divorced. After all, they'd only been dating for two weeks, and only eloped because they couldn't have escaped together any other way.

"Mom wants you to accept Bruce better than you do," she says, "and to understand that even Dad accepts Bruce because he just wants Mom to be happy."

"I guess he's better than some of the other guys," I say. "Remember Charlie?"

I know Mom and Bruce are happy now. I know that every time I see them in their ridiculous matching shirts and matching belted jeans, getting ready to go out line-dancing. Mom and Dad didn't choose to just stick it out, and that's okay. I just wish Dad could have changed a little bit. I don't like how he's so alone, how he puts himself into solitary confinement like that.

"Dad should be closer with us," I say. "He doesn't have to be alone so much like that."

"His friends are around. His golf buddies," Laura says. "He's fine."

She suggests that now I should go and do my run around the lake, and she will stay back with the kids so that I don't have to run with that clunky stroller.

"Or I could take Simeen," I say, "if I could try out the jogging stroller." She shows me how to use it and helps me get Simeen belted in. The lake is more than a mile around, but I manage to run the whole way without stopping. It's not easy, and I still wonder when it will get easy—when, if ever, I will experience that state of flow, that runner's high. When Laura and her baby come back into view I look down and see Simeen sitting up in the jogging stroller with a look of euphoria on her face.

Letters

Two of the letters arrive the same day from New York City. Holding the letters, I let myself imagine a bidding war. After admiring the postmarks and return addresses of the publishers, I tear open the first envelope and see immediately that it's a form letter. And so is the other one.

One of these rejections refers me to the new self-publishing arm of their company. It says my novel is a perfect candidate for self-publishing. For vanity press.

Then the literary agent letters arrive, those who bother to send me form letters refusing their services but wishing me the best of luck in my literary future. I line these letters up against a wall and study them all. The code that emerges from the collection spells out that I am nothing but a failure.

Wayzata Bay

I get Simeen strapped into her car seat and drive twelve feet to our mailbox, pull a stack of mail out of the box and plop it on the passenger seat.

It's Melinda's birthday, and she's flown to Minnesota to celebrate her "dirty thirty" with me and a few other people. Most importantly, me, her best friend, she says. After all of this time, after all of her success and how far apart we are, she still thinks of me as her best friend, even though all we do is email and trade packets of articles and gifts (ninety percent from her to me).

Naveed is helping Matthew fix his catamaran and Firoozeh has asked to have Simeen for the day. Goli Joon is at Firoozeh's place, and now that everyone is slightly more open about the affection between Goli Joon and Mr. Noury, he's over there helping in the community garden plot.

I hand Simeen to Firoozeh, and compliment her on some thriving basil plants. She picks off a leaf and orders me to smell it. "Fantastic," I say. Mr. Noury nods at me as he winds the vines of the *kadoo tanbali*—the lazy squash—around a stake. A big yellow blossom radiates from the end of one vine.

Mr. Noury turns to ask for some help with the plant from Goli Joon. He calls her his little basil flower, in rhyme:

Goleh rayhoon-am, Goli Joon-am.

Goli Joon inspects the pumpkin vines, her fingers moving along the curlicue tendrils, pulling a shriveled yellow blossom toward herself to free it from the rabbit-proof fencing.

"The *kadoo tanbali* isn't really any lazier than the other *kadoo*," she tells me, as if she's picking up a conversation where we left off years ago. "It just needs more space and time to become what God wants it to be."

I nod, liking what she says, wishing she may be talking about me.

"And look," she said, pointing at a little green pumpkin orb growing under the shriveled yellow blossom. "A flower dies, but a baby is not far behind."

Nobody else is there in the beach parking lot, so I sit in the car waiting, getting madder and madder and wondering if Melinda is going to screw me over this time or not.

The stack of mail sits on the passenger seat, so I glance through it as I wait. There's one more publisher letter in there. This one has a Minneapolis return address and my heart rises in my chest. A *local* publisher, maybe they will like my book better than those New Yorkers. It is, after all, a Minnesota story.

But it's another rejection, albeit this one is not a form letter. The submissions editor writes that he likes some things about my novel, and even wonders if I have any other novels that I would like to submit. There are some flaws in this manuscript that make it impossible for him to currently evaluate for publication.

I throw the letter on the floor and look around for Melinda, hoping that she doesn't come. A boat ride doesn't sound fun anymore. As I'm about to drive away, a limousine pulls in to the parking lot and Melinda jumps out.

"Hey, like our wheels?" she asks. She explains that some others wanted to meet at Lord Fletcher's; she's planning on avoiding DWIs and thought a limo would be a better start to her party than a taxi.

I think for a second and then remember that I do not want to bring my purse on the houseboat. I still mourn the loss of my pink and green Wayzata tote bag and Ray Bans that fell into Lake Minnetonka one summer during high school. I don't want my car keys and wallet to join them.

There's a space under my passenger seat where my purse fits perfectly. I look around to see if anyone is watching me hiding my valuables, but the only lurker is a smug looking cat on the retaining wall of Wayzata Boatworks.

Melinda offers me a drink in a crystal goblet, and I take just one sip. There are no red Solo cups in Melinda's world. Just new music and exclusive liquor in crystal drinkware. "It's artisanal tequila," she tells me, pronouncing it the right way now, instead of *artesian*.

The chauffer takes us to Lord Fletcher's, where Melinda, her friend, and I share a lobster-bite appetizer plate on the lakeside patio as we wait for our party boat to pick us up.

The first person I see waving from the boat coming in to dock is not the person I expected to see. When Melinda said it was a friend with a houseboat, I thought of another guy she knows. It turns out that it is that guy's boat, but the person waving is not him. It's Kurt, and another guy besides the boat owner. No other women.

It's been years since I have seen Kurt, but he's wearing the same shirt I've seen him in a hundred times. It's his long-sleeve red Coca-Cola jersey, with the rip in the arm at the left bicep. The rip is much bigger and there's a hole in the shirt at the clavicle and the hem is undone. I think, this shirt wouldn't get him into Lord Fletcher's, but it doesn't matter because he isn't getting off the boat. We're getting in.

I turn and whisper to Melinda. "You know I can't see Kurt! I've promised Naveed, and I've kept my promise."

But I board the boat, and she hisses, "I'm glad Roger doesn't make all the rules in our relationship."

I'm mad, but I don't turn around and get off the boat. I don't know why not. I just don't want to let Melinda be right about Naveed making all the rules.

But then somehow, probably because I see the irony of how Melinda is actually the one to think she can make all the rules in our relationship, I dish it right back out for once. One deep breath, and then a swallow, and then, "And I'm glad that Naveed isn't an embezzler like Roger."

When her jaw drops, I add, "I'm just afraid that could end badly."

Melinda's face goes blank in disbelief, but she's perfectly composed, her face seamless. Instead of responding, she seems to make a decision to pretend I did not just talk back to her, and walks to the stereo to load up her CDs into the stereo system and unload her fine tequila.

The boat is moving. It's too late to turn back.

I haven't been in a boat on Lake Minnetonka since the early 90s. It doesn't feel like anyplace else in Minnesota. I quickly kill the feeling of being misplaced and let myself feel like I've been scrubbed clean and dressed in a white tennis sweater, like I belong here in this scene straight out of *The Official Preppy Handbook*.

Kurt's eyes light up to see me, and he offers me a hit off a joint right away while he complains that Chantal took away his bong this morning and he had to go to the gas station to buy Zig Zag rolling papers. "At least she didn't find my stash," he says.

I think about asking him what he's been up to, because I don't have any idea about how he's making a living or anything. But I stay quiet. The less I talk to him, the less guilty I feel about breaking my promise, breaking the rules. I don't even smoke the joint.

As I take my second-ever sip of *good* tequila, a voice breaks through the stereo system to announce a tornado watch for Mower County, a few hours away from here. Nobody changes what they're doing. It's nothing here. The sky has some sun peeking through the clouds. It's not even raining. I think of my family, all of them. The tequila is smooth, and I know it would help me to fend off the panic attack I feel setting in. But fine tequila is not my thing, so I set it down.

The panic attack isn't because I'm worried about a tornado half the state away from here. It isn't because I'm breaking anybody's rules. I just know Goli Joon needs for us to all be together when there's a tornado watch, even if it's for Mower County, or Madelia, or even for the Mariana Islands.

We're supposed to be home together when tornadoes threaten places that begin with an M.

"Melinda," I say, addressing her but looking at her friend who owns the boat, "I want to get off the boat. Can we please cruise over to Wayzata Bay, so I can get my car and go home?"

Melinda says, "Chill out, little Valerie. We'll go back later." Her friend looks at me and shrugs, as if a decision has been made and there's nothing to be done about it.

Kurt rolls another joint, this time with weed from a different container—an old metal film canister that I recognize from our years together in the 80s. He lights it and passes it to me, but I tell him no, that I'll try some later.

I take a deep breath, and Kurt puts his arm around me affectionately—I know that is all. I have not felt his strong weight-lifter arm around me for more than a decade. I have an urge to reach one arm over to that rip in his Coco-Cola shirt, to feel the resistance of his bicep when I try to squeeze. To know that it has not softened over the years. To be assured that we are all forever young. But I turn away from him and get up to look over the water.

The voice comes over the radio again. "It's still not for anywhere near Hennepin County," Kurt says, and he gets up to take a piss off the side of the boat. I go to the back of the boat, and look out over the bay and at all the other boats. I try to imagine the people on those other boats—who are they and what are their lives like? All rich and happy, I'm sure. Then something comes into my head—something my writing teacher had said.

What was it? That I needed to develop *a personal interest* in others?

No, it wasn't that. It wasn't even personal. Now I remember. She said I should start with *a professional interest* in others, that the world doesn't revolve around me, that everybody has feelings.

That if I could not see that personally, as a writer I could at least begin to see it professionally.

I try to imagine the people on the boats again, as who they are without their boats and their money, about a time when maybe they were hurt, a time when they felt failure or loss. Or felt alone, or stayed silent like Savi with her depression that I had not been either personally or professionally interested in enough to detect.

Then I look at Melinda and see her offering more of her expensive tequila to her friend, hungry for approval. She needs so badly to impress people, to be admired. I distance myself from her for a moment, forgetting the hurt between us and assessing her more objectively.

Things aren't going well for her. Not really. Maybe if I could stop taking things so personally...

The letter on the floor of my car comes to me at that moment, interrupting my thoughts. I suddenly realize: It isn't a rejection. I write these letters to agricultural scientists all the time at work—it's not a rejection, it's a "revise and resubmit," and they might even be interested in *Shoedog.*

I know what I need to do, and how I need to revise.

And maybe, how I need to start living. My teacher told me months ago—it's simple: *Take an interest in people.* That's all there is to it. All the rest are just bullet points.

Melinda cranks her music louder. The boat had been anchored in the West Arm, but now we're heading under the bridge to Crystal Bay. I close my eyes and try to imagine Lake

Minnetonka—*Big Water*—before white men came, without all the mansions and motor boats.

We pick up speed, going about the fastest the houseboat can travel. Noerenberg Gardens, where Naveed and I got married, comes in to view. I know this means we're near Quentin's house too. But I can only see the houses on the peninsula from a distance and I'm not sure which is his from this far away and when it's been so long since I was there. All I see is manicured shoreline, flowers in pots, boats tied to their docks and covered with striped Sunbrella awnings.

Melinda is dancing around on the boat to her new music— something I haven't heard before. Melinda is always playing something I have not heard before. I can't hear myself think. We keep moving, past the site of my wedding and into Brown's Bay.

Kurt is moving from the railing on the other side of the boat to the little fridge, pulling out a brown bottle of beer. Melinda brought the beer too. It's a kind I've never heard of before. Always something I've never heard of before. She tells Kurt it's brewed locally. It's a *microbrew*. In five years, this will be nothing unusual, but in 2001 the only local small batch beer I've heard of is the kind guys like Matthew brew in their basements.

Although I didn't smoke the joint, I pick up the end of it from the built-in ashtray and sniff at it. Kurt offers me the lighter, but I'm bracing as the boat picks up more speed and then comes to a sudden stop. The waves from the inertia slam the boat. I fall down on the bench and just lie there for half a minute, a little nauseated.

And then I know where we are. We're in Wayzata Bay. The far side of it, but the boat starts moving again, and I see the mansions I've been ogling for my whole life: the mansions where I've babysat, the mansion where our high school class always had our last-day-of-school parties, the mansion where my next-door neighbor boy moved after his father's once-small company went public.

I look out over the big bay. I can see Wayzata beach, and very far away and small, the small park playset shaped like a sailboat. *Simeen would like to play on that,* I think. She's getting so big. I see the dot that is my car, behind the garden that's kept up by the Wayzata Garden Club.

It looks far, but not impossible. I have swum in the middle of this lake before.

The water looks warm. So warm. So silent—there's none of Melinda's loud, new, experimental music out there. Just a long, calm swim to the beach, to my car, to my baby, to my love. To Goli Joon, who would have heard about the tornado in Mower County and worried that it was bearing down on Minneapolis. I imagine her...no, I sense her.

I look to the waves and I sense Goli Joon upon them, as if I'm high even though all I have had are two sips of tequila. She's blessing me from somewhere invisible, wafting smoke from her wild rue all around me, whispering a prayer into my ear. I'm imagining it; I must be high from the second-hand smoke of Kurt's joints. But it seems so real and my nausea builds. I can smell the smoke of the wild rue. The scent of rosewater hits me too, as if it is emanating from Lake Minnetonka.

This momentary hallucination hits me with the knowledge that Goli Joon is not going to live much longer. We've been told again and again by the doctors that her heart has held up impossibly long already.

I need to get home.

I slip off my sandals, climb up on the ledge and quietly lower myself into the lake. There's a gentle splash as I land in Wayzata Bay—resting home of my old pink and green tote bag and my Ray Bans, resting home of a million lost things.

First, it's breast stroke, the quietest stroke I know to get away from the boat but make headway without making an embarrassing scene. Then I move to back stroke, and look back toward the boat. Nobody looks out searching for me. How long will it take them to realize, I wonder, and then I realize: I don't care.

I swim. And when the beach doesn't come any closer and I realize I may have misjudged the distance, I float on my back to catch my breath. I think of the ten-foot sturgeon of Lake Minnetonka legend and hope it does not come to bite my foot.

I turn my head and see the cat that had been on the Wayzata Boatworks retaining wall earlier, and I realize that if I'm close enough to see that cat, then maybe I'm close enough to start swimming again. After a little rest, I think. But I can't fall asleep. Maybe it would be good if the legendary sturgeon exists. If it would come gliding along and rescue me.

The clouds are getting darker, and I think *that's good, the coming rain will keep me awake so I can swim.*

Or, maybe that rainbow will keep me awake.

A banding of colors swirls together like marbling paints, and then floats away into a marbled sky. The crisp Sunbrella fabric stripes of color come in and out of focus, and the scent of the wild rue and rosewater I've been imagining swirl away back to shore.

Where did these moving rainbow ribbons of color come from, sailing toward me in this big water?

As I float above a million lost items in the waterbed of Lake Minnetonka, and while a houseboat cranks its music louder across the bay, a canvas catamaran flutters and swerves my way. It clips along on the waves of Wayzata Bay, and I begin to swim.

Acknowledgements

I have the luck to have two especially talented writers as friends: Kathleen Cleberg and Pauline Chandra Graf. They have treated *Roseheart* with love, enthusiasm, and their usual imaginative spirit that I know I take too much for granted. Thank you, Pauline and Kathleen.

I also owe my gratitude to Jennifer Erdem, a most loyal friend whose sense of humor astounds me, and to friends from the University of Minnesota Master of Liberal Studies program and The Loft Literary Center.

Other longtime writers, teachers, and friends have generously read my work and provided extensive feedback: Paulette Alden, Mary Beskar, Cynthia DeKay, Shadon Ghassemlou, Walt Jacobs, Mary Carroll Moore, Bita Payesteh, Allison Sandve, and Aimee Viniard-Weideman. Special thanks to Cynthia for also enlisting beta readers, to Sally Thompson for copyediting, and to Justin Clifton for answering the panicked call to get my text "back on the grid."

For encouragement and unconditional support, I thank my entire family. While *Roseheart* is a work of fiction, and no character is intended to represent any real person, it is born out of my experiences. My live-in mother-in-law, Zari Behbahani, was a transformational person in my life, for example. My own mother, Leslie Hakkola, is my model of strength and resilience. Like Valerie's father in the story, my father, Elliot Kjos, has always told me, "Education is always worth it." Thank you, Dad, for investing and believing in me.

Sisterhood was a minor theme in this story, and my sisters are a major part of mine. I don't know how I would live without you, Jennifer Fackler and Susan Woodward.

Many authors thank their partners for reading dozens of drafts and being their front line of reader/editor. I'd like to thank my husband, Mohammad Dehdashti, for *not* reading my drafts. It was better that way. You did exactly what I needed you to do: support me in my dream, and make up for my neglect of our children.

For a debut novelist, it's a blessing when a reader takes a chance on a new name. If you enjoyed *Roseheart*, please tell a friend, write a review, or mention it on Facebook or Twitter. A new writer needs nothing as much as to know her readers exist.

CPSIA information can be obtained
at www.ICGtesting.com
Printed in the USA
FFOW02n1354290615
14715FF